Anna Apparent

Nina
Bawden

Published by VIRAGO PRESS Limited 1995
20 Vauxhall Bridge Road, London SW1V 2SA

First published in Great Britain in 1972

Copyright © 1972 Nina Bawden

The right of Nina Bawden to be identified as the author of this
work has been asserted by her in accordance with the Copyright,
Designs and Patents Act 1988.

A CIP catalogue record for this book is available from the British Library.

Printed and bound in Great Britain by
Cox & Wyman Ltd, Reading, Berkshire

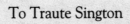

To Traute Sington

Part One   *CRYSTAL*

One autumn evening in 1940, when she was four years old, Annie-May Gates passed within a yard of her future husband, her future mother-in-law, and neither of them noticed her.

Not that this was surprising. It was war-time, the lighting was minimal and the station was alive, like an ant heap. There was just that feeling of endless, aimless scurrying and bustling; as if the ground itself were heaving in perpetual, pointless motion. It was only when the tannoy music was interrupted for an incomprehensible announcement that the swirling and the eddying stopped, that anxious, listening faces became briefly individual: a tired soldier with a pack, a young woman in a red coat, leading a straggling crocodile of mothers and babies and unaccompanied children.

Giles and Crystal Golightly were standing on the platform when they filed past to wait for the train. The children carried gas masks in cardboard containers, teddy bears, crumpled comics, bags of sticky sweets. Labels, pinned to their chests, announced their identities and destinations. Giles, noticing the labels, but with his mind on his mother, felt, for a fleeting second, that he was posting her like a parcel.

He said, 'But of course it's not absurd for you to leave London, dearest. What point would there be in your staying?'

His question was not even faintly ironic. There was no possible connection in Giles's mind between his mother and the women who manned the A.R.P. posts, drove ambulances while bombs were falling, worked in munitions. His father, Colonel Basil Golightly (chronically unfaithful and always compensating for it) had conditioned him to think of her as someone to be cosseted and cherished like some delicate and prized possession. The obvious course in time of war was to despatch her to safety like a piece of good porcelain or a valuable painting.

She said, 'All the same, I wouldn't go if Daddy hadn't insisted.' She gave a deprecating but complacent smile. 'He does worry about me so.'

'Well, of course. Stuck up there in Scotland!' Giles, who was aware (as his mother was not) of his father's sexual habits, was struck suddenly by the thought that the Colonel's concern might be exaggerated by some new occasion for guilt. Otherwise he would surely have sent for her to come to him, rather than suggesting she went to her own mother, in the country? The colour rose in his cheeks which embarrassed him; afraid she might notice and guess the reason, he stared past her at the waiting children. They stood in a tired, meek line and one or two of the smaller ones were snivelling. He thought, *poor kids* – and then of his mother's comfort. He said, 'I'm afraid you'll have a crowded journey,' and looked at her anxiously.

She was a very pretty woman in a restrained and ladylike way. ('Ladylike' was not a word Giles would have spoken aloud but it was a concept he would unconsciously employ when assessing a member of the opposite sex.) A smooth, oval face, wide, healthy, grey eyes, a barely lipsticked mouth. She was thirty-six but looked barely older than Giles, just eighteen and fresh as a lettuce in his stiff, new uniform. In fact (he was proud of this) people often took them for brother and sister. Even for lovers – when they'd had tea at the railway hotel, the waiter had found them an especially quiet table for two, in a corner. Remembering this, Giles blushed again.

Crystal said, 'Oh, the poor children! I shan't mind them.' She glanced at them with vague pity and thought of Giles, ten years younger, fair-haired and grey-flannelled, waving goodbye. She said, with sudden emotion, 'If you were that age, darling, I wouldn't send you away like that.'

He answered without thinking. 'You did, to school.'

She looked at him, shocked, and he felt guilty at once, though he hadn't meant to hurt her. But she was so sensitive, it was difficult not to. He began to wish the train would come and then felt guilty about that, too. Heaven knew when he would see her again!

He said, 'I know that wasn't quite the same thing!' Of course there was all the difference in the world between a rich little boy, off to his good school, and this sad, raggle-taggle lot. Had it *felt* different, though? The worst thing was leaving one's mother, though naturally one couldn't admit that. Apron strings were a bad thing to be tied to – he could remember his father saying something of that sort and his childish bewilderment: he had never seen his mother in an apron. He hadn't cried, at least not in public as some of those quite big boys were doing (there was one fat, unattractive child with jade green snot streaming unchecked from his nostrils), but recalling his own, hollow sense of loss at much the same age brought a sympathetic tightness to his throat.

He said, 'I expect they'll be all right once they get where they're going, railway platforms are always the worst part,' and felt better.

She put her gloved hand on his arm. 'Darling, did you *hate* going away?'

Her eyes were moist, and for a moment he had an impulse to tell her (after all, he might never see her again!), but she said, 'I can't think you did, you always seemed happy, but it upset me quite dreadfully. I used to sit in your room and cry for hours after you'd gone. It felt so empty.'

He said, 'Poor sweet,' and touched her cold cheek. She looked solemnly into his eyes for a second, then smiled and sighed. 'I should have had ten children, Giles, then I wouldn't have been such a silly.'

He said, 'Listen a minute.' The voice over the tannoy sounded as if the speaker had a gag in his mouth or was shouting through fog. 'Not ours, is it?' Crystal said, but people had begun to run down the platform. A laden porter jostled them and Giles put an arm round his mother. He said loudly, 'Careful, now!' The porter glanced at him and jerked his head. 'You'll have to move along, the coaches this part'll be reserved for the children.'

The train was shunting in backwards. The slowly moving connecting rods gleamed, then a sharp hiss of steam rose, hiding them. The carriage windows were obscured. Some of the people who had run down the platform passed them again, hurrying back. 'Which way did he mean, to move along?' Crystal said, but the porter had gone and there was no sign of another. Only anonymous strangers with intent, worried faces, pushing past them. Giles kept his arm round her shoulders.

He said, 'There's no hurry, there's plenty of time.'

He thought, *Not long now,* and felt an extraordinary sense of relief as if a heavy weight had been lifted from him. The day had been a bit of a strain, perhaps; he could admit it now. Now it was over and he had nothing to do except catch his own train, join his unit tomorrow. And he was looking forward to it, he didn't know what was going to happen next but he was looking forward to it, whatever it was. It was all, quite suddenly, so immensely exciting that he could hardly endure to stand still another minute. Everything was exciting, the whole business of war and movement and not knowing exactly where you would be tomorrow. He felt so strong and eager and energetic that he was quite sure other people must feel the same way. Even those kids, one or two of them, anyway, must be finding this fun, a new and marvellous adventure . . .

The children were boarding the train. A young woman in a red coat, standing by the carriage door, was swinging the little ones up. Giles caught her eye; although she looked tired, she grinned at him cheerfully. He took his mother's case and swung it lightly as he led her down the platform.

The train was longer than he had realized and most of it seemed set aside for the children's evacuation. The only unreserved coaches were full already; the soldiers, sprawled across the seats, looked as if they had been settled in for hours. And even the corridors were filling up: quite elderly women, he was shocked to see, were sitting uncomfortably on their suitcases.

He said, 'Try the other end,' but as he wheeled her round, they met other voyagers, surging back. He forced forward, against the tide, peering in through the smudgy windows. Some of the reserved compartments seemed only three-quarters full; children took up less space than adults. He found one with an empty window seat and put the suitcase down to open the door but a uniformed man – a guard or a porter – slammed it almost on his fingers. 'These coaches are reserved for special passes,' he said, looking angry, or perhaps only harassed. 'Never mind, I can catch the next train,' Crystal said.

Giles felt his heart sink. But he smiled down at her. She said, 'Really, I can quite easily . . .' but he had caught sight of the young woman standing alone by an open door and watching him. He hurried Crystal towards her. He said, 'D'you think you'd have room for my mother?'

The girl nodded and moved aside. She was a year or so older than Giles, perhaps, but not much more. The way she smiled at him acknowledged their joint youth so brightly and openly that it was almost a sexual invitation. Or so it seemed to Giles. He caught his breath: that was another thing to look forward to!

Crystal was saying something. He didn't know what; didn't want to know. He whispered in her ear, 'You'll be all right here, better than with the coarse soldiery,' and helped her in. There was room for her case on the rack, a seat by the window. The girl got in behind them, waited in the corridor. A whistle blew.

Crystal kissed him on the mouth. She said, 'My darling, take care!' No time for more, luckily – he was very conscious of the girl, standing there. Not that Crystal fussed over leavetakings (coming from an Army family she was used to them), but she had been sad, shutting up the flat, and he had seen tears in her eyes in the taxi. He said, 'You take care of yourself, that's more important,' and stepped back, off the train, brushing past the girl as he did so. Their eyes met and hers were very lively and friendly. He thought, *I could have kissed her too*! The train began to move and he ran beside it, watching the girl through the smeary glass and waving and smiling. Crystal, standing by the open window, was astonished by the brilliance and gaiety of his smile.

And also a little hurt. He looked so happy and free and *she* felt so bereft, suddenly. It had been a dreadful day, leaving the flat and all her pretty things and now Giles was gone, too. A tired depression came down on her spirits and the journey seemed unlikely to lift it. The carriage was dimly lit, only one blue bulb in the centre, and the bigger children were making such a noise, shouting and giggling and roaring up and down the corridor. Crystal felt her head begin to ache. The girl in the red coat smiled at her and said, 'They're excited, that's all, they'll give over later.' She was clearly too busy to quieten the noise; there were so many smaller children who were crying or clamouring to go to the lavatory. Crystal wondered if she should offer to help but the girl seemed so competent and she was also afraid of being rebuffed: children were always unpredictable and these were much wilder and rougher than the ones she was used to, almost a different race, with their ill-fitting clothes (either too large or shrunken) and their running noses and their raucous voices. The young teacher's voice was 'common' too, but Crystal, whose ear was carefully tuned to differences of accent, placed her a social notch above her charges. She seemed a 'nice little person', she would even be pretty if it wasn't for that frizzy, permed hair, and she was certainly kind: when she had settled most of the babies with comics or sweets or thumbs in their mouths, she sat opposite Crystal with one particularly inconsolable little boy on her lap. He had been crying softly ever since the train began to move; now, as the girl cuddled him and talked to him gently, only an occasional, helpless sob shook him. He looked about six and was thin and wretchedly pale with huge, dark, luminous eyes that roamed desperately round the carriage. 'What beautiful eyes,' Crystal could not help saying. The girl smiled, rather blankly, and the little boy began to wriggle on her lap. She tried to hold him still, to soothe him, but he wailed, 'I don't want to be safe without Mummy,' and began to cry again, and kick. The girl stood up and carried him into the corridor. Crystal watched her, walking up and down and holding his head against her shoulder.

She stared at her reflection in the glass window beside her until it began to mist and blur. The child's sad little statement had made her eyes burn. For a moment she could have wept for him; then his unhappiness became a kind of fiction, to turn to her own use. She thought, *I don't want to be safe without Basil or Giles.* It didn't have quite the same pathetic ring but she felt, she was sure, the same desolation and loneliness. Growing older didn't make you less vulnerable; you could feel as miserable at thirty-six as you did at six or sixteen. And there was no one to comfort *her* – even Giles, who was usually so sensitive, had not understood what a wrench it was to leave home . . .

When the girl came back, the little boy was asleep. She sat down, carefully turning his face from the light, and smiled at Crystal. 'They're all dead tired, that's half the trouble, we've been on the move since this morning. Most of the time just hanging about, that's been the worst part. And most of them don't understand what's happening or why, and the parents haven't helped much. D'you know what this kid's Mum said to him? When she put him on the bus this morning she said she was coming on the train too and she'd meet him at the station.'

'Maybe she couldn't bear to tell him the truth,' Crystal murmured, and the girl tossed her head. 'Then she ought to be shot. Oh, that's silly, but it's the sort of thing makes me so mad! Poor little rats, they've got enough to bear without being lied to as well.'

Though she knew it to be ridiculous, Crystal felt a stab of jealousy. All that young, indignant sympathy – and none of it for her! She said, 'One mustn't exaggerate. Children's emotions are very ephemeral, it's the mothers that feel it. My son went to school when he was seven and I know how I felt! And of course for these children there's a good side, too. I don't mean just escaping the bombing, but it's a wonderful chance for them to get out of the city. Where do you come from?'

'Stepney. Creechly Road Juniors and Mixed Infants,' the girl said, rather shortly. She looked at Crystal with a sudden gleam of battle. 'A bit of a slum but they don't know that, do they?'

Crystal thought the poor girl was probably tired. She said, gently, 'Well, then. Fresh air, good food, woods and fields to run round in . . .'

'Cows and manure,' the girl said. 'I was evacuated last year, with my training college. I'd never been to the country, only to the seaside, and I hated it.' She stopped, frowning; her eyes darkened and she looked much younger, suddenly. 'I think I was scared, really. It was so hot and still to begin with and so dead dark at night, and everywhere so empty and *waiting* – as if something awful was coming.'

She was looking quite white, Crystal thought. She said,

brightly, 'I expect it was just that at that time no one knew what was going to happen. The phoney war feeling.'

The girl smiled uncertainly but her eyes remained shadowed and fearful.

'What else could it be?' Crystal said. 'It's bound to seem quiet, after town life, of course. But I had the *happiest* childhood in the country!'

Not that her homecoming, this dark night of war, was particularly cheerful. She had trouble getting a taxi at the station and the driver was surly when he found he had to drive up an unmade road that the rain had turned into a swamp in places. And when she arrived, there wasn't much welcome, either. It was a year since she had visited her mother and the condition of the cottage dismayed her. Dust everywhere, chairs hidden beneath piles of books; used cups and plates on the table, several encrusted saucepans standing in the hearth. And her mother, wearing an old, moth-holed cardigan fastened across her flat chest with a huge safety pin. As Crystal looked round the room, she began patting and pulling at her clothes. Crystal said, 'Mother, you've been ill! Why didn't you tell me? I'd have come long before!'

'Afraid of that,' her mother said in a queer, mumbling voice; then flushed and added, more clearly, 'I didn't want to worry you.'

'Oh, how silly!' Crystal said, speaking gently, though the old irritation had begun to rise up in her. All her childhood, dirt and muddle; her mother deep in some book while the dinner burned on the stove! Turning up at school prize days, hatless and vague-looking – Crystal had always felt so sorry for her father when she met them, arriving together. He was so well-dressed himself, such a handsome man, who liked women to look pretty. She remembered the expression on his face, the first time he had seen her in a grown-up ball gown. He was taking her to a charity dance

for her sixteenth birthday treat; she came down in her new
green dress and pirouetted round, watching him, and herself, in the mirror. When she stopped, he came to stand
behind her; their eyes met in the glass and he smiled,
white teeth gleaming under his black moustache. She took
a white rose from a vase on the table and turned to him but
he caught her hand and said, 'I don't need that, you're the
flower in my buttonhole.'

It took so little to make him happy. Wearing nice
clothes and smiling at his jokes. Her mother made no effort
to please him, never had, as far back as Crystal could
remember. She bought clothes only when her old ones
wore out and never went to the hairdresser. Even as a girl
she had been much the same: old photographs showed the
same faraway look, the same wild, spiky hair. Why they
had married seemed a mystery. For her money, someone
had once said, in Crystal's hearing, but Crystal always
ignored unpleasant gossip and so the mystery remained:
her father, so gay and outgoing, her mother only caring
for her books and her music . . .

The piano was open but hopelessly out of tune. Crystal,
who didn't play but who had inherited her mother's ear,
winced as she touched the keys.

'I don't bother now,' her mother said. 'It's that wireless
you gave me. There are so many good concerts. I'm not
up to the standard.'

Crystal was hurt. She had given her mother a new
wireless on her thirtieth birthday. (She liked to celebrate
her own anniversaries by giving presents; besides, it
reminded her mother, who forgot them.)

She said, 'But dearest, that's not the same thing! I know
you play wonderfully well, but you never thought of yourself as a professional, did you?'

'I suppose not.' Her mother's hollow cheeks flushed.
'But I find it's true what the Greeks said. The best is the
enemy of the good.'

12

That odd, half-mumble again, as if she were talking to herself! Of course that was it, Crystal thought, she's been alone so much. No one to talk to, no point in cooking for herself – she had got so much *thinner*, her eyes looked enormous!

Crystal refused to feel uneasy. She said, 'I'll take my things up. Then we'll have something to eat and sit by the fire and talk.'

'I've got your room ready,' her mother said.

So she had, after a fashion. The high, iron bed was made (though the sheets were unironed) and there were flowers in a jam jar. And a photograph of her father as a very young Captain, smiling at her out of a silver frame. Her mother had put all his pictures away when he died; she'd been up to the attic to fetch this, to please her daughter. *Poor old soul*, Crystal thought, and vowed to be tactful. She would ignore the mess the cottage was in, at least for a day or so. It wasn't really too bad, perhaps – at least, by her mother's standards!

But looking into her mother's room after she'd washed – *peeping in*, she thought tenderly, *like a child coming home* – she saw the worst yet: all in a shambles, a chair overturned, an unemptied chamber pot under the bed . . .

She closed the door quickly. She felt pity for her mother, for herself (what a wretched end to a tiring day!) and then, a sudden, dark wave of panic. She thought, *As if something awful were coming*, and then, immediately, *Oh, that silly girl on the train*! There was nothing frightening here, only an unexpected degree of disorder. It was just as well she had come before things got too bad! Downstairs, her mother started to sing in the kitchen; the true, sweet voice, rather cracked now, sounding old. . . . Of course she *was* old, Crystal thought, that was all it was; people got old, there was nothing to panic about. . . .

But it wasn't all. A week later, Crystal came home from shopping (she had found the larder almost empty except for tins of baked beans and dusty jugs of stale milk) and found her mother asleep in her chair. There were raised spots on her cheek, like red pennies, and she was snoring heavily. She was hard to rouse but when she did wake she seemed well enough except that her speech was a little slurred and when she stood up she moved stiffly. Although her voice improved, after tea, she still seemed to be dragging one leg.

Crystal wanted to call the doctor at once but her mother said Will Davies was too busy to be bothered with an old woman's rheumatism. Doubting this diagnosis, Crystal tried to insist – there was so much could be done, nowadays, to help minor ailments. And when her mother remained obstinate, went to see the doctor herself.

An old man with a veined, knobbly face, he had been due for retirement the year the war started; now his young partner was in the Army and he was running the practice single-handed. He listened to Crystal and then said, brusquely, 'She drinks, you know.'

Drank himself, Crystal remembered, rather indignantly. That grog-blossom nose! She was sitting facing the window; shutters had been closed outside, for black-out purposes, and she could see her reflection in the glass, had been watching it, in fact, most of the time she'd been talking. Now she saw that Dr Davies was regarding her covertly, with shy admiration, it seemed. She crossed her pretty legs, tilted her head in a way that she knew showed off the vaselike curve of her cheek, and thought of the time (years ago now, before her father died) when she had been staying with her parents and had been taken ill with pleurisy. Will Davies had visited every day, more frequently than had really been necessary; his hands had shaken when he examined her chest and there had been such a look in his eyes! Perhaps he was still a little in love with her, Crystal thought, and her indignation faded. She said, 'Of course she doesn't, what nonsense! Only her old

14

home-made wine from time to time! Stone jars of it, glug-glugging away all over the house, elderflower, bilberry – horrid stuff, to my mind, but hardly a vicious tipple!'

The doctor said nothing.

Crystal said, 'To tell you the truth, I'm afraid she may have had a slight stroke. I didn't say so before because I know how doctors hate patients to say what they think is wrong! But I would like you to see her. And since she won't come to see you, I'm afraid Mahomet must come to the mountain! Pretend it's a social visit – or that you've come to see me. After all, you have done before!'

She laughed, inviting him to recall what must be a tender memory for him. But he only frowned and tapped his long, yellow teeth with the end of his pencil. After a pause he said, 'Were you ever a patient of mine?'

The frown and the hesitation were deliberate. Will Davies remembered the occasion perfectly, could date it, in fact: that summer fourteen years ago, the year his wife died. He had loved her passionately; they were both in their fifties but there were still times when they could hardly wait to get to bed. When she died (suddenly, in the cold, early spring) he missed her in every way, but the sexual loss, for a man in his profession, was particularly agonizing: the bodies of his young female patients became a torment to him. He had never once lapsed, thank God, never even (he hoped) betrayed himself, but there had been a few girls who had guessed. Amy Haines's daughter – what was her name now, Golightly? – had been one: spoiled, silly tart, sitting up in bed in her frilly flimsies and baring her breasts almost before he was inside the room. She knew his trouble all right and enjoyed seeing him sweat – it was clear from the way she watched him, from that arch, sly smile. He should have sent his partner, of course, why hadn't he? Wanted to prove himself, perhaps. Or just unwilling to miss a chance of getting his hands on those tits, he thought disgustedly,

15

sitting at his desk after Crystal had gone and putting off summoning the next patient. Then he thought, *Oh, be honest!* He'd gone because Amy wanted him to and he was very fond of Amy (loving his wife hadn't made him less susceptible in that way; more so, if anything) and she had been so worried about the girl. And he had been worried about Amy, a nervy, fragile creature who had already begun to drown her sorrows. Not very great sorrows, perhaps: her husband wasn't a bad chap, simply a military muttonhead (the Army, to its credit, had cottoned on and retired him early), but a cross for a clever woman to bear. Pity the girl hadn't turned out more her sort, instead of a pretty flibbertigibbet; a disappointment for Amy – maybe it was guilt over that made her overdo her concern. He remembered (clear as yesterday, suddenly) coming into the cottage kitchen and Amy's flushed, anxious face looking up from the stove. She was stirring something, some fancy sauce to tempt her daughter's appetite. She'd said, 'Oh Will, it's no use, *everything curdles*,' in a tone of such exaggerated despair that he would have wanted to laugh if he hadn't seen the tears in her eyes and known they were not for the spoiled sauce but for a deeper failure: neither her husband nor her daughter wanted what she had to offer, all they wanted from her were the things she did badly. Poor Amy, he thought now, as he pressed the bell on his desk, all that talent, all that wit and intelligence lying unused; Lord, how the human race does waste its resources. . . .

It seemed to him that his next patient underlined this point. He had never seen her before but he placed her as soon as she opened her mouth: the cockney whine hurt his ears, as her situation hurt his mind. Most of the evacuees in his area, mothers with babies or children alone, had come from the worst slums of London or Birmingham; a pitiful army whose arrival had made him aware of a kind of poverty he had not known existed. Children with lice, children with rickets; most of them chronically underfed. This young woman could have been a beauty, he thought, if she had not been so thin (by country standards her face was almost emaciated), though her child seemed better cared for than most he had seen; a solid little girl with red cheeks and straight, black hair.

Perhaps her mother was a cut above the average: certainly there was considerable intelligence in what Will Davies was oldfashioned enough to think of as her 'fine' dark eyes. And though for him her dreadful accent was a stumbling block to regarding her as a thinking, reasoning, human being, her purpose in coming to see him seemed to bear this judgment out.

The little girl had a bruise on her forehead. It was nothing much (her mother, sweeping back the child's fringe for only the most cursory of examinations, knew this as well as he did), the real complaint was how she had got it. 'She fell down the stairs on the way to the toilet, missed her way in the dark. I say dark, it was pitch! Not a light in the place – nine o'clock, she turns them off at the mains! The child should be asleep at that hour she said when I told her, but Annie-May's got a weak bladder and she's particular, not like some kids who'd mess their beds and think nothing of it. No convenience in the room neither, just a bed and a Bible – Mrs Gates, she said, when I come, I'm taking you in because we're all God's creatures, I hope you appreciate that, if you don't, I've put a Bible by your bed to remind you. I hope you'll read it and keep the child quiet because of my nerves and as you know the Government don't pay much so I'll trust you'll give me a hand in the house to make up . . .'

'She' was a Mrs Herbert Fitch. Will Davies did not attend her because she employed a doctor in Shrewsbury but he had looked after her long procession of maids who had come to him, ostensibly suffering from some minor ailment or other but really from Mrs Fitch, who drove them

17

to the brink of hysteria with her prurience, her meanness and her slave-owner's mentality which had, in recent years, acquired a convenient, religious gloss: she seemed to believe (or managed to suggest, anyway) that entering her employment was akin to taking holy orders. She had told one girl (not, it was generally thought, misquoting deliberately), 'Who sweeps a room as for My laws . . .' and another, who was hopeful enough to ask for a rise in wages, that she could not expect to serve both God and Mammon. This maid, the last, had left some months ago, and, since she was unlikely to be easily replaced now that the war offered alternative employment, Will Davies did not need to be told why Mrs Fitch had elected to perform her Christian duty and take in a mother and baby.

The young woman did not need to be told either. And was having none of it. 'I'll be buggered if I'll be used as cheap labour, not by her, anyway. I don't mind giving a hand, I'm not so fond of sitting on my backside, but she'd have a chain round your neck soon as you showed willing. And even if she wasn't such an old bitch, it 'ud kill me to stay in that house, bitter cold, and all those pictures of dogs eating pheasants, enough to put you off your food. Not that there's much of *that* to be put off! Lukewarm tinned pilchards was what Annie-May had for her dinner today and bread and marge for tea *and* the larder door padlocked! I don't mind for myself, I've lived on bread and scrape before, but it's not good enough for Annie-May!'

There was no point in letting this go on. Will Davies could produce tales about Mrs Fitch beside which locked larders and lights out at nine were mild eccentricities. But what could he do? He said, 'Have you been to the billeting authorities, Mrs Gates?'

'Miss. Miss Mary Gates.' She spoke loudly and looked him straight in the eye.

He said, 'I shouldn't make too much of that, we're rather oldfashioned round here.'

18

She said, more gently, 'I just wanted to be straight with you because I want to ask a favour. The billeting people can't help. I'm lucky to have a roof, they say, and you can see their point – they've got kids sleeping on mattresses in the Church Hall. So I thought I'd best be independent, get some sort of job where I could live in with Annie, and then, the person to try 'ud be the doctor. I mean, going about, you might know of somewhere . . .' She paused, looking uncertain, as if, now she had got it out, the request seemed presumptuous; when she went on she sounded younger, more vulnerable. 'I'm strong, I daresay I could help on a farm. I wouldn't want much, just the board, and a few bob on top to get clothes for Annie-May.'

He looked at her. The child was half asleep, sucking her thumb; her mother's arms enclosed her. . . . For a sentimental moment, it came to him that he had room in his own house but he dismissed the impulse to say so. His housekeeper was old and inclined to be crotchety; he sensed that this young woman's character might not be mild enough for peace. It appealed to him though, she seemed honest and sensitive – last time he'd visited the Fitch mausoleum, that gory gallery of game birds had made him wince, too.

He said, 'They're small farms round here, family concerns, not much call for hired help. But I'll ask around, if you like.'

Her response was immediate. She only said, 'Thank you,' but with such a smile! It made him see what she could have looked like, if her life had been easier. He thought, unfairly perhaps, *That spoiled girl of Amy's . . .*

When he called on Amy Haines, nearly a week later, Crystal was glad to see that her mother made no fuss, seemed to accept that this was a social call. To bear out this pretence she chatted a little before excusing herself – she was making jam, the garden was full of fallen apples

19

and it seemed a pity to waste them. From the kitchen she could hear them talking, and, once or twice, her mother's laugh; a delightful, unaffected sound, almost girlish. Listening, it struck Crystal that this was the first time she had heard it since her arrival and this upset her suddenly. Not that she minded for herself, but it brought back how seldom her mother had even smiled at her father's jokes! They weren't always very subtle, perhaps, but he enjoyed them so much himself, it seemed almost cruel not to share them. He never reproached her, the nearest he ever got was to say, 'Lighten up old girl, lighten up, what's on your mind?' And once, one dreadful day, she had answered, 'Lord Chesterfield's remarks on the laughter of fools.'

Standing over the stove, stirring apple jelly, Crystal remembered the bewildered look on her father's face, the pain in his eyes.

Will Davies came into the kitchen. He said, 'I'll be on my way now.'

She went with him to the gate. As soon as they were out of earshot he said, 'I think you were right. She seems to have recovered, only a bit of what she calls heaviness left in one leg, but that may go too. Even if it doesn't, she's come off fairly lightly. I've told her to take things easy, but don't worry if she doesn't. She might as well wear out as rust out!'

Crystal was shocked at this casual approach. Surely there was something more to be done? A regime to be followed, some special diet? She said, 'There's one thing I do know, she shouldn't have alcohol. After what you said I've been keeping a weather eye open and it does rather add up! The elderflower mid-morning, the raisin in the afternoon, and a number of "little glasses" in the evening. Quite a bit of tippling, really! And some of these country wines are quite absurdly strong, aren't they?'

She laughed merrily but he didn't smile. He said, 'Yes, I suppose so.'

She said, 'Well, then. I think a bit of sternness is called for, isn't it?' Thinking how old he looked in the clear, autumn sunlight; fiery red face and pale, old eyes and grizzled, shaving-brush hair.

He said, slowly, 'She hasn't many pleasures. She's had a hard life, she might as well enjoy what's left of it.'

As advice this seemed sentimental rather than professional. But it was the other point that roused Crystal. 'What hard life?' she could not help saying, though she knew exactly what he was thinking of and thought it too bad of her mother! Not that she had ever complained but it was the impression she gave. Or had given, when her father was alive. The silences, the martyred withdrawal! She said, 'She's never been poor, or even ill, until now. If she wasn't happy with my father, it was her own fault. She despised him, that was the root of the trouble and she never attempted to hide it. Oh, I know he wasn't an intellectual, but that doesn't mean he couldn't be hurt! And he was, often – I'm their daughter and I saw it! He'd come bouncing in with some funny story – like a big, jolly dog with a bone to lay at her feet – and she'd cut him off in the middle. Just turn away.'

Tears came into Crystal's eyes. She made no attempt to hide them.

Dr Davies took his fob watch out of his pocket, opened it, looked at its face through his eyeglass, snapped it shut. He said, 'Your mother is a clever and a serious woman.'

'Then she should have managed him better. I could always twist him round my little finger!'

'I don't think your mother sees men as objects to be manipulated.'

He spoke so coldly that Crystal was astonished: it was almost as if he were criticizing her! She smiled at him forgivingly to show that she knew he had no such intention and thought the colour deepened in his face. He coughed and said, 'Well, whatever the rights and wrongs, there's no point in taking it out on her now!'

Did he really think she was likely to, Crystal thought, and then, at once, *Oh, poor old man, perhaps he does*! Her little outburst had alarmed him; he wasn't to know she felt better after it, cleansed of enmity towards her mother! He was getting into his ancient car; she followed him to make some reassuring remark, but, bending to look through the window, saw that he had passengers in the back. The woman was very ordinary, cheap hat and shoddy-smart coat, but the child was enchanting, a rosy little girl with eyes like black cherries. When Crystal said, 'Hallo,' she put her plump hand over her eyes and peeped through her fingers. 'Go on, Annie-May,' her mother said. 'Say hallo to the lady.'

Driving away, he apologized for being so long. He could have stopped at the cottage later but it was on the way to the farm he was taking her to, he had other calls to make further on and he liked to spare his old car as much as he could. Growing old himself, he had begun to think of it with tender anthropomorphism as another ageing creature with creaky joints. 'She's getting on,' he said. 'She gets a bit blown on the hills.'

'Oh, we didn't mind waiting. Annie-May and I don't often get the chance of a car ride, do we Annie?'

'Bit of a rough one, round here.'

'I think it's lovely,' she said. 'Annie-May and me, we've never bin in the country.'

He watched her in the mirror. She looked such a townee in that silly hat, where did she think she was going, dressed up to the nines? Oh, probably only wanted to make a good first impression – his irritation didn't arise from her unsuitable clothes but from his own doubts. Owen was a decent enough old chap, running his small farm with the help of his children: a son from one marriage, a girl from another. But the boy was said to be wild as a hawk and the girl a dim wit: she'd had a child recently and there was gossip about its paternity. He wouldn't have paid much attention ordinarily, he prided himself on not making moral judgments, but it occurred to him as he eased his old car over the ruts in the road that he had, in a way, done so now: if this young woman had been respectably married, he might not have suggested this somewhat unconventional household. Not that any alternative had turned up; only old Owen who had come to the surgery to get liniment for his bad back and mentioned that things were not too easy at home. The girl was vaguer than ever ('a bit lighter up here' Owen had said, tapping his forehead), and her aunt, Owen's sister, who had been staying a while had gone home to Chester. He had jumped at the offer of help, even offered fifteen shillings a week if she would see to the poultry. . . .

He said, cautiously, 'They're simple people, you know. And I'm afraid you may find yourself a bit out in the wilds.'

'Where else could I go?' she said, but quite cheerfully.

'I mean, if you don't like the look of the place, you're in no way committed. It's a hill farm, a bit rough, I daresay.'

'Oh, we're not expecting the Ritz,' she said. 'Are we, Annie?'

He could not know how little she expected, how little she was prepared to settle for – she would have settled for the terrible Mrs Fitch if the stupid woman had not locked the larder door and rationed Annie's milk. Nor, luckily for his peace of mind, the extent of her plight: she had fourteen shillings in her purse and no one in the world to turn to. Her parents had not spoken to her since before her child was born and she had not seen Annie-May's father since the night he impregnated her in an alley behind the local dance hall. He was drunk, she was sixteen years old and too frightened to stop him. He hurt her and made her bleed but when it was over she was not really worried: her girl friend told her that nothing ever happened the first time, and, anyway, it was always safe standing up. When time disproved this theory, the same friend knew an abortionist. Her refusal was part economic (she hadn't got the ten pounds) and part instinctive: she was by nature maternal. She longed for her baby, even before the first, fluttering movements, and with her birth embarked on a long love affair that more than compensated for what was (at that time, certainly) a desperate situation. Not that she saw it as desperate; everything is comparative and her life had not, up to then, set much of a standard. She had never starved, but her parents had lived on the edge of want for so long that it had drained their spirit. Home was a harsh, cold, defeated place; leaving it, there was almost nowhere to go but up. She hadn't climbed very far but she counted herself fortunate: she found a place as a cook-general in a cheap boarding house before her pregnancy began to show, and by the time it did, had proved herself so strong and willing that her employers saw that charity would be to their advantage. They didn't make life easy but they made it possible, and Mary, who had not been taught to hope for more, was grateful. She had been exploited – worked to the limits of her young strength – but with Annie-May in her arms she had never felt lonely or poor and now, bouncing about in the back of the doctor's old car, she thought herself lucky. They were not only safe from 'that Hitler' but they were going to live on a farm, fresh milk and eggs and country air for Annie, and, since she would call herself Mrs Gates, no one to name her a bastard. A new life beginning . . .

The next six months were the happiest she had ever known. She took to old Owen as he took to her. His children had disappointed him, his sullen, idle son and witless daughter, and he liked Mary Gates for her pluck, her bright, tough perkiness, for the way she sang round his house. And he grew fond of the child. When Mary heard from her father that her mother was dying (though she had written to her parents, this was the first reply she had had) she had no doubts about leaving Annie with him while she went home to see her. To do anything else was, anyway, out of the question: there were nightly air raids on London.

She left an address. When she didn't come back, old Owen wrote, but got no answer. He did nothing else. He was old and stubborn. He knew what might have happened but preferred to think he'd been made a fool of. Or preferred, perhaps, to hope.

A new life had begun for Crystal, too. She was so used to being put first, fussed over – Basil had taken over where her father had left off. Giles's birth had been the only real occasion when pain and fear had touched her and Basil had continued to be gratifyingly appreciative of the terrible anguish she had endured on his account. On Giles's birthday he always sent her roses and an expensive present with a card that said, *Thank you for my son.*

Her mother seemed to find this peculiar. When the birthday came round, eight months after she had come to the cottage, and Crystal was distressed because there was not even a letter from Basil, Amy Haines said, 'But it's Giles's birthday, isn't it, not yours?'

Crystal explained but her mother's face retained a mulishly blank expression as if she did not wish to understand. Her only comment was that she hoped Giles had got the socks she had sent him, though later in the day she seemed to regret this grudging attitude and, before she went to bed, kissed Crystal quite affectionately, and said, 'Don't worry, dear, I'm sure you'll hear from Basil soon, I expect he's busy.'

If Basil was, he didn't say. When he wrote he spoke of the war and its – to Crystal – tedious progress. Indeed, there were long periods when she quite forgot about it. No daily papers were delivered, and though her mother listened to the wireless, Crystal was far too busy. She cooked and cleaned and trudged the two miles to the village to shop until a neighbouring farmer offered her the loan of a pony and trap. She had never worked so hard in her life and though she didn't complain, wished, as the months went by, that there was someone to see and admire. She wrote gallantly humorous letters to Basil (Your little wife has found her War Work with a vengeance!) but even he did not seem to appreciate (or at least his replies did not comment on) the extent of her sacrifice: buried in a wild part of the country with only an ailing old woman for company. Not that Crystal was bored, even superficially (that deeper level, staleness of spirit, was one she didn't know existed), largely because every day of her life was a drama in which she played the chief part and always gave a delightful performance. Since it charmed her so much, she was sure it must charm other people: bowling along in the trap, enjoying the slap and creak of harness, the smell of horse sweat and leather, she was convinced that every farm boy she met was secretly in love with her.

She met Annie-May one wet afternoon outside a small general store some miles from the village. The shop was an old lean-to against the wall of a cottage; it had one fly-blown window displaying tinned foods of such apparent antiquity that it made Crystal shudder to look at them, but the widow who owned it also sold black market butter and Crystal called for a pound once a week.

As she got down from the trap, the little girl was pulling the rusty bell to summon Mrs Purvis. Crystal gave her a friendly smile but she didn't respond, only looked sullen. She was wearing a woman's cut-down dress and Wellington boots that seemed too large for her. When Mrs Purvis came, she waited silently by the door while Crystal bought her butter and spoke about the weather. Mrs Purvis cut her short – rather rudely, Crystal thought. She said, 'What d'you want, Annie-May?' and the child began to cry. Not loudly, but with little, suffocated gasps, open-eyed. Crystal said, 'What's the matter, dear?' Her concern was genuine but she could not help being conscious of her charming kindness: when Annie continued to weep, she knelt gracefully on the dirty floor and took out her handkerchief. Mrs Purvis said, 'Lost the money, Annie-May?' The child shook her head; her chest began to heave like a bellows. 'Oh, poor baby,' Crystal murmured, and put her arms round the small, stiff body. 'Come on, it can't be so dreadful!' The little girl looked at her for a moment, dark eyes dilated and fearful. Then she whispered, 'They allus send me for things I can't say.'

Mrs Purvis said, 'What is it then, butter or bread?'

The child's face convulsed as she struggled with the dreadful consonant.

Crystal smiled. She pulled aside the white napkin covering the butter in her basket. The child shook her head. Crystal rose to her feet and picked up a loaf from the counter.

Annie nodded. Crystal said, 'Then why not say *loaf* another time? Think of another word when you're stuck, it's always the best way!' She turned to Mrs Purvis. 'I used to stammer quite dreadfully when I was young. I can remember the *agony* – M's were my worst thing! Mummy and money – goodness me, I stumble even now when I think of it!' She had, in fact, a slight hesitancy still and thought of it as rather charming. She smiled at Annie. 'You know, the first teacher I had was called Miss Murdoch! I simply couldn't get it out! She used to make me stand up in front of the glass and say, blow it out, Crystal, *blow* . . .'

The child received this engaging confidence so blankly that Crystal wondered if she were quite all there mentally. She had slightly slanting brown eyes and a pale little monkey face – it had shocked Crystal how seldom the country children she saw were healthy and rosy-cheeked. All that terrible white bread, she thought, watching the two carrier bags being filled. Mrs Purvis rang up the till, then rubbed an apple on her apron. 'There you are, Annie.'

Annie smiled briefly. She put the apple in her pocket, picked up the bags. Not a heavy burden, of course, but clumsy; she looked small and encumbered as she left the shop. The two women followed her; while Mrs Purvis locked the shop door, Crystal watched the girl trudging away, head down against the fine, stinging rain. 'She could be pretty,' she said. 'Rather an unusual face! If only someone would wash her hair!'

Since the parents were presumably known to Mrs Purvis, she laughed, to show this was not a serious criticism. Mrs Purvis did not reply. Like many country people, she seemed disinclined for friendly gossip: Crystal had been living with her mother for over two years now, and still felt she was looked upon as a 'foreigner'. She said, irritated by Mrs Purvis's vague, muddy stare, 'Though the stammer is more important, of course! You'd think her mother would send a note. I suppose she doesn't realize how distressing it is for the child, perhaps *I* only do because I suffered so much myself. It really is terrible what children go through!'

Though Mrs Purvis nodded, her expression was politely mystified as if Crystal spoke some unfamiliar language. By the time Crystal had climbed into the trap, picked up the reins, and turned to smile goodbye, she had disappeared into the cottage.

Crystal clicked her tongue at the pony and the trap's iron wheels rattled along the road after the small, almost vanishing figure: it was not very late in the day but the rain had brought the dark early. Poor little waif, lugging those awkward bags, alone in the chilly murk. Crystal drew up alongside and said, 'Like a lift?'

The pony's hooves slipped on the wet road. Annie stopped and looked up. 'Hop in,' Crystal said.

But the child stood quite still. Her mouth was pinched tight. Crystal got out of the trap, took the bags of bread and said, gently, 'Come on, sweetheart, I'll take you home.'

Annie started as if she had used some unexpected or evocative word; when her next question was answered, Crystal understood why. She asked where she lived and the child replied, 'London'.

'You're an evacuee, are you? So am I.' Crystal lifted her into the trap. 'But I meant, of course, where are you living now?' Had been living for some time, presumably; the child spoke in the local accent, a musical lilt.

'Owen's farm. Up th'lane.' She pointed; they were almost upon it. A stand for milk churns and a narrow opening beyond it, so narrow and steep that Crystal had difficulty turning the trap. It was like going into an underground tunnel: hedges so ragged and high that branches laced over their heads. The lane was deeply scored by tractor wheels with a spine of grass down the centre: the trap lurched from side to side. Crystal said, 'Do you like living in the country?'

The child shook her head. Crystal thought, poor little soul! She had heard so many stories in the village about the misfortunes of foster parents, dirty urchins from the slums with lousy heads, unused to proper beds or even to sitting at tables for meals, but *her* heart had bled for the children! She said, 'I know how you feel, it's all so different from London. I feel a bit lost myself sometimes. All those cows instead of people and the birds waking one up in the morning!' She laughed her pretty laugh. 'Still, there are nice things, too. I expect you like collecting eggs, don't you? Lovely and warm from the nest?'

No answer. She sat, legs dangling in those absurdly loose Wellingtons, face averted. Not an immediately attractive child, Crystal thought – almost certainly poor

Farmer Owen and his wife would have a few depressing tales to tell! She said, reproachfully, 'I know when *I* was a little girl, I would have loved to live on a farm!'

Possibly not on this one though, she admitted when it came into view. The hedges here had been cut down, savagely hacked almost to ground level, and apart from a few wind-flattened trees there was no other vegetation to soften the bleakness of its position on the side of the hill. It was bleak architecturally, too: a brick box with ill-kept outbuildings and a yard deep in mud. No sign of life, not even a light in the window this dull evening, but as Crystal checked the pony a man emerged from the wainshed and came towards the gate. He was tall for a Welshman, and, as far as she could see in the half-light, extremely good looking, if in a rather unusual way – his forehead and nose being set at the same angle, so that they seemed to flow into each other without any break. This bone formation gave him a high, proud look. Like an Aztec, Crystal thought – and then knew she had the wrong word: she had been thinking of the figures on Etruscan vases, of helmeted men with spears. But she thought of him as the Aztec from then on. It seemed to express something about him.

As he approached the gate, Annie seized the carrier bags and tumbled out of the trap, leaving the door swinging. Not even a glance at Crystal – she slipped through a gap between the gate and the butchered hedge and ran towards the house. The man said, to Crystal, 'What's she been up to?'

His tone suggested that it was Crystal who had been up to something. Or at least had no business here. He stood waiting, head thrust forward, thumbs thrust into the waist band of his trousers. For a moment she felt a flurry of fear – his oddly menacing stance, the gathering dusk, the lonely dilapidation of the place – but wholesome indignation dispersed it. She had only wanted to help, gone out of her way, and no one had thanked her; the child had not even looked back. She said, 'I gave her a lift from the shop, it's such nasty weather. Would you please open the gate, I want to turn the trap.'

He stood for perhaps half a minute, grinning broadly, as if something about her request (her crisp, middle-class tone of command, perhaps) had amused him. When he finally unhitched the gate, she had begun to feel flustered. There was not enough room to turn in the yard, and when she tried to back the pony began to dance, throwing his head up and down. The man came forward, taking his time. He said, 'Gently now, pretty,' and laughed at Crystal over the pony's arched neck.

She smiled her thanks, at ease now as she was always at ease with men when they did things for her, and then, seeing the appraisal in his eyes, felt a familiar excitement stirring. Sex for her was almost entirely an indulgence of the mind; bed with Basil (there had been no one else) had never come up to the expectations aroused by her fantasies which were centred, not on rape, exactly, but on the threat of it, a titillating, romantic terror. Sometimes her father would figure in these imagined scenes – touching her breast with a trembling hand and turning away with a sigh – but since some inward censor would not allow him to play a more violent role, her partner was usually some new acquaintance, a comparative stranger. He did not need to make overtures in reality; since Crystal knew herself to be desirable, she believed all men desired her, and, when her mood was right, could see in the simplest act of courtesy, a dark, unspoken passion. She did not immediately suppose, because this farmer had quietened her pony and turned the trap that he wished to leap upon her and tear her clothes, but later that evening he began to figure in her dreams. Living with her mother she had grown short of what she thought of as 'candidates'. The local farmers all seemed cast in the same unexciting mould, brick-faced, bow-legged, and Owen was the first man she had seen for months who had moved her sexually: something about him, his pointed teeth, his curious, light eyes, had provided the right element of fear.

Annie-May was afraid of him too, though less pleasantly. He had never struck her, or no more than a casual cuff, but she kept out of his way as his father's old dog did (creeping away from the fire when his step was heard at the door) and for much the same reason: they both knew he hated them, they had been his father's pets and he had hated his father.

Annie-May was seven years old, nearly eight. She could remember 'Granpa' Owen more clearly than she remembered her mother who had gone away a long time ago (back to London, Granpa had said) and he had only died last summer: she had found him lying in the stackyard with flies on his face and his old dog shivering beside him.

She had not been afraid of Uncle Owen then. He and Ant'Owen did what Granpa told them, and she was his 'little maid'. She ran to find Uncle Owen in the cowshed (Ant'Owen was no use, she was silly) and he came stumbling up the yard with his mouth open.

He took no notice of her. She ran to the dairy and hid there for a long time, singing under her breath to comfort herself until she heard the dog whining outside and opened the door. She looked in the stackyard but Granpa was gone; she went indoors with the old dog pressed close to her legs and they were having tea as if nothing had happened. Uncle Owen said, 'Leave that bloody dog outside,' and then, 'What are you snivelling for?'

She said, 'Granpa's dead,' although she was really crying because of the way he had spoken to Prince, who was always allowed in, by the fire, and he said, 'Not your bloody granpa.'

He was a frustrated man, full of grudges. He was twenty-seven years old and had been treated like a serf; all his life he had never had money of his own in his pocket.

His father had been a tyrant who despised his children, the girl because she was simple, and Owen because he had fathered her baby and several others in the locality. Old Owen paid three paternity orders monthly, signing the cheques in his son's presence and saying, 'There's your wages, boy.' When Owen asked to be made a partner, his father said, 'Silly young fool, can't control your prick, how d'you expect to manage a farm?'

Owen stayed because the place would be his one day. It wasn't much, but it was better than nothing. He clamped down his resentment when his father was alive: when he died it broke loose with no focus except the dog, Prince, and the child the old man had been fond of.

He could have got rid of Annie. That his father had chosen to keep her when the mother walked out was no business of his. But to say that is to assume a world of rational behaviour which the Owens did not inhabit. Besides, though idleness and inertia also played their part, his main reason was simple: although Annie-May was only seven she was more use about the house than his half-sister.

For several weeks after his father's funeral, he did not lay a finger on her.

Annie-May wet her bed. She woke in the night with a pool beneath her and pulled the pillow on top to soak it up. In the morning it was dry but smelly. She left the blankets thrown back to get rid of the smell and Ant'Owen came in and saw what she'd done. She must have told Uncle Owen: when he came in for his tea he dragged her upstairs and rubbed her face up and down on the stiff, fusty-smelling sheet. Then he hit her hard, one side of her face then the other, and said she was to take her tea in the yard, if she sat at the table it would put him off his food. Ant'Owen gave her a slice of cold bacon and she went outside with it, but it was mostly fat and she threw it away.

The bed smelled horrible. She covered the sheet with the blanket and put some of her clothes on top but she could still smell it. She had bad dreams and when she woke the blanket was wet and her clothes, too. It was raining, she hung them out of the window to wash them clean and take the smell away, and, later in the day, crept up and put them back on the bed. They smelled wet and furry but not of the other thing.

Uncle Owen wouldn't let her eat with them. She said she was hungry and Ant'Owen giggled. She gave her some bread and said, 'Don't let him catch you.' She was frightened of Uncle Owen, too; he slapped her round the face when his dinner was burned and threw the ruined saucepan out in the yard. Annie-May took it into the wainshed and cleaned it out with her fingers. It was nasty but she was so hungry.

She was hungry all the time. She woke in the night and crept down in the dark. There was food on the table, bread and dripping. She crammed it into her mouth so fast that it stuck in her throat and made her gag. She was so afraid Uncle Owen was watching from the shadows.

He watched her all the time. If she was in his way he punched her, as he kicked the old dog when he got under his feet, which he couldn't help doing; he was going blind, poor old Prince. Annie hid from him when she could, listened for his stamp on the sacking outside the door, his step on the stair. She grew quick and sly. She began to stammer.

That made Ant'Owen laugh. She would make Annie try to say the words she found hardest and laugh and laugh till her face went red. Sometimes she would put food on a plate and say, 'Go on, say please,' and when Annie-May couldn't she would laugh and tip the food into the pail for the pigs. Most of the time, though, Ant'Owen wasn't too bad to her as long as she washed the dishes and kept the baby quiet and went down to the shop when she asked her.

She didn't like going to the shop, partly because of the stammer, and partly because Mrs Purvis would ask her questions like, 'Anything wrong, Annie-May?' that she didn't know how to answer. She always nodded because all that she knew to be wrong was that she couldn't stop wetting her bed; it was that made Uncle Owen so angry with her and she couldn't tell anyone that. It was so disgusting, *she* was disgusting; she smelled all the time. When the lady gave her a lift back from the shop, she was horribly afraid she would smell her and be disgusted, too. So she sat as still as she could, tucking her hands between her legs and holding herself tight to stop the smell getting out from that part of her.

That was how she must have lost the ring, pulling her hands out from down there, suddenly, in fright, when she saw Uncle Owen. It was a pretty, green ring Granpa Owen had bought her a long time ago and it had fitted her then because her hands had been fatter, but lately it had got loose on her finger. When she found she had lost it, she went to the orchard at the back of the farmhouse to cry. She ate the apple Mrs Purvis had given her and then some of the apples that had fallen from the trees. They were unripe and maggoty, but she ate them for comfort.

They gave her a pain. Late that night she woke with it and drew her legs up. The pain ebbed and then returned, paralysing her. She began to gasp and moan, not so much because of the pain, but because she knew what was going to happen.

The next time Crystal went to fetch the trap, the farmer's young son was waiting for her. Unlike many of her imagined conquests, he really was in love: a secret, burning, adolescent passion, sweating palms and foolish grins. 'You lost something?' he said, scarlet with pleasure because he had found it for her, and smiling idiotically. He put the ring in her hand, a chip of green glass in a metal setting.

Crystal was going to hand it back, laughing; then she guessed whom it belonged to. The child must have dropped it when they were jolting along in the trap. She said, 'It's not mine, but I think I know whose it is, a little girl I made friends with. It's not worth anything, you know, but I expect she'll be thrilled to have it back. Children do value their little treasures!'

A sweet memory came into her head of herself on her wedding day, wearing under her high-necked dress, not the pearls Basil had given her, but a blue, bead necklace her father had won for her once, shooting wooden ducks in a fun fair. She had told him she was wearing it, in the car on the way to the church, and his eyes had filled with tears. He had won a toy rabbit for her at that same fair, he reminded her, but she had forgotten that. It was such a long time ago, she had been only nine years old. 'Ah, you were my girl then,' he said, so sadly that it made her cry a little. Poor Daddy, she was leaving him for another man – he would think about her and Basil tonight! Thinking of how he must feel about *that* made her tremble with excitement. She pressed his hand and he returned the pressure; they sat, holding hands all the way to the church. Like a pair of lost children!

He had never thought Basil good enough for her. And though she and Basil had laughed over this, she could not help feeling, secretly, that Basil really was lucky. She was prettier than anyone else she knew: sometimes, after a party, she would gaze and gaze into her mirror, enchanted by her flushed skin and laughing eyes. She had once read *War and Peace* (leaving out the boring campaign sections) and for some time afterwards thought of herself as the young Natasha, innocently wanton, deliciously gay. Everyone liked her: her hairdresser and her dressmaker were always complimenting her on how young she looked, how well she had kept her beautiful figure. If some of the women she knew were more reserved, it was only jealousy on their part. Which was her mother's trouble, of course. It might seem incredible that an old woman could be jealous of her only daughter and it had been a long time before Crystal could bear to face up to it, but once she had done, she had to admit it was the only explanation of her mother's critical attitude. Watching Crystal, her mother must be constantly reminded of all she had missed in life; understanding this, Crystal told herself she must ignore the occasional tart remark, even what seemed, sometimes, deliberate unkindness.

This wasn't always easy. Take the day she found Annie's ring, for example. She came home in the late morning and found Will Davies sitting with her mother. He had an almost full glass of wine in his hand but as soon as Crystal came in, he drained it down and said he must go. She saw him out, and, watching him walk down the path, thought that he stooped more than usual. She closed the door, smiled at her mother, and said, pityingly, 'Poor old man.'

Her mother stared. 'Why do you always call people poor and old? Do you really feel so very young and rich?'

The remark had a clipped, stagey contempt as if it had been long rehearsed. It was this, the thought that her mother had been nursing some cruel grudge against her, rather than what she actually said, that made Crystal gasp. She said, 'I suppose I do. Is that wrong?'

Her mother did not answer for a minute. When she did, she spoke in a mumbly, old woman's voice. 'No, of course not. Only – only it makes you vulnerable.'

She was ashamed of herself, Crystal saw. She said, 'Wot, me?' in a comic, cockney voice and laughed to show that she knew her mother had not really meant to hurt her.

But her mother didn't even smile. Her discomfiture must have gone too deep. She stood up, slowly and stiffly, said that the postman had been, there was a letter from Basil behind the clock, and left the room.

Crystal heard her slow footsteps climbing the stairs.

Her mother rarely went to her room in the daytime now; it cost her too much effort. Crystal thought, *poor old soul* – and checked herself. Had she been guilty of patronage? She had not meant any harm, she had felt nothing for Will Davies but kindly pity (which was generous of her, really, considering the curt, dismissive way he often treated her) but when you were old that might be hard to bear. Youth gone, hope and love, nothing left but pain and aching legs – bad enough, without being reminded of it! Crystal's eyes brimmed. She had been at fault, she could see; she would do her best to make amends. Cook something special for lunch and talk cheerfully as if nothing had happened. Perhaps Basil would have something to say that might interest her mother, help to build a bridge between them . . .

But there was nothing in Basil's letter that she could possibly repeat. Crystal had to read it twice before she understood the contents, and even then she did not really take them in. It wasn't true, it was some cruel joke. She left the letter lying on the table and walked in the garden to recover from the shock it had given her. The blood, drumming in her ears, made her feel giddy; she leaned on the gate and forced herself to breathe slowly and regularly. Of course, it must be a joke! Not of Basil's, Basil loved her, but some spiteful stranger! Had it, in fact, been Basil's *writing*? She had read the letter so quickly. Perhaps it had not even been addressed to her but written by someone else to some other woman and delivered in error? That she had not noticed any discrepancy could be explained by her state of confusion when she had opened it: she had been more distressed by her mother's unexpected attack than she had been prepared to admit. She hurried back into the house with a bright, unnatural smile on her face, but without picking the letter up from the table, she could read the beginning of it. *My dear Crystal* . . .

She was Basil's dear Crystal. He made a great point of

that. His affection for her was unchanged; all that had happened was, he had discovered he was capable of feeling more. He didn't mean sex, he had had his affairs (and while he was on the subject, wanted to thank her for never reproaching him) but this was the real thing. What he felt for his A.T.S. girl was something quite different from anything he had felt before. He could not envisage life without her and felt that it would be unfair to Crystal to try. Since he knew now that he could not offer her anything worth having, the honourable course was to leave while she was still young enough to find happiness, as he had done . . .

And so on. Crystal began to see that there was some slight foundation for her idiotic delusion in the garden: this letter might really have been written by some total stranger. It was so carefully thought out, so worked over, that it had the air of a specimen in some quaint, Victorian manual, *Letters For Divers Occasions*. On leaving your wife for your True Love, the right note to strike was pompous righteousness. Thinking this she laughed and threw the pages onto the fire; when the edges began to brown and curl she had an impulse to snatch them out and read the letter again but, as she stretched down her hand, the paper flared.

It blazed like her anger. Looking at herself in the mirror above the fireplace, she saw that her eyes appeared becomingly dark in her pale face. They were also bright and dry. Quite tearless.

She felt no desire to cry. She was too bitterly angry. Not because Basil had made a fool of her but because she had allowed him too. She had been so blind, so naïve – she saw herself, suddenly, beaming complacently down the years, and the vision humiliated her. What a ridiculous spectacle she had made! Had made *of herself* – she wouldn't blame Basil. To blame him would be to put herself in the weaker position and she refused to do that. Oh, she would be proud and obstinate! She had suffered a terrible insult:

the only way to respond was to put on the best performance she could manage.

Giles, coming down to the cottage ten days later on a
forty-eight hour leave, was impressed by it at first. He had
come straight from seeing his father, who was also on
leave and in London with his mistress, a woman of thirty
with a big nose and sweet, spaniel eyes. The three of them
had dined together. Basil had been anxious and adoring
and sweating profusely and Giles had been slightly disgusted: it seemed undignified, at his father's age, to be so
much in love.

He thought his mother came out of the situation better.
He had been nervous on the train, expecting martyred
looks, hysterical scenes, and was grateful to find her calmly
smiling at the station. She said nothing about his father in
the taxi, nor during the early part of the evening. Instead,
Giles talked about what he was doing, but, although she
seemed to listen, her expression was stiff and unnatural
and after a while he began to feel he had nothing much to
tell, that his Army life, which seemed so full to him, was
really rather boring. And, when this feeling had overcome
and silenced him and she asked questions about things he
had already told her, he knew she had not been listening at
all.

But when his grandmother went to bed she seemed to
relax, sat girlishly at his feet and told him to turn out the
lamp: it was cosier, she said, in the firelight. It was, in fact,
very pleasant in the shadowed, warm room; watching the
gleam of his mother's hair, close to his knee, he wished he
had brought his current girl friend with him. It would be
romantic to make love on the hearth in front of the leaping,
log fire. Thinking of it, he sighed, shifted restlessly in his
chair and reminded himself that even if he had brought her,
they couldn't have done it, not with his mother there.
Besides, the whole point of coming to the cottage was to

comfort her. That was what his father had said when he wrote and asked him to go. 'You might be able to comfort your mother.'

Not that she seemed to need it. She talked lightly, almost gaily. She warned him to say nothing to his grandmother. 'I'm afraid she'll be terribly shocked by Basil's behaviour and I suppose it's cowardly of me, but I feel the one thing I can't bear, at the moment, is to hear him abused!' She said, 'Your poor father!' with a small, rueful smile.

Giles thought, the old girl's taking it well. (She had not aged perceptibly: *old girl* only measured the change in his attitude towards her.) But later, he was chilled. She could not feel as little as she pretended; surely at major crises in one's life it was more important to behave with truth than with dignity? Her composure made her appear cold and shallow; he began to feel, in bed that night, and increasingly the following day, that he would have respected her more if she had admitted she was suffering, had wept, railed against his father. He was aware that he was condemning her for behaving in a way that had been a relief to him and this finally shamed him: standing on the station platform at the end of his leave, he hugged her awkwardly and said, 'Don't be too brave about it, Mum, don't bottle it up, you've every right to be bitter! After all, he's had the best years of your life, as they say!'

He felt this was magnanimous. There was still time for her to make a scene; the train was not due for ten minutes. But all she said was, 'Please don't call me *Mum*! You make me feel like a charwoman in a flowered apron and a badly fitted corset!'

It irritated him. He had offered her his shoulder to weep on, been prepared to endure embarrassment if it would ease her, and all she could do was to sneer at charwomen! Oh, not sneer, perhaps; she had spoken too unthinkingly. And that was, in a way, even worse: her remark was typical of a class attitude that now seemed to Giles quite tasteless.

Didn't she know the world had changed? Giles, who thought he knew it had, said coldly, 'Well, you are my mother, aren't you? Not my girl friend. And it's no moral virtue of yours that you've never had to work for your living!'

Her astounded expression goaded him. She didn't even see what she had done wrong! 'I mean, to say something like that – don't you *see* how frightful it is? I mean, I've got a friend whose mother's a charwoman – not now, she's working in munitions now – but she was before the war.' This was a lie, or partly a lie: the friend's mother had kept a sweetshop before it was bombed in the blitz, but she was the first working woman Giles had known socially. Thinking of her, and knowing he was adapting the truth to suit his case, increased both his guilt and indignation. He went on, 'She's a marvellous woman, she's worked hard all her life, not *wasted* it, keeping her figure and having her hair done, and I admire her for it!'

She said helplessly, 'Giles, darling . . .' He was being preposterous, of course, but he had hurt her. She smiled at him brightly and bravely to show he had not, and this alienated him further. He said, in a cold voice, 'Oh, I'm *sorry*. I didn't mean to be beastly.'

She ignored his tone – it was only awkwardness. The poor boy was so upset by what Basil had done; he could think of no way to express his unhappiness and was lashing out wildly at the one person he wanted to comfort! She said, 'Of course you didn't, my darling. Your old "Mum" isn't cross. Now let's kiss and be friends.' He hesitated, then bent his head. She held his face between her small, soft hands, and kissed him several times on the mouth. She said, 'You mustn't worry about me, you old silly billy. It's not such a terrible situation, you know!'

But it was terrible to her. The worst part was the shame. When the train had gone, one thing Giles had said went on ringing in her head like a knell. That phrase, *The best years of your life*. Of course he had meant it as a joke, but did he really think her old? A passed-over, middle-aged woman? She had refrained from asking him how old Basil's mistress was. It was too degrading. But her mother would want to know when she told her. And she would have to tell her some time, she couldn't pretend for ever. But she shrank from it. It seemed that once her mother knew, she would be quite defenceless, exposed. She had always resented her for being so happy, so pleased with her life – *So you think you're so young and rich?* – had always criticized her for taking care how she looked. An obsession, she had once called it. Crystal had been fixing her hair a new way; she had asked her mother if she liked it and her mother had said she hadn't noticed any difference, she didn't share Crystal's obsession with personal appearances. Crystal had answered, laughing, 'It's not an obsession, darling. Basil likes me to look pretty and I like to please my husband.'

Hearing this innocent, foolish sentence echo in her mind, made Crystal tremble and gasp. Oh, how her mother would crow! She thought, *I can't bear it, I want to die . . .*

She sat, bolt upright, in the back of the taxi. When they reached the bottom of the lane, she paid the driver and walked slowly homeward in the cold, blue dusk. She stopped at an open gate and went a few steps into the field. She was shivering from head to foot; she was so imprisoned, so knotted up with rage that it seemed that only some violent act could release her. If the grass had not been so wet, she would have thrown herself down, dug her fingers into the earth. She pictured herself doing that and it eased her a little. Then she saw herself going into a public house and picking up the first soldier who smiled at her, having a drink with him, then going into a field like this one and lying passive beneath him while he tore off her clothes. She gave him Farmer Owen's Aztec face.

She went to the farm a week later. It looked less desolate on this second visit. There was no one about, not even a dog to bark, but there was a dim light in a downstairs window. The gate was open and she led the pony into the yard and tethered him. It was a cold, clear, late afternoon and the muddy ground was hardening into frosty ridges that crackled under her feet. She knocked on the door with her knuckles and after a minute it opened. A woman stood there, holding a Tilly lamp. She was quite young but very pale and somehow dry-looking: there was no shine to her hair or her eyes or her skin. She stared at Crystal. Crystal said, 'Good evening, Mrs Owen. My name is Golightly. I brought your little evacuee home the other day and she left something in the trap.' She waited. Mrs Owen said nothing. Crystal spoke more loudly. 'May I give it to her? Can I see Annie?'

The woman said, 'Tom . . .' She turned and scuttled away. Crystal followed her, through an outer kitchen into the main one. The man sat by the range fire, stockinged feet stretched out. The woman said, 'Tom, she wants Annie,' and he looked up. Not at Crystal, at his wife; something seemed to pass between them. Mrs Owen set the lamp on the table. It was the only light and it was inadequate in the big room; the ceiling and the corners remained in shadow. What was revealed was very plain and poor: a scrubbed table, a high-backed settle on which the man sat, one rug on the flagged floor. Not even a rug, an old dog: as Crystal came into the room it lifted its flat head, weaving it round like a snake. Crystal was startled by this strange motion until she saw its blind, milky eyes. She said, 'It's all right, old chap,' and Owen looked at her then. He said, 'What d'you want Annie for?'

It was absurd how suspiciöus he sounded. Shyness made him rough, probably. Crystal smiled graciously, conscious of how she must look to him, of the difference between her and his sad, pale wife.

44

Crystal said, 'It's nothing much. I found her ring. It must have slipped off her finger.'

'She's in bed,' Mrs Owen said. 'Annie's in bed.' She didn't look at Crystal. She was rubbing her hands up and down the front of her apron and watching her husband.

'Oh dear, is she ill?' Crystal said. Neither of them answered her. 'I mean, it can't be much after five o'clock.'

'We're not town people,' the man said. 'We settle in early.'

He laughed in an excited, boyish way. He looked so much younger than his wife, Crystal thought; country women seemed to fade so quickly. And this one looked so beaten down – standing there with her mouth hanging open. Clearly there was unlikely to be any social offer from her! Perhaps she should say she would like a cup of tea. They might be pleased if she suggested it; perhaps they felt she was too stuck-up, too *posh*, to sit down on the settle and drink tea with them. Though she didn't really want to. Not from fear of boredom – why, she could make friends with anyone! – but because of an odd uneasiness she couldn't place. As if she had suddenly found herself in a strange country where she didn't know the customs or the language. Perhaps it was the old dog, she thought. Few of the farmers she knew allowed dogs in the house, and none of them would keep an animal in such a state of decrepitude: blind, with livid patches of bald, scaly skin on its back. It made her own skin creep to look at it.

'Well, then,' she said, beaming impartially at husband and wife. 'If you'll just give it to her.'

She put the ring on the table among the dirty crockery. Neither of them offered to show her out. She had to stumble through the outer kitchen (smelling of sour milk and old rags) in the pitch dark. So dark that by contrast it still seemed day outside; then she saw it was the moon that had risen, full and clear and bright above a bare, black tree. The pony was standing, patient head drooping; she patted his nose, unhitched the rein from the post and began to back the trap.

Something moved behind her, in the wainshed. A dog, or a cat? She turned and saw the child watching her. She said, 'Hallo, Annie,' but the little girl flinched as if from a blow, lifting one shoulder, and ran towards the back of the shed. 'Funny little thing,' Crystal said, aloud. She hesitated; then followed her. The shed was high and long, full of farm equipment. Crystal looked behind the tractor, under a cart, and then saw the loose box at the far end. It was dark inside, the moonlight did not reach here, but Crystal thought she heard breathing, the rustle of straw. She laughed softly and said, 'Come out, Annie, what are you hiding for?' but the child didn't speak. Perhaps she wasn't there after all, only a rat scuffling. Crystal said, 'Annie?'

No answer. She sighed, opened her handbag, found matches. The yellow flare revealed the child crouching on an old mattress in a corner of the loose box, wide, wild eyes staring. Like a trapped little animal, Crystal thought, a dog in a kennel – there was a pile of old sacks beside the mattress, a tin bowl with what looked like food in it . . .

The match burned her finger. She dropped it, stamped it out under her foot. In the blackness that followed what she had seen seemed improbable: she could almost believe she had not seen it. She said, in a carefully bright voice, 'Why Annie, what are you doing here? I thought you were supposed to be in bed.' And then, more softly – a conspirator's whisper – 'It's all right, silly one, I won't tell.'

Won't tell what?

'Leave her alone,' the man said, behind her.

She turned. He was standing between her and the moon, a hulking, black shadow. She was alarmed for a minute, then indignation restored her. How dare he creep up on her!

She said, 'What's she doing there? In that *stable*?' And

began to laugh, partly from nervousness and partly because, as she put the question, she saw there must be some perfectly reasonable answer. The child had been put to bed (been naughty, perhaps) and had slipped out without anyone hearing and run to her hidey-hole, her private place . . .

But Owen said, 'She shits the bed. You can't ha' that in a house, can you now?'

He sounded calm, almost amused. Crystal stammered, 'B-but you can't. I mean it's m-monstrous. It's . . .'

'None of your affair, is it?' Owen finished for her. He moved forward a pace or two. She could smell him, sweat or dirty clothes, perhaps both; a sharp, leeky smell.

He was close enough to touch her. He kept his hands hitched in his trouser belt and grinned. She could see his teeth shining. He said, 'Come on, now. You're a fine, smart 'oman, you don't want to worry your head over a dirty little cunt like that.'

Crystal said, 'How dare you use that word to me!' The outrage made her tremble; her legs felt weak.

He laughed aloud. 'Ah, come on,' he said, softly and coaxingly as he might have spoken to a nervous horse but with an undertone of cheerful contempt that she guessed he would only have used to a woman, 'you know what it is, don't you, you know what it's for?' He laughed again, confidently, and her own rising excitement frightened her.

She shouted, 'Don't you dare touch me.'

The child began to whimper. The man swore and pushed Crystal aside. He went into the loose box. The child cried out, a short, cut-off scream, then there was a crash as something – not the child, Crystal thought, oh God, not the child – was hurled against the wooden partition. But perhaps it was only that the man had stumbled against it in the dark because almost at once Annie ran out, blundering into her. Crystal caught her shoulders to stop her falling and the child looked up, into her face. 'Please Miss,' she whispered. 'Oh, please . . .'

The little, hoarse, imploring voice steadied Crystal. She had not been physically afraid (she could not believe this man would dare to harm her) but she had been irresolute: nothing in her life had prepared her for a situation like this. But now, suddenly, it all seemed quite straightforward. She said, 'All right, Annie, it's all right. Go and get in the trap.'

The man lurched out of the stall. He made a grab at the child but Crystal pushed her behind her. She said, 'Really, this is *disgraceful*.'

Something – perhaps the irrelevance of this shrill, indignant comment – checked him briefly, long enough for Crystal to seize Annie's arm and run for the trap. Or perhaps he did not understand that she meant to take the child with her: it was not until they were both safely aboard, Annie huddled on the floor and Crystal standing, holding the reins, that he appeared at the pony's head, seizing the bridle and cursing in a way that excited and terrified her. If excitement was uppermost, it was largely because the moon gave the scene such a dream or film-like quality, making everything darkly shadowed or hoarily silver. Then the pony reared, the trap bucketed crazily, and anger drove out everything else. She grabbed the whip from its stand and lashed at him, missing him the first time but flicking his face the second. He reeled back, vanished briefly, and then, as she turned the trap out through the gate, appeared at the side, wrenching the door open. Crystal dragged on the left rein and the pony danced sideways, bringing the trap swinging round so that he was caught between it and the gatepost. She heard him cry out, knew what she had done, what she had meant to do, and didn't care; when she looked back and saw him, staggering up from the ground, she felt only a pure, fierce exultation. She whipped up the pony and careered down the lane like a charioteer.

She didn't slow down till she reached the main road.

When she did, she found she was trembling so much she couldn't stand any longer. She sank on to the seat, letting the reins lie loose on the pony's sweating back, and said, 'Safe now! Up you get, duckie.'

The little girl stood up slowly, staggering with the slow, rocking movement of the trap. Dark, fathomless eyes fixed on Crystal; it was as much to escape that unblinking stare as to comfort the child that she pulled her down beside her and held her, lightly encircled in her arm. She said cheerfully, 'Well, that was a fine old bit of excitement, wasn't it?' It seemed a fatuous remark as she made it, but what else could she say? What the child must have gone through in that place was unthinkable. She could not bear to think about it.

She was not the only one whose sensibilities were tender. Will Davies, examining Annie and finding nothing wrong except a mild degree of malnutrition and a bit of gastritis, found the situation painful. Though no blame attached to him, of course. He had seen old Owen in the town just before he died and been told Mrs Gates had left. Since the child was not mentioned it was natural to assume she had gone with her mother.

No blame, in fact, could be made to stick on anyone's door. The Owens had kept Annie out of kindness, most people would say. Maybe they had even done their best. If their best was inadequate, what point would there be in bringing it home to a poor half-wit who was bound to be charged with her brother? Even he was probably more ignorant than wicked, Crystal decided. If to see the Owens in this kindly light was perhaps a grotesquely charitable effort, it seemed to Crystal tidier. After all, a police action for cruelty was not really feasible: her evidence alone might not be enough and it seemed a fearful thing to question Annie. Crystal said, '*I* can't bear to think about it, no child should be made to!' She was in a high-flown, exalted mood. She insisted on taking responsibility for Annie, at least while the family was traced.

'Are you sure you can manage?' her mother asked, after the first, dreadful week. The child was filthy in her habits, wetting the bed, defecating in the corner of her bedroom, shy and wild as an alley cat. She would not eat at the table but grabbed food from her plate and ran into the garden. Amy Haines was afraid of her. She was frightened by the dark, empty look in the child's eyes and by her sudden, unpredictable movements: the old woman would come into a room and Annie would dart past her, out of some hiding place, almost knocking her over. Amy was afraid of falling: coming down the stairs was a nightmare. She could not tell Crystal, could not be so selfish, but she felt too old, too tired, to live with this small, wolfish animal. 'Suppose they can't find her mother?' she said to her daughter.

'Let's cross that bridge when we come to it,' Crystal said. 'If she doesn't turn up, if no one does – and let's face it, she's not the only evacuee whose people have vanished – I can hardly abandon her, can I?'

'Basil may have something to say about that.' Amy saw a faint hope here.

'Basil doesn't really come into it. You may as well know, Mother. I've decided to leave him.' Crystal smiled. 'Or not go back to him, rather.'

Amy was shocked by the way she said this. So cold and smiling. 'But why? I thought you were happy. Basil adores you . . .' And when Crystal shrugged her shoulders, she added, 'Poor Basil . . .'

'Why poor?' Crystal said. It amused her to get a bit of her own back. 'D'you think he'll lose so much, losing me?'

Amy began to cry. For herself, not for Crystal's marriage. She was ashamed of her weakness but she couldn't help it. Through her tears, she saw that Annie had come into the room and was watching her. No expression on her face apart from a kind of cold watchfulness. No child should look like that, Amy thought, and felt a strange uprush of fear. Was it just for her old, brittle bones? She dabbed her eyes and said, 'Well I hope you know what you're doing.'

Crystal's motives were not obscure. She had lost her role in life and seized on a new one. The more exacting the task, the better it would compensate for her sense of outrage and failure.

She was marvellous with the child; no less so because that was how she saw her behaviour. To act in a way that would be seen to be admirable had become the main spring of her life. She had not undergone any great conversion, not 'changed', merely altered her course. The stage might be a different one, even the audience – Will Davies, her mother, the welfare authorities instead of her hairdresser – but the pleasure of applause remained the same. And, in a way, it was a part that suited her better: she had a great deal of energy, a capacity for endurance that had lain unused until now. Single-mindedness, too: she understood that Annie's presence was hard on her mother, and why, but refused to admit it. 'I'm afraid she's a little bit jealous,' she said to Will Davies. 'I suppose it's natural, poor old soul, she's had all my attention so long, she can't bear to share it.'

Will Davies knew that this explanation was simply one that suited her, but not how to reply. He didn't like Crystal any better than he had ever done, still found her smooth self-confidence repellent, but he had to admire her for what she had taken on. And he was unsure how Amy did feel. Not jealous, she hadn't a jealous bone in her body, but she did seem to him to have grown suddenly, almost wilfully, very old. Even petulant. He asked her if having the child in the house worried her and she snapped, 'No, of course not. But to my mind, Crystal has taken an asp to her bosom. It'll bite her if she don't watch out.' It was unlike Amy, that spiteful remark. But it explained why she stayed in her room. She was an old woman, sulking.

He said, to Crystal, 'Be patient with her.'

'I am patient,' Crystal said.

Patience was necessary to success and she did not intend to fail. A month, and the little girl was clean in the day, even, occasionally, dry at night, and ate her meals properly. Another, and she hardly stammered at all and had begun to laugh, although she sometimes stopped abruptly as if the sound astonished or alarmed her. Like a baby donkey, Crystal thought, surprised by its first bray. Six months, and she seemed, outwardly, a happy, normal child. Only the watchful look remained.

At his grandmother's funeral, Giles was startled by it. Standing in the front pew of the church with Crystal, he looked round for some reason during the service and met Annie's eyes, coldly glaring. And later, at tea, dutifully filling cups and passing plates, he was conscious of the child, standing close to his mother's chair and watching him. It made him uncomfortable. 'She's only jealous, darling,' Crystal said when he mentioned it. 'She doesn't want to share me! It's rather touching.'

He wondered if she were really touched or if it simply fed her vanity. It would irritate *him*, he thought, that silent, clinging shadow. Oh, there was nothing to put a finger on, she did what she was told, fetched this, fetched that, went to bed the moment she was told, but with a kind of sullen, automatic obedience, like a prisoner with no will of her own. Or as if obedience were not natural to her. 'She's not *sullen*,' Crystal said. 'You should see her smile! Of course she's a bit quiet, what do you expect? She's upset by Gran's death, they were tremendous friends, you know, and she *found* her, half in and half out of bed! A cruel shock for the child after all she's had to bear! But she's been very

sweet, such a comfort to me. Almost motherly, really!'
Crystal laughed; she and Giles were sitting by the fire
with a bottle of whisky he had managed to buy and she was
a little drunk. 'That sounds queer but it's true. The day
Mother died, I was sitting here, in the chair, feeling – well,
as you can *imagine*, no husband to turn to, you miles away –
and she came up and put her little arms round me. She
didn't say anything, just held me close and tight, almost as
if I were the child and she were my mother! She's very
sensitive to one's needs which is surprising, really, after all
she's been through. I mean, you'd have expected her to be
blunted. But she can't do enough to please . . .'

To Giles, who was also slightly drunk, these words had
an ominous ring. He said, 'Poor child, I suppose she has to.'

'What do you mean?'

'What I said.'

Crystal put her glass down. Her eyes shone. 'Do you
mean that my affection for her – or at least, whether I keep
her or not – is dependent on *her* good behaviour?'

'Isn't it?' Giles leaned back in his chair, smiling, stroking
his newly grown moustache with the stem of his pipe and
feeling very old and cynical.

'Of course not.'

'*She* must think it is, mustn't she?'

'Oh, Giles!'

She sat stiff in her chair, cheeks ruddy with whisky and
anger. Giles saw they were about to quarrel and felt his
heart thump. But the prospect exhilarated him, too. He had
provoked it: he was sufficiently like his mother to know
what would get under her skin. She honestly wished to
behave well but she liked her good behaviour not only to
be seen and appreciated but to be seen to be perfect. To
suggest that Annie might feel insecure in spite of her
efforts was to diminish them. Giles understood this because he shared the same strain of self-regard. He felt it to
be a failing in himself and it annoyed him in his mother.

He affected bewilderment. 'Why do you say, *oh Giles*, in that indignant way?'

'You know quite well, do you think I'm a fool? Oh, perhaps you do, you're not the only one, your grandmother always thought that! You were saying that all I've done for that poor child has been worthless!'

'I never said anything of the sort.'

'Then why are you smiling like that? In that smug, knowing way?'

'I'm sorry. I didn't know I was smiling.'

'How can you be so cruel, darling?' Tears brightened her eyes. 'I've tried so hard and it's not been easy with Mother ill these last weeks, I can tell you. Do you think it's all been for *my* benefit?'

'No . . .' He pulled a face and lit his pipe, watching her through the smoke as he puffed away. 'Though if you think that cap fits, you're quite welcome to wear it.'

'Oh don't be silly smart. Making points! Giles, this isn't like you!'

Which was really, of course, what this was about. Not about Annie, but because they were both disappointed. He was no longer her uncritically adoring son and both had lost something. Her loss might be more permanently painful but he was young and felt his acutely. He had loved her so much; loved her still, but she now seemed so ordinary! He felt let down and it made him judge her harshly.

They quarrelled for perhaps half an hour, not unenjoyably. Neither was sober, both had the kind of minds that are made nimble by anger and they enjoyed the exercise. When they went to bed, they kissed goodnight as friends.

Giles slept at once. When he woke he felt refreshed, wide awake, as if he had slept for hours but when he looked at his watch it was only just after midnight. Something had woken him. Drink, he thought, but he didn't feel drunk. He sighed, turned over, thumped his pillow, then listened.

Someone was moving about; he heard a board creak, the whine of a door hinge. His mother, he thought; hurt, unable to sleep. Mulling over some of his stupid remarks, probably! He muttered, 'Oh dear, oh dear, oh dear,' – a curious, old-maidish trick of his when remembering something embarrassing he had said or done. He sighed again, got out of bed and pulled his trousers on.

He went downstairs, braces dangling. The light was on in the kitchen. Annie stood by the table. He said, 'What are you doing?' though there was no need: there was the open tin, the child's mouth solid with funeral plum cake. He said, half-amused, half-grumbling, 'Do you know what the *time* is?' and she gulped and swallowed, staring at him with such terror and anguish that he was appalled. He said, 'Oh, for Heaven's sake,' and took a step towards her. She gasped and backed away, trembling.

Crystal called, from the stairs, 'I'm coming.' She came into the kitchen, fastening her dressing gown. She said, 'I heard her come down. All right, it's all *right*, Annie-duckie.' Crumbs mixed with spit were dribbling from the child's mouth; Crystal took a handkerchief from her pocket and wiped her face gently. She said, 'I thought you'd stopped this, silly one. I forgot your beddy-byes biscuit, was that the trouble?' The little girl leaned against her, hiding her face. Crystal said, 'And then Giles frightened you, did he? *Naughty* Giles! But he didn't mean to, you know, I expect you frightened him, really. I expect he thought you was burglars!' She spoke in the deliberate, cheery voice she usually employed to dismiss unpleasantness, and it irritated Giles: remembering the desperate look on the child's face, it seemed inadequate. Annie began to cry, pressing her face into Crystal's side. She went on weeping as Crystal led her upstairs, and for some time after her door was closed.

Giles was in bed and almost asleep again when his mother came in. She sat on the edge of his bed. He looked at her and saw for the first time that though she was still beautiful, she no longer looked younger than her age. This softened him and he smiled. She said, 'It's by way of being a precautionary measure on her part, this night foraging. The Owens starved her, you know.' She laughed, rather awkwardly.

Giles hadn't known. His mother had told him very little, only that Annie was an evacuee who had been badly treated in her billet and that they now knew her mother was dead. He said, 'How frightful,' not quite believing it.

Crystal said, 'Yes. The whole thing!' Again that queer, awkward laugh. 'But I suppose one mustn't exaggerate. She was neglected by *our* standards, no doubt about it, and she was obviously very unhappy, poor mite. But they were very limited people. I expect it was ignorance, really.'

'*Starving* her?' Giles said.

'Well. One says that. I don't imagine they ate like kings themselves! One mustn't blame people, Giles, that's something I've learned these last months. One must try to be generous, however indignant one feels. The greatest of these is charity!' She sighed and smiled. 'I don't feel any bitterness towards your father, you know. I meant to tell you that last night, but instead we had that silly quarrel. And all about nothing. I lay awake, thinking about it, after I went to bed, wondering what had gone wrong between us and trying *not* to feel hurt about some of the things you had said. And then, after a bit, I began to see why you'd said them and I wasn't hurt any more . . .' She touched his face and lowered her voice. 'Giles, darling, you're my dear, sweet son, nothing I do or feel for Annie can take away from what I feel for you. There's enough room in my heart for you both.'

Giles was silent. Guilt kept him silent. He wondered if she were still rather drunk. Her eyes had a glazed, solemn look. She picked up his hand and held it between both of hers. She said, 'We have to make a decision, Giles. I want it to be a joint decision, it would be unfair to you otherwise. Annie is my "evacuee" at the moment – I actually get twopence halfpenny a week from a benevolent government! But when all this business is over I suppose some other arrangement will have to be made. If I am to keep her.'

Giles was wondering why she hadn't said 'this *war*'. It was a word she hardly ever used, he realized, avoiding it the way other people avoided 'cancer' or 'shit' – something not to be mentioned in polite society.

Crystal said, 'You *must* say what you think, Giles. After all, you'll have to live with her too! There's room in the flat for the three of us, but it's not just a matter of space, is it?'

Giles had no intention of living with his mother after the war, but it seemed hardly the moment to say so. A picture of her, alone in the flat, rose up and reproached him. A child would be better company than a dog or a cat . . .

He said, 'Of course, it's a splendid idea! I've always wanted a sister!'

Crystal gave Annie a photograph of Giles in his uniform to keep in her bedroom. 'There you are! Your big brother!' Annie didn't really want it, staring at her with that fixed smile. Giles himself had frightened her, all men frightened her. But Crystal expected her to be pleased so she said, 'Thank you, Crystal.'

'Goodnight Crystal, goodnight Giles.' When Crystal had tucked her up in bed and kissed her goodnight, she gave her the picture to kiss. Annie disliked the feel of the cold glass on her lips. God bless Crystal and brother Giles and Doctor Davies. God bless me . . .

One night she said, 'And Granpa Owen.' She didn't know why she said it, the words just came out of her mouth. 'What made you think of him, suddenly?' Crystal asked, but she couldn't tell her.

Crystal had been fixing the black-out frame in the window. Summer was over and it was nearly winter again. She twitched the cotton curtains straight and came, smiling, towards the bed. She seemed very pleased about something.

'I tell you why, Annie-duckie! You're not frightened to think about that time any more! You were fond of Granpa Owen, you want to put him in your prayers, but you couldn't do it before because thinking about him made you think of all the rest of it and that frightened you. Do you think that's it?'

'I don't know,' Annie said.

She wasn't sure what Crystal wanted her to say. Watching her carefully after she had said, *I don't know*, she saw her smile fade and knew that had been the wrong thing. She creased up her face, wondering why, and Crystal said, 'Don't be so solemn, duckie,' and took her in her arms. She hugged her tight, so tight it was almost uncomfortable, and then she held her away and looked steadily into her eyes as if she were searching for something. Annie began to feel shy and uneasy, she wanted to look away but she didn't because Crystal was being serious and when she was being serious about something she liked her to sit still and listen. So she fixed her attention on the two Annies, reflected in Crystal's eyes, and then looked higher where the hair sprang from her forehead like wheat from a snow field.

Crystal said, 'Look at me, Annie. What I mean is, when something bad has happened to people they often can't bear to think about it for a long time, they shut it away in their minds and pretend it hasn't happened. It's quite a good thing to do, really, a bit like covering up a bad graze or a cut on your knee, you cover it up with a piece of plaster so it can heal. But once it *has* healed, you take the plaster off, don't you?'

Annie hated pulling plaster off. Crystal always did it for

her, very quickly in the bath. But she hadn't cut herself since that day last summer when they had been gathering bilberries on the hill and she had fallen off a stone wall. She didn't know why Crystal should want to talk about this now but she saw, by her flushed, eager face, that it was important to her.

Crystal said, 'We've never really talked about Uncle Owen, have we? We don't really want to talk about him now, except for one thing.' She paused, flushing even more brightly: Annie, watching closely to stop herself thinking about Uncle Owen, saw that there were two red, wriggly marks high on one cheek, like tiny bits of thread under the skin. Crystal said slowly, 'I don't want you to grow up hating him, Annie. Not because he wasn't *horrid* to you, though even that wasn't his fault, really, he didn't know any better. But because hating someone is bad for *you*, it turns you bad *inside*. And I want you to be a whole person, Annie, happy and good!'

Annie said nothing. She felt nothing; only her stomach tightened as if she were going to be sick. Perhaps that was the badness inside her; thinking about that, about her stomach going bad like a rotten, squidgy apple, she felt terrified, suddenly.

'Do you see what I'm getting at?' Crystal said. 'You don't hate Uncle Owen, do you?'

She was looking closely at Annie, as if she could see through her skin. Annie put her hands over her stomach to hide it: Crystal would never love a bad person, someone whose insides were smelly and horrible. She shook her head and smiled stiffly.

Crystal smiled too. She kissed Annie. 'There's my good girl.'

She was Crystal's good girl. Crystal's daughter. But she could remember her own mother now. Not much, just a series of snapshots in her mind. Herself sitting in a chair with fat, short legs sticking out and her mother tying her shoe laces. Her mother's dark hair falling from a white parting on the top of her head. And her mother feeding the chickens in the field, white apron blowing, and the young, white chickens, fluttering like pigeons. 'Come on, Annie-May, see them having their dinner.' The young chickens were tame, they would peck corn from her hand. She liked that but it scared her, too. Her mother laughed and said, 'Don't be scared, Annie-May, it's only a tickle.'

Her mother laughing and teasing her and making her angry. Stamping her feet, waving her arms, face red and roaring. And her mother laughing and laughing and saying, 'Oh, Annie-May, what a *temper*.'

Now she was Crystal's good girl. Not bad Annie-May with a temper. 'She doesn't look like the same child,' Mrs Purvis said when they met her in the village. 'I wouldn't have recognized her.' Sometimes it frightened Annie to think she had changed so much. And other times she knew she had not really changed at all but was only pretending to be someone nicer and better and that frightened her more. She was afraid of being found out.

She loved Crystal. She dreamed of dying for her, rescuing her from fire or from drowning. At school, one of the older girls said, 'You think your mother is beautiful, don't you?', giggling in the playground, and Annie hurled herself on her. She was big now, strong and heavy for her age, and the other girl, taken unawares, went down thump on her back. Annie twined her fingers in her hair and banged her head on the concrete.

The form mistress kept her behind after school. She said, 'I'm afraid you're a very aggressive little girl. This isn't the first time. Do you know what aggressive means?'

Annie nodded. It meant bad. She was bad. Her face set, solid and sullen.

The form mistress sighed. 'I don't know what Mrs Golightly will say.'

'Don't tell her,' Annie whispered. 'Please don't tell my mother.'

Crystal said, 'Don't cry, darling one. I know it wasn't your fault, you'd never start a fight.'

But the child was inconsolable: Crystal had never seen such tears! 'I did,' she said. 'I did, I *did* . . .'

Crystal held her on her lap, though she was really too big now, and stroked the hot forehead. 'Nonsense, sweetheart, I know you better than that!'

She was sure of it. Annie was a timid and sensitive little girl, just as she had been. And of course the village school was unsuitable for a sensitive child: all those rough children fighting like wolves in the playground! And the staff so limited, so lacking in understanding. She had had quite an unpleasant scene with the form mistress. She had said, 'I know you've been good to Annie, Mrs Golightly, but you can't make a silk purse out of a sow's ear,' and looked triumphant, as if she had said something original and penetrating! It was too ridiculous – if Crystal had not been so angry she would have laughed – to suggest Annie had made trouble of this kind before, just because she wanted a scapegoat for *this* occasion. It was victimization, and Crystal had said so. 'I can only tell you that I know *my own child* better than you do. And if you persist in these malicious lies about her, I shall report you to the education committee!'

She really did feel Annie was her child now. Oh, she had never been half-hearted, but perhaps it had needed an incident of this kind to bring home the real strength of her feeling. Had it brought it home to Annie, too?

She wanted to do something, say something, to mark the occasion. She held the girl tight, mopped her tears. When the sobs quietened, from exhaustion, it seemed, rather than any real lessening of distress, she kissed the poor, puffy, stained face and said, 'Anna! I'm going to call you Anna!'

It was something she had had in mind for some time. 'Annie-May' was impossible, of course, but even plain 'Annie' had stuck in her throat. It was so common; a servant's name. Ann was more dignified, but Anna more romantic. She had already begun to call her Anna in her letters to Giles.

The child was looking bewildered. Crystal explained patiently. 'You're *my* girl now, aren't you? So I thought it would be a good idea to give you a new name. So that everyone will know!'

'But I'm *Annie*,' she said, with more energy than Crystal would have thought possible, after that long crying fit. The colour rose in her cheeks and her eyes had a withdrawn, stubborn look.

Crystal laughed. 'But Anna is a much prettier name, don't you think? It even sounds like a prettier *person*!'

Part Two *TOTTIE*

Giles's wife, Tottie – her name was Charlotte but Giles called her Tottie, inventing what seemed to him a charmingly eccentric diminutive – had a story she told about Auschwitz. She had been there two years when she was sent to a shed at one end of the camp for selection. The women were told to strip and run past the doctor who glanced at them briefly before motioning them to stand at one side or the other. One look, a slow, tired movement of his hand. Though it was rumoured that the fit were to be sent on a transport to Hamburg, no one knew their precise destination. Only those who were rejected had no doubt of theirs.

Tottie had three friends with her. These four girls had been together since the beginning. They were all young (Tottie was within two days of her twenty-first birthday), strong, and still hopeful. One had her mother with her, a powerful, pugnacious woman in her late forties who had a job in the kitchens and regularly stole food for them all. Clothed, she had a heavy, chunky look, like a solid and useful piece of machinery; naked, she appeared fat, soft and helpless, an ageing woman with sagging breasts. But she was plucky; she straightened her back, tucked in her belly and followed her daughter past the doctor, running like a girl, on her toes. He hesitated for perhaps a second – it was a brave try – before he waved her to her death. She didn't move; simply stood there with a look of amazement. He looked up, frowning, and her daughter ran back and put her arms round her. She was a slender girl, gracefully angular, like a young doe. She said to the doctor, 'Please let her come with us, she is my mother,' and he looked at her, at her tear-filled, doe's eyes, and shrugged his shoulders . . .

When Tottie reached this point she would often pause, her usually lively face almost expressionless, her eyes suddenly inward-looking and thoughtful, producing in her audience a curious uneasiness. What was expected of them? It seemed dreadful to be self-conscious about making the right response, as if this were merely an unaccustomed social situation, but it would be worse to make the wrong one. What did Tottie feel? What did *they* feel? Horror, of course, compassion – but also this strange, inhibiting embarrassment. Tottie would observe them for perhaps a minute without a flicker in her clear, green eyes; then her mouth would twitch, her whole face assume a wicked, laughing mobility. 'And so . . . they went through the rest of the war together, and then to Canada, and she was free to get on with ruining her daughter's life the way it was obvious she was always going to do . . .'

Giles disliked hearing this story. He wasn't stupid, he understood it was to some extent a defence, as were other stories which made Tottie's war sound more like life in some jolly boarding school than in the death camps of Europe, but it offended his susceptibilities. Tottie's history was terrible; thinking about it kept him awake at night, sweating in the darkness while she slept peacefully beside him. It shocked him to hear her speak lightly of what she had suffered.

She said she had been 'lucky'. Lucky to have been young and a girl. Lucky to have no children. Lucky to have been sent, initially, to Theresienstadt with her widowed father, instead of to one of the Polish camps like earlier transports from her town. Privation is easier to bear if you get used to it gradually, and, though they were not fully aware how much worse off they might have been (and even that ignorance was a kind of safeguard since fear of the future did not cast such a dark, backward shadow), it was possible to live in Theresienstadt with some measure of dignity. Possible, that is, for those who could work. Tottie's father was a publisher, but he had some skill with his hands, enough to learn to mend shoes and even to find some pleasure in it. He had been born poor, made his way, and the journey had tired him, perhaps: certainly he was less unhappy as a cobbler in Theresienstadt than might have been expected. No more struggle, and what he had come to was not, after all, as bad as he had feared. There was even a kind of freedom in this, for a tired, frightened man.

Too tired – he had ceased to fight and his body betrayed him. He contracted tuberculosis and was sent away 'for treatment'. Since the authorities had laid down a kindly-sounding directive that there should be 'no family separa-tion' Tottie went with him to Auschwitz. He died there; Tottie survived. In 1944 she was sent to Hamburg to work in the ruins of the city and she survived that. She would not have survived long in Belsen but her luck held: the Allies liberated the camp ten days after she arrived there.

Giles's regiment was in the neighbourhood. A detach-ment was sent with a small Intelligence unit. No one knew what to expect: they were simply sent to liberate a camp. They entered, innocent as children, through a light, wooden gate with criss-cross wiring like the entrance to a zoo and found ten thousand unburied dead and thousands more dying. The dying lay in their own excrement, or, trying to crawl away, fell on top of the living who were too weak to push them away, and died there. There was a smell of ordure and of burning.

Giles entered this charnel house a gentle, serious, civilized, and largely ignorant young man. He wasn't 'changed' by what he found but he measured life differently after. It seemed that the standards he had been taught to judge by were as remote from life as the rules in a children's game.

He thought, at first, I shall never forget this. I shall

never allow myself to forget it, I shall think about it, remember it, every day until I die; I shall tell my children, and, if I live long enough, my children's children. And when he did begin to forget; when he realized that several days had passed without a single thought of what he had seen there rising up in his mind, he felt a terrible guilt. He had eaten, made love, dug his garden and sat afterwards in the warm sun on the pleasant grass; enjoyed the kindly surface of the world as if it had never opened, shown him the pit beneath. It shamed him. He wanted to remember; he would force himself to, and then would be doubly shamed because the memories that came most clearly were the ones it was easiest to speak of. Like one dying old man who clung to him with tears; offered him, variously, a 'secret treasure' buried under a tree in Bavaria, a job in his importing firm, and an introduction to an English peer, if only he would promise to get him a few slices of bread and a pint of soup a day.

It was understandable, of course. Explicable. The old Jew remained in his mind because he had seen him as human. Sad, wretched, even undignified perhaps (those bizarre offers made in dying desperation), but still human. As so many had not been. You could not look at a pile of bodies, charred flesh and naked bone interleaved with railway sleepers to facilitate burning and see human beings with doubts and hopes, wives and children, aunts and cousins, bits of poetry in their minds, snatches of songs. You saw only facts, numbers, terrible statistics; a problem of disposal.

Tottie was human, of course. Though in a way, finding her in this place added to Giles's sense of disorientation. The first time he saw her she was sitting at a table in one of the huts, eating an omelette. She was clean, she was young, she was even decently dressed: she and her friends had raided the clothing store the night the S.S. had left. She spoke English well, behaved with a calm competence that seemed wonderful to Giles: she was a haven, a miracle, a reassurance that life could go on.

He needed this reassurance. His decent, comfortable world had cracked wide open and he was terrified. It was not simply that life would never be the same again, but that it had never been what he thought it was. He was ashamed of feeling like this, of course: surrounded by so much bottomless horror, to recognize his own emotions seemed an indulgence. The first night Tottie slept with him he clung to her and cried and she comforted him; both his terror and his shame. She said, 'Don't be ashamed to be shocked. It makes me feel safe, to be with a shockable man.'

He felt humble before her. This small, delicate, brilliant creature had seen so much, knew so many things he could never know. Or at least could never understand fully. But it seemed important to him to try: he felt this was the most important thing that had ever happened to him and he wanted to understand it. He questioned her endlessly, sometimes it seemed with an almost prurient curiosity but it was not really that: he was asking not what had happened, but why.

Tottie could not tell him. How could she? A river had burst its banks and she had simply been caught up, swept along in a torrent. All she had had time for was to keep her head above water.

How could anyone explain it? Not historically, but in human terms. It seemed to Giles that the only place to look must be in his own heart. Since it was men who had done this, all men must be capable of it. *He* must be, how dared he think himself different? The more he thought, the more convinced he became. When he and Tottie were living together – he attached to, she interpreting for, the War Crimes Commission – he would sometimes wake her up in the night. He had been thinking. In different circumstances he could have done this, or that. It was hard work searching for comparable evils in his innocent life but he had once bullied a younger boy at school and found pleasure in it; he had often had fantasies . . . 'Everyone has cruel impulses, it's just that the society *I* was brought up in taught one to restrain them.' He said this at three o'clock one morning, sitting up in bed in a large, velvet-curtained room in the Dolder Grand Hotel in Zurich.

That was in 1947. Tottie had told him that when she was in the camps, she and her friends had spent hours talking about what they each wanted to do most when they were free, arguing, quite heatedly sometimes, over whose idea was best. It had been a sort of game, a ritual to be looked forward to. She said, 'I suppose it sounds silly.'

It didn't, to him. It touched him to think of this group of girls lovingly discussing the freedom they might never have, lingering over details: what would most catch the essence of peace? He said, 'What did you choose?'

She laughed like a child. 'Spend a week at an expensive hotel, lying in bed all day long with a pink-shaded light and a bottle of wine and a box of chocolates and a packet of cigarettes.'

It disappointed him (what would he not have done?) but he took her to the Dolder Grand. They had a room with a balcony and an enormous bathroom, full of black marble. The light shades were apricot and he ordered champagne. He bought her a black lace nightdress (he had conventional tastes in women's underwear) but he did not make love to her because it had not been part of her picture. He left her in bed and walked the wide, clean streets of Zurich, eating bananas. He had not seen bananas for years; he bought a kilo and ate them one by one, sitting on the parapet of a bridge and dropping the skins into the clean, shining water. A policeman reprimanded him. 'It is forbidden to throw litter.' He was frowning severely: this was a real crime in his calendar. He said, 'I will warn you this time but I must tell you, there is a penalty.'

Giles apologized meekly but he wanted to laugh with joy. It seemed marvellous to be in a country where dropping banana skins was a serious offence. He finished his bananas and stuffed the remaining skins in his pocket. He went back to the hotel and found Tottie sleeping, with chocolate round her mouth.

He undressed and sat beside her. Her hair spread like a copper fan on the pillow. He wanted to make love to her but it seemed cruel to wake her. He went into the bathroom and she called to him sleepily before he turned on the taps.

They made love then, and afterwards bathed together, giggling and splashing each other in the absurd, black marble bath. They went to the opera and saw a magnificently grandiloquent performance of *Don Giovanni*. They walked by the dark, glistening lake. Everything delighted them, that night and the next day: the gold autumnal trees, the private funicular that carried them up and down the mountain between the hotel and the town; the wide, clean streets, the whole of the clean, rich, innocent city. Tottie said, 'Pinch me, Giles!' She closed her eyes and he pinched her arm; she opened them and said, 'No, I'm not dreaming!'

It wasn't until the evening of the second day that his conscience disturbed him. Tottie was hungry and they were eating early in the almost empty dining-room: at one point at least five waiters seemed to be hovering close to their table. A slight draught made Tottie shiver, and at once, one of the waiters brought a lace shawl and put it round her shoulders. Tottie looked at Giles with pure disbelief. He laughed and said, 'Anything else, my lady? Any little thing at all?'

She said, 'I haven't opened a door for myself since I came here.'

'You look like a cat. A lazy, comfortable, cream-filled cat!'

She sighed contentedly and began to eat her steak. Giles looked from her blissful face to the others around him, those solid, smooth, well-fleshed Swiss faces, and thought of the German city they had left a few days ago: the broken town and the pathetic, starving shadows in the rubble. They rose up before him like ghosts of his own guilt and the food on his plate sickened him.

Tottie said, 'What's the matter?'

He crinkled up his eyes in an artificial smile. 'Nothing. Not frightfully hungry, that's all. I'll get my second wind in a minute.'

He sipped at his wine and picked up his knife and fork. But his throat seemed actually to be closing.

Tottie watched him. She said. 'Don't, Giles. Not just to please me.'

She went on, eating with appetite, talking and smiling, but her face had changed: it was as if a light had gone. From her face, from the evening. When dinner was over they sat for a while in the bar; she drank three brandies one after the other, rather fast, and then said she was sorry but she felt very tired.

She slept as soon as they went to bed. Giles slept and woke. It was hot in the room and Tottie was leaning on one elbow, watching him. When she saw he was awake, she said, 'Do you really feel it's so wrong to be happy?'

There seemed to be a reproach in this question. He shook his head. He had drunk too much and his eyeballs ached: he was aware of them as pebbles of pain, rattling about in his skull. He said, 'Did you wake me up for that? I'm sorry if I spoiled your evening.'

His own pettiness did reproach him. He sat up, painfully smiling, and felt exonerated by the effort it cost him. He said that of course it wasn't 'wrong' to be happy, he had never, for a moment, meant to suggest that. After all, he had done nothing except leave his *dinner*! And that was quite involuntary, he had simply felt unable to eat, suddenly. Not that it did any good, of course, leaving the food on your plate didn't help anyone, he recognized that. Nor had it just been the specific contrast of himself sitting there stuffing his face while others were starving – though it wasn't *over* sensitive, surely, to be affected by that? – but something more general. A kind of disgust with himself that had been growing throughout this last year. And a kind of shame. The more he learned about the terrible things that had been done, the more he found himself condemning the criminals who had been responsible for them, the guiltier *he* had begun to feel. How could he be sure that in their position he would have behaved differently? Oh, he wasn't a sadist, a pervert, but he wasn't a natural martyr, either. For every monster, there were hundreds of ordinary men who had simply carried out orders. Ordinary, frightened men with wives and families – what else could they do? Become victims themselves? What would *he* have done? Could he really sit here, in comfort, hand on heart, and swear he would not have behaved as they did? Of course he couldn't. He was every bit as wicked – or frail, it hardly mattered what you called it – as they were. As capable of evil. All he had lacked was the opportunity. That was a terrible thing to face. To look at what had happened, at those fearful crimes, and see, not other people's wickedness, but your own, laid bare . . .

He began to feel exhilarated. His eyes had mysteriously ceased to ache. He became aware that he was enjoying himself, admiring a poignant phrase here or a subtle point there, but he was not ashamed of this because he knew he meant everything so very sincerely. Talking about it had made it plain; led him to the heart of the matter.

He was quite hurt when he saw Tottie was smiling at him with a kind of sad tenderness. She said, 'No one is naturally good or bad, perhaps. I suppose if you had been brought up differently, twisted and maimed in your mind, then you would be different. But you weren't and you aren't, Giles. So it makes no sense, what you're saying. You are the person you are and you could never have tortured or degraded *anyone*.'

It seemed to Giles that in some subtle way she was attempting to diminish him. To suggest he knew nothing. He said, haughtily, 'You haven't understood me! I suppose the truth is, you don't want to, don't want to feel there is any connection between someone like me and those bastards in the camps. I'm not deriding that, it's natural you should want to feel safe. But you simply cannot divide the human race into good and bad. Of course I wouldn't hurt a fly, sitting here in comfort in the Dolder Grand, but then why should I want or need to? All I was trying to say was that given certain circumstances, I conceivably *could*. There is a dark side to us all!'

Afraid that this last remark might sound a bit high-flown, he retreated onto more personal ground and told her how he had bullied little James Platt at his preparatory school.

If the memory had not haunted him as persistently as he now suggested, it was something of which he had always been honestly ashamed. James had been in his first year when he had been in his last, and had slept in his dormitory. He had a father who wore rings on his fingers and a mother who had admired Crystal's mink wrap one sport's day and said she knew a good skin when she saw it because her husband was in 'the trade'. That remark, the rings, the 'common' voices, the fact that James was small and shy and clever, fixed him in his role of victim. Nothing terrible happened: this prep school was, for that date, an unusually watchful and kindly institution. The worst, until Giles's last term, was arm-twisting, teasing, derogatory remarks. Then, one Saturday, James went out with his parents, ate too much ice-cream, and was sick in the dormitory just after lights-out. 'I suppose it made me mad,' Giles said. 'He didn't make any attempt to reach the

jerry, just sat up and spewed over everything. I called him
a greedy Jew-boy. He was Jewish, you see, we used to
tease him about noses and so on. So I got out of bed and
called him a Jew-boy and he looked up at me with tears
running down his face and the sick coming out of his mouth
and something came over me. A sort of feeling of power
and disgust. He didn't seem like another boy, but like
some kind of filthy animal. I rubbed his nose in the mess
and said, "Go on, you sicked it, you eat it", and the frightful thing is, he actually *did* – oh, not much, just one *lick* – I
suppose he was terrified, poor little rat . . .'

Tottie said, 'What are you trying to prove?' She was
leaning back against the bed head: pale, pleated, apricot
silk behind her copper head. Her eyes were bright and cold.

Giles was excited. Telling this tale had excited him. It
was substantially true – except that young James had not
been Jewish. Or if he had been, Giles had not known it.
But he felt only a fleeting compunction: the lie didn't alter
his point, only sharpened it. He said, 'Don't you see? I felt
everything a torturer might feel, I behaved like one!
There's only a difference in *degree* . . .'

Her face puckered. She began to cry, sitting with her
head pressed back against the pleated silk. She said, 'Oh
Giles, oh Giles,' and it was as if she said, 'Alas, alas . . .'

Her tears produced an oddly pleasurable sensation in
him. He didn't want to analyze it. He told himself he was
appalled. He kissed her wet eyes, her soft, hot mouth. He
said, 'Oh, I'm sorry, I'm sorry, my love.'

She went on, weeping helplessly. He wondered if he
should tell her he had lied about James being Jewish but
couldn't quite bear to. It was irrelevant, anyway; it wasn't
why she was crying. He said, 'Darling, I'm frightfully
sorry. I really am a rotten swine.'

She flipped in his arms, like a fish jumping, and made a
curious, smothered sound, a sort of choked, muted howl.
He thought she was choking for a moment and then

realized it was laughter. She was laughing and crying. He held her away from him, so he could look into her face, and she sniffed and gasped and said, 'Oh Giles, don't pretend to be something you're not, what's the point? Except as a kind of *exercise?*'

He sighed, very deeply. It seemed that he had been making a valid and important point and she had wilfully misunderstood it. Oh, perhaps not wilfully! Like all women she was simply incapable of following an intellectual argument. (This had been his father's creed and Giles had not yet met a woman who disproved it.) Thinking like this made him feel tender towards her, and guilty. He rocked her and said, 'Hush, my love. My little love.'

But she continued to cry, softly and sadly. He had never heard anyone cry like this before, as if out of some bottomless pit of despair. There had always been anger behind his mother's tears. He said, 'It's all right, my baby, I've got you.' But she felt like a stranger, suddenly. He was sitting in this bed with a stranger in his arms. The thought frightened him. He tightened his hold and said, 'It's all right, I love you, I never want to let you go.'

She moaned, her face against his chest. His pyjama jacket was wet. He said, 'I'm asking you to marry me.'

She coughed and lifted her head. Her eyes were wet, shining green, like glass under water. She said, 'No.'

He felt an enormous relief, then terror. He said, 'Don't you love me?'

Her face screwed up as if with pain. Tears had dried, leaving rough, grainy streaks on her skin. He touched them and said, 'Like a salt pan. Oh, I do love you so!'

She was holding his hand against her stomach. She was thin but her stomach was soft. She said, 'We love the wrong things in each other.'

'That's just fancy talk.'

She didn't answer. She was looking very sad. He said, roughly, 'Who's talking for exercise now? You know that's absolute rubbish.' He couldn't bear the sadness in her face. It seemed to reflect some sadness within himself, some doubt, perhaps. He thought, what of it? Everyone loves out of some unconscious need. He crinkled his eyes and the corners and laughed, theatrically. He said, 'I'll be de-mobbed soon. Going home. Everyone wants a bit of loot to take back, I want *you*. My green-eyed Sabine, my slave girl.'

He smiled at her until his face ached, until she smiled back. He said, 'You will have to marry me, you know. Or my mother will be most *frightfully* shocked.'

Crystal often said, when describing her daughter-in-law, 'She doesn't look in the least Jewish!' Crystal was not anti-Semitic (how could anyone be, nowadays?) but she was of a class and a generation that had been used to making jokes about the Chosen Race and found this awkward habit hard to shed. Of course that sort of thing was absolutely out now, utterly tasteless, but she still could not help being glad, privately (she always said *privately* when she was admitting this to other people) that Tottie's nose was not hooked. Not that she would have dreamed of saying so to Giles. She was tremendously careful not to mention the word 'Jew' in his or Tottie's presence; sometimes, indeed, went to almost grotesque lengths to avoid any related topic, like pork, or Hitler. When she knew Tottie was coming she ordered no bacon so that the girl should not be embarrassed by having to refuse it. And on one occasion, at a dinner party she was giving for Tottie and Giles, she launched suddenly, and for no reason it seemed, into a long story about a sailor who had had his first sweetheart's name tattooed on his chest and suffered discomfort in later amatory adventures. While she told this apparently irrelevant and presumably apocryphal tale (though Crystal claimed to have ques-tioned this sailor and been told, 'It's quite simple, Madam,

I wear vests in bed', it seemed unlikely to have been a personal experience) her guests listened, for the most part, with bemused politeness. But Giles, who had seen old Major Prewitt staring at the blue identification number stamped on Tottie's arm, understood his mother's tortuous mental processes and felt angry and humiliated. It shocked him that Tottie should sit there, so calmly smiling at her glass.

'I expect she thought he might ask me and that I might not want to talk about it,' she said, in the Tube, going home.

'She doesn't want it talked *about*. I'm sorry, but I find that kind of attitude *frightful*!'

Tottie said, 'I don't see why your mother should be embarrassed at her own dinner table.'

He was in no mood for sweet reason. 'Your being Jewish embarrasses her.' He lowered his voice to say this, although the carriage was empty except for one old man at the far end who appeared to be asleep.

'Perhaps it does,' Tottie said. 'But it's a small thing. I don't mind, Giles.'

'I mind for you,' he said sternly. This was painfully true. It seemed to him that until he met Tottie, he had never really encountered any anti-Jewish feeling. Now it seemed to surround him, he was aware of it all the time, was amazed how many otherwise decent people made slighting references as a matter of course. It made his blood boil, but Tottie hardly seemed to notice. When he taxed her with this, she said she did notice, but she was used to it. And it was only a thoughtless custom; there were cases in which a difference of degree really did mean a difference in kind, and this was one of them. She said it didn't make her angry, only tired, sometimes.

She was looking tired now; pale, and swaying tiredly with the movement of the train. He put his arm round her and wished they had taken a taxi instead of the Tube, but it was an expensive ride from his mother's flat in Maida Vale to their two rented rooms in Knightsbridge, and his gratuity was almost gone. He was not really worried about money, merely embarrassed by the thought of possible penny-pinching. His mother had only enough for herself and for Anna: his grandmother's estate had proved smaller than had been expected and Crystal had refused to take anything from Basil apart from the flat and the furniture. 'I won't be pensioned off,' she had said, 'put out to grass like some used-up old mare!' Giles had thought this rather gallant at first but now, sitting uncomfortably in the train and feeling generally irritated with his mother, he thought it looked more like pig-headedness: it made it awkward for *him* to approach his father should the need arise. Not (he had to admit it) that there would be much point in doing so. Basil's family (all those retired admirals and generals and their weather-beaten wives) might have status but their money was in trust funds and land, and Basil himself had retired six months ago and was living with his nice, plain wife in a cottage on a cousin's estate, digging his garden and playing golf, and looking for some untaxing and gentlemanly part-time job. No, if he got stuck, the man to turn to was Uncle George, his father's banker brother. Although when they had lunched together the other day, there had been a slight restraint, an odd coolness in the atmosphere. Giles had sensed it, but couldn't think why; returning to it now, he was still unable to pin it down. It was nothing to do with Tottie, Uncle George was too intelligent to be swayed by that kind of prejudice as he was too sensible to be put off because Giles had said he was hoping for a more adventurous career than banking – publishing, perhaps, or the B.B.C. 'Not much money in either,' George Golightly had said, gouging away at his gums with an ivory toothpick (like most of his family he tended to be uninhibited in his public behaviour), and Giles, averting his eyes from what he found an unpleasant sight, had answered, cheerfully, 'Oh, money isn't all that important.'

Which it wasn't, of course. Although Uncle George, after extracting a stringy remnant of lamb from between his back molars and depositing it on the side of his plate had said, 'My dear lad, that's a young man's remark,' Giles had still been convinced of the truth of it. Was convinced of it, now. Really, it had been silly not to have taken a taxi: Tottie could have been at home and in bed by now. He felt protective towards her, as if she was his weary child. He tightened his arm round her and said, 'When I get a job, I think one of the first things will be to buy a car. A good, pre-war job – an old Bentley, or a Delage. Ronnie Baker's got a Delage – d'you remember, he brought us home in it after the Hasselton party last week. White sports saloon with an aluminium body and a Cotel electric gear box. He got it for almost nothing, I believe, from some Fleet Air Arm type's widow. 1939 vintage, laid up on blocks during the war, absolutely *marvellous* value.'

Tottie was smiling and yawning. He said, 'Oh, I know cars are *boring*. Sorry. But I was really thinking of you.'

She put her hand up and touched the side of his face. She said, 'You know, Giles, your mother tries very hard not to be what you think she shouldn't be. She means so very well.'

Giles snorted so loudly that the old man who was sleeping further up the carriage woke up and looked at them suspiciously.

'It's important,' Tottie said. 'It really is *frightfully* important.'

It amused him, that 'frightfully'. She had picked it up from him as she had picked up a number of his verbal mannerisms, like saying, '*Jolly* good', and 'Let's have an *enormous* drink.' But she was looking very serious, so he didn't smile.

He said, 'All right, if you say so.' His annoyance with

Crystal had diminished, anyway. Thinking about cars had helped; it was something he had always found soothing. And she had, it was true, been very decent to him and to Tottie, giving them her double bed when they stayed with her their first weeks in England and sleeping in what used to be the maid's room herself, supplying them with scarce pre-war linen when they found a place of their own and giving these dinner parties, even if the other guests were hardly exciting, being mostly those old Army friends who had remained 'loyal' as she put it, after his father's defection. As Basil's family had not: although Crystal had not actually said so, Giles had noticed that she never spoke about any of them. Not even about Uncle George, who had been a regular visitor to the flat in the 'thirties when Basil had been at the War Office – a young, jolly, bachelor uncle who was also an admirer of his mother's, Giles had sometimes thought. But Uncle George had not asked after her when they met for lunch, and, when Giles mentioned her, he had nodded, no more. In fact, now Giles thought about it, it was from that moment that there had been a change in his manner. Not a chill, exactly, simply an odd feeling of withdrawal, as if this were a subject he did not want to discuss. Though Giles had half recognized this at the time, he had ploughed on – at the back of his mind, perhaps, the idea that it might cheer Crystal up if Uncle George took her out sometime, to dinner, or a theatre. He had said that though she was putting a good face on it he was afraid life wasn't much fun for her, a woman alone, and with that child hung round her neck like an albatross. Uncle George said, 'Yes, the child, that's a curious business,' and for a split second Giles had thought he was going to say something more, but either he was wrong, or his uncle changed his mind, because almost as soon as he had spoken he put the toothpick back in his waistcoat top pocket and swung round energetically to catch the wine waiter's eye. There was an elaborate fuss about a special brandy (unlisted, in short supply), and when this was over and they were sitting with the liquid gold gleaming in fussily warmed goblets, Uncle George had launched into a monologue on the Romance of Banking. It was a subject near to his heart; he spoke of his merchant bank as of an adored wife or mistress. Perhaps this was why he had never married, Giles had thought, sipping his brandy and listening to his uncle with amusement and affection. It would have been like committing bigamy.

Remembering this phrase, he smiled now. And then thought, *A bit unfair, really, to have called poor Anna an albatross!* Certainly his mother did not seem to think of her as a burden, was obviously fond of her, but though she would never admit it, Giles suspected that she might be disappointed. She expected (as he did himself) a proper reward for effort and Anna had turned out so ordinary; a null, pale, submissive child whose only distinction was that she was rather big and clumsy for her age. Giles could not remember what her age was, exactly, only that she seemed large for it. Devoted to his mother, of course, watching her all the time with immense, dark, solemn eyes, but surely Crystal had hoped for more than a shadow of herself, an echo? Oh, perhaps not, Giles thought. What did he know about it? About his mother and her needs? He ought to be grateful to her for not imposing them on him the way some women in her position would have done; the way, if he had thought about it beforehand, he would have expected Crystal to. The child had probably helped in that way, given her an alternative to focus on, but she must also have made a considerable effort to deny her own nature: ever since he came home she had not once demanded anything, seemed to expect nothing from him except that he and Tottie should come and eat an excellent meal from time to time. And all he could do was to criticize her for being over-sensitive on Tottie's behalf . . .

He said, 'I suppose you're right. She does try. The

trouble is that I think she ought not to have to! She ought to be able to treat you quite naturally!'

'I can see why she finds it hard,' Tottie said.

Crystal had been to see the film they had made in Belsen. She had taken Anna with her. She said to her, 'This film we are going to see will explain what the war was about.' Children were not allowed into this cinema but Anna was tall enough to pass as an adult. Indeed, with her hair in a wispy bun and wearing one of Crystal's coats (they had had great fun dressing her up) she looked, to a casual glance, like a middle-aged woman.

The film affected Crystal very badly. When it was over, she hardly knew how to get out of the cinema, her legs were shaking so. As they came down the stairs into the foyer she caught a glimpse of herself in a gilt-framed mirror and saw she looked white as a sheet. The last time she had felt so terribly shocked had been when she was very young and had seen a child with no legs and no arms being wheeled along in a barrow. But her father had been with her then; she had only time for one look before he whipped her up in his arms and held her face against his cheek. He had carried her like that all the way home. He had said, 'My poor chick, my poor baby.' Now there was no one to comfort her.

They went into the nearest café. Crystal ordered tea. She said to Anna, 'Cake or ice-cream?'

'I'm not hungry.'

'Oh, come on, darling. Surely you can eat something?'

The waitress looked at Anna, pencil poised. Anna shook her head. She was looking stolid and bored.

'A plate of buttered toast, I think. Not that it will be *butter*, I fear,' Crystal said. She thought how extraordinary it was that she should be sitting here, calmly ordering tea. She smiled bravely at the waitress and said, 'I suppose life must go on.'

The girl had a blank, moon face with a tiny nose that tilted up at the tip, displaying dark, hairy nostrils. She sighed heavily as she wrote on her pad as if Crystal had insulted her by expecting to be served, as if all life was a burden. Crystal felt like saying, 'You don't know how lucky you are!'

Across the table, Anna gave a long, exhausted sigh, and fainted.

She lay on the ground, crumpled against the table legs. Crystal knelt beside her, straightening her limp, heavy limbs. The waitress said, triumphantly, 'I thought she might be going off. We've had a lot of that. You been in next door?'

Crystal said, 'Will you get a glass of water, please?' She stroked the hair back from the damp forehead. Anna's eyelids were fluttering; she gave a little moan. Crystal said, 'It's all right, honeybee.'

A man said, beside her, 'If you've taken her to see that film, I'm not surprised. A child that age!'

Anna opened her eyes and struggled to sit up. Crystal laid her head on her lap. A hand came down with a glass of water and she held it to Anna's lips. 'Just a sip now.'

Another voice. A woman's. 'You ought to be ashamed of yourself.'

Crystal looked up. Several people were standing round. A ring of hostile faces. She felt quite sick with shock. She said, in her crispest tones, 'Kindly give my daughter room to breathe.'

'Oh, la–di–da, is it?' the woman said. 'Well, all I can say is, you ought to know better.'

Crystal gasped. If Anna had not been conscious, she would have denied taking her into the cinema. Not that she had done anything wrong, but it was mortifying to be attacked by these dreadful people. Tears pricked her eyes.

Anna said, 'Don't speak like that to my mother.'

She was sitting up. She was still very pale but her eyes

were angry. She said, 'It's only my period. I always faint when I have my period.'

Crystal helped her to her feet. Someone brought a chair but Anna shook her head. She held Crystal's arm, but not, it seemed, to support herself. She said, 'I don't want to stay here with all these stupid, rude people.'

Crystal almost laughed. It was comic, really: the angry child and that idiotic woman, looking so disgusted because the word 'period' had been mentioned! Like an outraged camel! She smiled gently and said, 'Perhaps someone would be most awfully kind and find us a taxi?'

She said to Anna, 'That was sweet of you, darling. A *good* lie! I mean it wasn't true, was it? You haven't started?'

'There's a girl at school has and she faints.' Anna was staring out of the taxi window. Her expression was stolid again, almost sullen. Though Crystal squeezed her hand, there was no answering pressure.

Crystal began to cry. 'Darling, don't be angry with me. I suppose I shouldn't have taken you. I just thought you should know – after all, there were little girls your age in the camps. Younger, even . . .'

'Please don't cry,' Anna said.

'I'm sorry, darling, I can't help it. It's all been so awful. Am I *such* a bad mother? Should I have protected you, pretended those terrible things hadn't happened?'

Anna said, 'Please don't cry. Not about me. It's all right. I'm all right. I mean it's not as if I didn't know. I knew about it before I went, after all.'

Crystal mopped her eyes. 'Of course. Bless you, darling, you are a sensible child. And I'm such a silly. Forgive your silly mother for crying.'

'I'm sorry about the faint,' Anna said.

She had more colour now but her eyes had a dark, withdrawn look that took Crystal back. Annie-May had looked like that! She said, 'Anna-duckie, give me a little smile.'

Anna smiled.

Crystal said, 'That's better. That's my girl. Now as soon as we get back you're to go into the garden and forget all about it! A bit of fresh air will soon blow it away!'

Their first-floor flat had no garden but there was a convenient bomb site next door, overlooked by the kitchen window. Crystal watched from this vantage point as Anna made her way across the foundations of the demolished house, now almost hidden by nettles and willow herb, to the square of cracked concrete and the bit of wall where she always played the same game with her tennis ball, a complicated ritual of bouncing and catching and hand-clapping. She was never bored by this game, playing it sometimes for an hour or more in the relentless, tireless way a younger child will rock its cot: it seemed, Crystal thought, to fulfil the same rhythmic need. But today when she reached the wall she stood motionless in front of it, her head bowed; stood there so long, so still, that when she eventually moved back and began to bounce the ball, Crystal was conscious of a quite ridiculous relief. Of course there had been no real need to worry, children recovered from distress so quickly, the memory of that dreadful film would soon fade from her mind. Watching her play her solitary game, a plump child in a pink frock, Crystal wished *she* could forget as easily! It had been pointless, perhaps, to torture herself! As Anna had said, she knew it all, really – after those letters Giles had written she had been unable to sleep properly for weeks! Moving about the kitchen preparing supper, she thought of a good phrase. 'With an imagination like mine one doesn't need the truth!' She spoke aloud, watching her reflection in the kitchen mirror, and smiled wanly.

When Tottie came, she enfolded her in her arms and said, 'My poor child . . .' And, as soon as possible, the first time they were alone together, made her little speech. 'You don't have to tell me what you've been through. With an imagination like mine, one doesn't need the truth!'

She was surprised by Tottie's well-dressed composure. She had expected someone crushed, beaten. But she liked her. She had been afraid her son's wife would make her feel old (she felt her age, forty-five now, to be an unbearable humiliation), but at the end of their first evening, Tottie looked at her, a long, appraising look, and said, 'Giles never told me how beautiful you were.' And they had enough in common to be easy together, sharing not merely a feminine interest in clothes but in quality, in good shoes, leather handbags. Tottie appreciated her sacrifice in turning out her linen chest: when Crystal gave her a pair of embroidered sheets that had been part of her trousseau, she held them against her cheek and said, 'They smell of civilization!'

Crystal laughed. 'Oh, Tottie, you do me *good*. My mother always made me feel it was so *trivial* to care about nice things. When they were bombing London, I used to lie awake at night and worry quite dreadfully – all my pretty glass and china left behind in the flat – and then feel ridiculously guilty because I knew she would despise me. But I couldn't help it, it really was important to me. You can understand that, can't you?'

Tottie smiled.

Giles said, 'Oh, God!' He had been lying on the sofa, reading. Now he sat up energetically. 'How can you expect her to understand, mother! Tottie had rather more important things to worry about during the war than a few old bits of crockery.'

He spoke with measured indignation but it seemed to spring from a deeper, more generalized hostility. Crystal felt this, as she had felt it on other occasions, and it embarrassed and hurt her. What had she done to deserve it? It was as if everything she did or said was being weighed and found wanting. She felt she hardly dare open her mouth! Giles had been such a sweet, loving boy. Why had he turned into this carping stranger? Oh, she could understand that he blamed her because she had had such an easy life, had not suffered like Tottie – she could view that attitude with indulgent amusement. But not this constant, nagging criticism. It generated such resentment she felt she could hardly contain it.

It needed a focus. She would not blame Giles: she was determined to be a loving, generous mother. Nor Basil: too obvious a target. But someone had to suffer for her bewilderment and pain. Only Anna loved her truly, and she was only a child still; she felt herself growing old, deserted not only by Basil but by Basil's family. Though she had behaved as well as she knew, given Basil his freedom when he had asked for it, not one of them had bothered to write to her. Of course she might have expected it; they had never liked her, had always treated her badly. It was so unfair. She had come to them, confident and open-hearted, and they had turned their backs on her! She remembered the day of her wedding: not one of them had said how beautiful she looked. And when her father had said, to Basil, 'Look after my precious girl,' she had seen Basil's Aunt Azuba, the Admiral's widow, turn away to hide a smile. That smile had spoiled the first night of her honeymoon. She couldn't eat a mouthful; she had cried and cried. It had been so cruel to smile like that, and it wasn't just Aunt Azuba; they all seemed to think her father's love for her was a ridiculous thing! And all Basil could say was, 'Perhaps they do think it a bit unusual. Trouble is, they all beat *their* children.'

Basil had never understood how important it was to her to be lovingly accepted; how much it hurt, when they visited his family, that no one admired her clothes or her hair or asked her opinion about anything. She was nothing to them. They stayed with his deaf Uncle Simon at his draughty old house in Bedfordshire and he had asked her, 'What do you do?' She had said, 'I'm Basil's wife,' thinking he would smile, as her father's friends would have done, and say 'Lucky fellow,' but he had simply drawn his heavy eyebrows together and growled, 'It wasn't information about your sexual habits I was seeking, girl. I was asking what you did in the daytime.' She had stood up to him bravely, 'Being a wife is a full time job,' but he had not heard her, having laid down his ear trumpet to signify the end of the conversation, and he would not have understood if he had. They were all such busybodies, meddlers, do-gooders, sitting on committees, running this and that. Obsessed with their own importance – even when Giles had been born, only Basil's brother, George, had taken the trouble to visit her in the nursing home!

There were so many old sores to be re-examined. And one more recent. She had thought George was her friend! She had once allowed him to kiss her in a boat on the river at Richmond. Only once, but she had felt, afterwards, that they had a rather special relationship. She had written to him when Basil left her, a gently noble letter. He had not answered, was too distressed, she supposed. And when she came back to London she had gone to see him at his office. Not just to renew their friendship: she wanted to send Anna to a good private school and hoped some provision could be made from the family educational trust. George had listened, frowning and scratching his ear (he had aged dreadfully, she thought, grown almost gross) while she explained her financial position and how anxious she was about the child, but in the end he had sighed and said he was afraid nothing could be done. Anna was not a child of the family. 'She is my child,' Crystal had said, and he sighed again and said, 'Yes, but not Basil's.' He picked up a match and inserted the tip into his ear while he said that if she and Basil were still living together, even if they had been living together when Anna first came to her, it might have been possible for the trust to stump up, but not in the circumstances. After all, when she took Anna on, the marriage had been virtually over.

'And whose fault was that?'

He removed the match from his ear and examined it. 'That's not the point, Crystal.'

His dry voice angered her. That dry air of superiority!

'Excuse me, but I think it is. Your brother left me. I let him go because it was what he wanted, let him go free as air! I've taken nothing from him, George, not a penny! I'm not asking for anything for myself now, only for Anna. Oh, I know she has no legal *right*, poor baby, but heavens above, George, there's enough money there!'

She did her best to laugh but inwardly she was raging. About a quarter of a million, Basil had once said . . .

'I'm afraid there's nothing I can do.'

Nothing he *wanted* to do. Oh, he had got dry and sour! And yet, he was younger than she was! Basil was fifty-two and George was eight years younger than Basil.

She said, 'You could do something if you wanted to, surely?'

But her confidence was sagging. Did she look as old to him as he did to her? She shifted in her chair, turning her face from the light.

He said, 'I'm sorry. But you needn't take my word for it, Crystal. James and Azuba are the other trustees – you can approach them, if you like.' He hesitated, looking at her, and then smiled. 'But I better warn you, old Azuba's pretty dotty. She picked out a hat in Harrods a few weeks ago, handed it to the assistant and said, "I'll have five dozen, please." She said afterwards she was thinking of the next thing on her list which was candles. But Harrods sent her five dozen blue felt hats. They must have thought she was equipping some private, female army.'

Telling this story seemed to relax him; perhaps he thought it would relax Crystal too. But it made her feel sick. Physically sick. This was one of the things she hated most about Basil's family: their fatuously tender regard for their own eccentricity. She folded her hands in her lap and lifted her chin. 'Thank you, George. When I want to go trailing round a lot of elderly madwomen with a begging bowl, I'll let you know!'

He was playing with a pencil, stabbing holes in a sheet of blotting paper. He said, 'Crystal, if you really are in financial difficulties, then the proper thing to do is to approach Basil. I know the arrangement was that he handed over the flat in return for an undertaking on your part that you wouldn't ask for alimony, but I'm sure he would help if you needed it. As much as he could, that is. His wife . . .'

'I would rather *die*,' Crystal cried. Oh, this was typical! Suggesting that there had simply been a legal bargain struck, that there had been no generosity on her part. She felt herself flushing with anger. 'I didn't come here to ask for charity, George. I came because I was a good wife to your brother for a very long time, the best years of my life, some people might say, and because I foolishly thought that his family might feel some small obligation towards me, since he left me for no fault of mine! I also thought you might be prepared to do something for an unfortunate child who has had very little chance in life, that you might at least have had the decency to try and fix *something*. Oh, I suppose I should have known better! My father always said if you want help, go to a poor man! Rich people stay rich by closing ranks and sitting on their money! But what *for* in this case? Tell me honestly, George. You know perfectly well that the reason there's so much money in the trust is that there have never been enough children to *use* it. All those crazy uncles and aunts you're so proud of – God knows why! – have barely produced a handful between them, have they? I suppose they're all sterile or impotent! It wasn't *my* fault that Basil and I only had one child, you know! And how about you, George? You haven't *any*. Which are you?'

She stopped. She had shocked herself. She had not meant to go so far but George had maddened her, sitting there with that wry, superior smile on his fat, jowly face. She felt so humiliated. She had come to him with a perfectly reasonable request and he had insulted her by suggesting she should go crawling to Basil. Treating her like a suppliant, she thought, standing up and collecting her bag and gloves. She wasn't sorry if she had hurt him, wiped that smile off his face.

He said, 'Basil's wife is pregnant, as it happens.'

She hardly knew how she got out of the office. Oh – she didn't sweep out, or burst into tears – she wouldn't give him that satisfaction! But alone in the lift she let out a low moan of rage and when she got home she felt quite ill with exhaustion. Must have looked it, too: Anna gave her one, frightened glance and made her sit down. She fetched her a glass of sherry and watched with a troubled face as she drank it. Poor child, Crystal thought, if only she knew what she'd been through on her behalf.

She said, when she had finished her sherry. 'You know, I'd forgotten how awful my husband's family are! An alien race of monsters! I've just been to see Giles's Uncle George on a business matter and I feel as if I've been visiting *Mars*. I used to think George was the best of the bunch but now he's as bad as the rest of them. If I'd ever had doubts about divorcing Basil, seeing George has put an end to them! Cold, cruel, self-engrossed – no one else of any importance except *their* family. When I married Basil, they made me feel as if I ought to think myself especially privileged, being elected to their marvellous club! And of course, I was only eighteen, I took them at their own valuation. I didn't see them for what they were, a lot of ruthless, rich people. I should have done, I suppose. My father went to see Basil's Uncle Simon at his club – Basil's parents were dead and he was by way of being the head of the family – and he didn't even offer him lunch, although my poor papa had travelled all the way up from the country to see him! And all Simon was interested in was what sort of allowance my parents were going to give me. My father explained that he was retired from the Army with only his pension to live on and my mother's little income, and Simon said, in that case, I was a lucky girl! Basil would have £400 a year besides his Captain's pay, and the family would provide for the education of our children. Oh, I know £400 a year was quite a lot then but it wasn't *riches*. But Simon made it sound as if this was a sort of prince-and-beggar-maid marriage, as if I was a *gold-digger*! My father made a joke of it, of course. He said, "Once old Simon gets to know you, he'll see how lucky *they* are!" Poor Daddy! He loved me so much, he used to call me the flower in his buttonhole! Oh, I had such a lovely childhood with him, Anna, so safe and protected, it was such a shock to find Basil's family so indifferent – so hostile, almost. Do you know, Basil wanted me to have his mother's jewels and Uncle Simon refused to hand them over? He said they were his grandmother's, family property – as if I wasn't Basil's *wife*! Basil was upset about it but there was nothing he could do, apparently. Didn't want to, I see now I'm older and wiser – he was always under his Uncle's thumb! He knew none of them liked me but he pretended not to notice. He said, "They're always like that, it's a kind of shyness, really." But it wasn't, it was *personal* – when Basil's cousin Sholto married, *his* wife got a moonstone bracelet, part of the famous jewels *I* wasn't allowed to have! Her father was a knight, that was it, they're such silly snobs, the Golightlys! And I was a nobody, so they could be as rude and dismissing as they liked! I'm sure that if Sholto had treated Amelia the way Basil treated me, there would have been no end of a fuss made. But I think they encouraged him! I didn't know it, I was so *trusting*, Anna, but I'm quite sure Aunt Azuba used to let Basil use her London flat for his sordid little affairs. Looking back, you remember things that seemed unimportant at the time and I remember when Giles was three months old and Aunt Azuba came to see him – for the first time, she hadn't bothered before – she brought a couple of Basil's shirts with her. She said, "You left them behind and I've had them laundered so you owe me one-and-six!" It was the meanness I laughed at, of course, and when Basil looked uncomfortable I thought he was just ashamed of his mean old aunt charging him for having his shirts washed, I suppose I thought he'd stayed there while I was in the nursing home, it's only *now* I see there was something else behind it. She'd lent him the flat to take his women to, it would be quite in character. She was an awful old tart, Aunt Azuba – it sounds a dreadful thing to say but there's no other word for her. She's eighty odd now so she must have been well over fifty then but I know for a fact that she had a number of lovers, some of them married men! I thought it disgusting but Basil was only amused. He used to say, "Oh, Auntie's a gay spark!" I suppose it seemed to him that his family were so superior it didn't matter how they behaved, they could just ignore decent people's moral values! When I said I was shocked he said that was priggish, he couldn't see any harm in his aunt having a good time if she could get away with it. Which was *his* philosophy, really, though I didn't know it, of course, I believed he was faithful to me as I was to him. I had come to him a virgin and I had never looked at another man. And all those years I loved and trusted him he was making a fool of me, destroying my happiness, and his horrible aunt was encouraging him, laughing at me, I daresay, behind my back, mocking my innocence. She'd have no respect for that, I can tell you! I remember her saying once, "Innocence is no more of a virtue than ignorance, to my mind." I thought it was just one of her cynical remarks but I see now it was really a dig at me, a sneer at my simplicity. *She* knew what Basil was up to, and if she did, you can be sure the rest of the family did too – that sort of news travelled fast on their grape vine! Oh Anna, it *sickens* me, looking back! Not that I didn't suffer at the time; I did, quite dreadfully, but I always blamed myself for not measuring up to what they expected of me. I was so *humble*, Anna, so young – you'd think they would at least have pitied me!'

These last words made her cry; quite enjoyably.

Anna said, 'Oh, I could *kill* them.'

She was standing in the middle of the room as she had been all the time Crystal had been talking. Her face was white and stiff and her whole body shook: she was hugging her arms across her chest as if she were cold or afraid. Had she frightened the child, Crystal thought. She said, 'Anna, *darling* . . .'

Anna gasped and rushed at her, falling on her knees beside the chair and enfolding her in a rib-cracking hug. Crystal endured as long as she could, then laughed breathlessly. 'Dear heart, I can't *breathe.*'

The child sat back on her heels and lifted her face. 'I can't bear it,' she said. 'How could they be so wickedly *cruel*? I hate them, I *hate* them. People who behave like that ought to be sent to prison. They oughtn't to be allowed to *live.*'

No fear in her eyes now, only anger. And such anger, such passion! Almost frightening, it was so out of character! Crystal had a moment of disquiet that came and went. It was gratifying, really. Faintly funny, too: this gentle child, breathing fire and brimstone! *My champion*, Crystal thought. She said, 'Don't let's get it out of proportion. Perhaps I overdid it a little. I don't quite know what made me go on like that. Something else hanging around, I expect.' By this she meant her period might be due. She couldn't be sure, she had been irregular, lately. The menopause, the final humiliation! She sighed. 'That's why I got so worked up, just chemistry. But I feel better now I've got it off my chest.' She smiled at Anna. 'Now it's all over and done with. Not another word! Especially not when Giles comes home. I've never talked to *him* like this and I wouldn't want to! So you understand, darling, don't you? Mum's the word!'

She laughed, to cover uneasiness. The expression on the child's face! Had she gone too far? Oh, it had all been true enough, in essence, but Giles would not understand that. Reported, it might sound different.

She said, 'I would hate him to know how I feel about his father's family. He's fond of them and I daresay he'll want to see them. I wouldn't want to make him feel it was disloyal to me, that would be wrong, wouldn't it?'

Anna said, 'He wouldn't want to speak to them if he knew.'

'Perhaps not. But we won't tell him, will we?'

'I shall hate him if he does speak to them,' Anna said. 'They ought to be *tortured*.'

'Darling, don't be vindictive. This isn't like you.'

She felt that. It was as if some stranger were sitting there. Not the things she had said, they were childish, but the feeling of violence behind them.

She said, 'Not like my gentle Anna!'

But the girl looked at her with a face like stone. She said, 'I'm not vindictive, Crystal. I just want to kill them for hurting you. I want to see them die *slowly*.'

Giles said to Tottie, 'You'll love Aunt Azuba. She's a real English eccentric. They don't breed them like that any more, the age of the individual is over. We've become so self-conscious, we can't do anything or say anything without doubting our motives. But Azuba was born before Freud, she's as old as *God*. She does what she likes and says what she likes – as direct as a child. Or a force of nature, like the wind! And old Simon's the same, and

Thaddeus – he's another marvellous character! He was in the Indian Army, spent all his life quelling riots, now he's retired to an old castle in Scotland and wears a *dhoti* all the time! I remembered seeing him in Princes Street, Edinburgh, once, and it was an amazing sight. This skinny old Englishman in a gown of white muslin. But he was quite unconcerned!'

Tottie smiled. Giles was so enthusiastic about everyone connected with him, except his mother. About the rest of his family, about his friends. . . . They were so kind, so intelligent; so liberal-minded in spite of being rich, so gaily inventive, though poor. Or, at the least, they had a wonderful, quiet sense of humour.

It seemed that he offered them to her like beautifully wrapped presents. She would never tell him that the contents were sometimes a disappointment. They were all so alike, Giles's friends, the young men he had known at school, or in the Army, and the girls they had married: good-tempered, well-mannered, sharing the same, unshadowed past. She did say once, early on, 'Giles, you make me feel so inadequate. Telling me how marvellous your friends are. It makes me feel I can never measure up!'

He looked puzzled. 'But sweetheart, I think you are marvellous, too!'

He did think so; he loved and admired her. But sometimes she felt like an exhibit. They gave parties in their two rented rooms; their guests brought bottles of wine and sat on the floor and Tottie provided simple food: a rice dish, a tossed salad. 'Tottie makes such amazingly good salads,' Giles said, urging his friends to take more than they wanted. 'You know, till I got married, I never knew that lettuce could be a gastronomic experience! And you must try the chopped herring. Tottie makes it from her grandmother's recipe, there are so many splendid Jewish dishes, but I think this is the best of them all.' And his friends would help themselves to salad and chopped herring and smile at Tottie with especially kind, respectful smiles: she was Giles's simply marvellous Jewish wife who had a terrible time during the war but was making a wonderful adjustment to her new life.

Tottie had never felt so conspicuously Jewish before. Her family had not been religious; although she had been aware of solidarity in the camps it had been more with other victims than with other Jews. But she saw that her Jewishness was important to Giles. He loved her, of course, but marrying her was also his personal answer to Hitler, his way of standing up and being counted.

Tottie did not resent this. He was so happy, so busy shaping his life, cultivating, besides his Jewish wife, other mild eccentricities to give it form and meaning. Since they could not afford a car, he bought a dramatically ancient bicycle which he rode round London; he wore discreetly flamboyant clothes, flowered ties and brocade waistcoats before they were generally fashionable; he fenced in their days with minor rituals ('It is the tradition in this family that the lady of the house always has breakfast in bed on *Tuesdays*') and invented a host of small, private jokes like saying, 'Come on lady, get your hat, stick and gloves', when it was time to leave a party.

She felt tender towards him. And also nervous for him: he seemed so vulnerable to her. When his things were moved from his mother's flat, she unpacked his old school trunk and found among the shrunken pullovers and rugger vests a notebook that was quite blank except for the first page where he had written, in a little boy's firm, black script, 'The Rise Of The House Of Giles Golightly'. Tottie did not cry easily, she shed no tears for Aunt Hannah, or her cousins, Ruth and Sara, for the roll-call of her dead, but she wept for the living Giles, sitting beside his black tin trunk with the notebook pressed against her chest; an absurd, bursting waterfall of grief for the sad, frail hopes of the world. From that moment Giles seemed much younger than she was, as if he were still no older than he had been when he wrote that heading in his notebook; she dreaded his disappointments as if he had been her child. To see him set off for interviews (dapperly dressed, riding his ancient bicycle), so young, so buoyantly hopeful, tore her heart; when she found a job before he did, translating educational texts for a small publishing firm, she walked the streets for several hours before she could bear to go home and tell him. And even when he was unfeignedly delighted, took her out to dinner to celebrate, told all his friends, 'Tottie has landed this simply marvellous job,' she continued to insist that it was nothing, a talent for languages was merely a saleable, easily measured commodity, nothing more.

It wasn't easy for her to be so self-effacing. She was naturally a buoyant character, cheerfully irreverent if not cynical. But she learned, early on, to rein in this side of herself. Shortly after they came to England, Giles took her to see his father. They spent a pleasant day with Basil and his shy wife, drinking sherry before a log fire and walking in the fir forest, but conversation faltered towards the end. They caught an earlier train back to London than they had intended and Giles was silent for some time, staring out at the darkening countryside. At last, he sighed. 'I suppose it's natural he should seem a stranger. After all, we've not met for two years, he's married to someone else. But I never thought we'd find so little to say to each other.' He rubbed his eyes with the back of his hand and sighed again. 'After all, I'd not seen my mother either but there's still some sort of emotional link, however bloody tedious it may be. But with *him*, listening to him going on about the golf club and old so-and-so, I felt – oh, *I* don't know . . .' He smiled at Tottie sadly. 'I suppose we've both lost our fathers.'

Tottie said, 'I'd have thought mine was gone more irrevocably,' and saw, at once, how much this hurt him.

She had not only written down his genuine sense of loss, but shamed him by appearing to compare it with her own. He gave her a look of penitent horror. 'Oh, darling, I'm sorry, that was unforgivably *clumsy*.'

She laughed and kissed him. There was nothing to forgive, she had meant nothing, simply spoken, thoughtlessly, the words that came into her head. But he could not forgive himself. She was so resilient, it was difficult, sometimes, to remember how much she had suffered, but he *ought* to remember! It was crassly insensitive to speak to her of *his* petty little woes! 'Oh God, I feel so ashamed,' he said, and sat with his head in his hands.

Incidents of this sort made Tottie tread warily. Giles was so thin-skinned. He worried about his friends, their jobs, their marriages; about the atom bomb; starving populations; earthquakes in Turkey. And he was not a hypocrite, weeping for the pleasure of it: he was honestly and honourably concerned about the unhappiness of the world.

'He is such a *nice* man,' she said to Ivan Winter, who ran the foreign department of the publishing firm she worked for.

Ivan gave her a sly, amused glance from the gold corners of his eyes. '*Nice*! Oh, that dreadful, English word! The *veather* is nice, food is nice, your husband is nice, now! What does it mean?'

Spoken in Ivan's deliberately retained foreign accent, it did sound absurd. Ivan, who had left Hungary in 1938 and worked for the B.B.C. throughout the war, could speak English almost perfectly but often chose not to: although he had changed his unpronounceable surname, he liked to think of himself as an exile.

'It's a useful word, I find,' Tottie said. 'It expresses something about the English character. But it could only be applied to an Englishman. *You* are not nice, Ivan.'

'I am glad of it. It sounds bland, like a milk pudding. But I would like to meet your paragon of a husband.'

'Sometime.'

'What are you afraid of? That I will laugh at him or seduce him? Which?'

Tottie shook her head loyally. But both suggestions had gone home. Giles was, superficially anyway, the type of public school, Empire-building Englishman that Ivan was most amused by; a type, he said, who behaved as if they still controlled the world but the arrogance of masters had been replaced by the insolence of upper servants. Giles would enjoy remarks like that (Tottie could hear him, saying to his friends, 'You simply must meet this marvellously witty new chum of Tottie's'), but he disliked homosexuals. He tried not to show his dislike (after all, they couldn't help being born that way) but he couldn't help how he felt, either: men like Ivan made him uneasy and uncomfortable.

'I would promise not to laugh,' Ivan said, watching her.

'There is nothing to laugh at, in Giles, but you would find something. You would laugh at your grandmother's funeral!'

Ivan rolled his eyes upwards and giggled. 'It wasn't my fault if I did. We were on holiday, my parents and I, at Lake Balaton. When we heard she had died, my father said, "What made her do that? She's never done anything like that before." '

Tottie laughed. She had heard this joke before, told years ago in Prague by her Uncle Franz about *his* father, but she laughed in recognition. Ivan often made her laugh in this way. She liked him for the familiarity of his jokes, for his merry malice and his easy kindness, and, because she also despised him a little (he was not, she told herself, a *good* man, like Giles) she felt comfortably at home with him as if they had grown up together.

Sometimes, after work, she went home with him to the

house off the Bayswater Road where he lived with a pale, sad-eyed Greek in his thirties, an ex G.I. who had gone to Oxford after the war instead of returning to America, and whose methods of earning a living appeared to be mysterious. Or Ivan was mysterious about them. 'Buying and selling, I suppose, greasing the wheels of the capitalist system in some small, productive way. He was trafficking in French horns when we first met, taking old ones out of the country and bringing new ones in. Now, I don't know and I don't *ask*, I'm afraid he might tell me and I am a timid man, I like to be on the right side of the law. Though to be honest, I suspect the truth may be legal and dreary and Nikos dresses it up for fun. You know what Greeks are, they can turn buying a loaf of bread into a cloak and dagger job!'

Whatever it was, it provided plenty of free time and money: Nikos seemed to spend a great deal of both at furniture sales and the flat was richly luxurious in a dimly lit, darkly curtained way – a startling contrast to the exterior of the house with its peeling paint and flaking stucco and unwashed milk bottles on the front steps. 'Why it's *beautiful*,' Tottie said, the first time she climbed the shabby stairs and entered this Aladdin's Cave, her involuntary exclamation so unmistakably genuine that Nikos smiled, his rare, slow smile, and looked at Ivan with sad pride. Her appreciation smoothed what might have been a bumpy passage: it was clear, in the beginning anyway, that Nikos was both jealous and afraid. Tottie did her best to reassure him by talking about Giles, treating Ivan more distantly in the flat than she did in the office, and carefully praising any new acquisition, a Queen Anne card table, a Buhl desk. Nikos was pleased, but largely because he hoped Ivan would be impressed: while he listened to Tottie he watched his love so hopefully that Tottie was saddened, sometimes. But Ivan preferred (or affected to prefer, in Nikos's presence) comfort to beauty. 'Persian carpets are all very well, but where's the *gin?*' Either showing off, or embarrassed by Nikos's devotion – perhaps a bit of both, Tottie thought, and was sorry for Nikos: as a person he seemed shadowy to her, part of her friend Ivan's background as a shy and silent wife might be, but his feelings were painfully real.

Not that the undercurrents of their relationship troubled her much. Since she had no designs on Ivan, she felt they were none of her business. She was simply content to go there once or twice a week when they could leave the office early; enjoyed the comfort, the drinks, the relaxed, gossipy atmosphere in which she could say what she liked, be silly if she wanted, without the feeling that she was falling short in some way, as, when she was with Giles, she feared she sometimes did. When Nikos was sure she did not mean to take Ivan away from him he began to press gifts on her in thanksgiving: lengths of cloth, foodstuffs that were still in short supply. She found it hard to refuse without hurting his feelings; would probably have taken, in the end, some of the things offered, if Ivan had not come to her rescue. 'Leave her alone, Niki. Her nice husband would be shocked if we sent her home with a load of black-market butter.'

That was part of it, of course (for Giles, who had never been hungry in his life, the words *black market* had an unqualified ring), but it wasn't all. Though she had talked about Ivan, 'my funny little Hungarian', disparaging him for reasons that were not quite clear to herself, she had not told Giles about her visits to the flat. At first out of loyalty to Ivan (Giles would find his domestic arrangements hilariously amusing) and later from a kind of self-protection. She was less certain of herself than she appeared to be. Without quite adopting Giles's standards, some of which seemed mysterious to her (she had bought clothing coupons on the black market and not told him), she felt them to be higher than her own and tried not to let him down too often. His wife being made a pet of by two homosexuals was how he would see *this* situation. He would be astonished at her lack of taste and assume she must be aware of it, or she would not have deceived him in the first place.

Not that she realized the extent of her deception, slipping into it easily over a period of months, until one day when she came home and found Giles had been telephoning her office for the past two hours. He had good news, he had found a job – and now the edge had gone from his triumph. 'When I couldn't get you at work, I thought you must have come home early – I raced the old bike all the way back,' he said, smiling sadly. 'You weren't here, so I rang the office again, and then, of course, I began to think something quite *frightful* must have happened.'

She could not have felt more guilty if she had spent those last two hours in bed with a lover. Even the truth, that she had been innocently giggling and drinking gin with Ivan seemed a terrible betrayal. She said, 'It was such a lovely day, I walked home slowly, window-shopping – oh, darling, I *am* sorry.'

She was near tears. For a second he looked surprised and then he laughed and kissed her. 'Did you see anything you wanted? Shall we go on a shopping spree? You have a husband with prospects now. Not managing director *yet* but you never know. Come on, lady, smile for me!'

The job was editorial assistant on a poultry trade magazine. Not what he had hoped for, perhaps. But what had that been? *Something useful and interesting* about summed it up. But as an ambition that was far too vague and diffuse, he saw now. Maybe he should have gone to university (with a degree he could have got into the B.B.C.), but he had felt too old when the war ended. And he had been riding high on a wave of simplicity and vigour that seemed bound to carry him forward into civilian life without loss of pace, into some splendid occupation tailored to his talents and ideals. Instead it had receded, not so much suddenly as imperceptibly, and left him, nearly thirty, stranded in a stuffy cubicle on the fourth floor of a drab office block, writing editorials about turkeys.

Giles observed this with amusement, not bitterness. At least it was more original than some of the jobs his friends had fallen into – advertising, or I.C.I. Betts and Billington was a large firm with a wide network of trade papers and Wilfrid Betts (Billington had died years ago) had assured him that there were good prospects of promotion. 'How many little Betts coming up, jostling each other for places on the Board?' George Golightly had said, but Giles decided that his uncle had got distinctly sour lately. Perhaps he was annoyed because his nephew had got himself a job off his own bat, without any help from him.

'The trouble with my father's family,' Giles said to Tottie, 'is that they are the sort of people who used to have influence. They can't believe that that's all over now, that the age of nepotism is dead.'

'I thought you told me Wilfrid Betts knew your Uncle Thaddeus,' Tottie said, rather sharply.

'Only by reputation. *His* uncle, Shanklin Betts, was a judge in Allahabad. He could hardly avoid knowing Thaddeus, everyone in India did. But that just happened to come out at the interview, it wasn't important.'

'Perhaps not,' Tottie said, after a tiny pause. She had developed an odd habit of watching him with a look of sad, puzzled concentration. She was worried about him, Giles guessed. If you love someone, you fear their failure more than you do your own.

It hurt, rather, that she should feel he might be disappointed. Because he wasn't: his ambition had never been to be powerful or famous or rich, but to live a decent, civilized life. Then it struck him, thinking about it, that this could seem to her a privileged attitude and he was ashamed of his blindness: he had forgotten that her need for security must be far greater than his. To reassure her, he bought a small house in Chelsea for more than he could really afford. Uncle George provided the deposit out of the family trust, a thousand pounds free of interest to be paid back when the house was sold, but the mortgage would have been crippling if Tottie had not been working too. 'Only for a year, I hope,' Giles said, 'then you can be a lady of leisure if you want to be.'

But it was two years before he got his promotion and then it was not quite what he had expected. He was made financial director of a group of Betts magazines at a salary of fifteen hundred a year, but he was not given a seat on the board. Wilfrid Betts took him out to lunch at the Savoy Grill and Giles told Tottie, later, that he knew from the moment he ordered the first course that it was bad news he was breaking.

'A dozen oysters instead of half a dozen. Old Wilf doesn't throw money about like that unless he's feeling bad about something. Though he hasn't got much to feel guilty about really. To tell you the truth, I was quite sorry for him, time he'd finished. The trouble is the collapse of the Empire, apparently. Not shrinking markets but the return of our natives! Young and not-so-young Empire building nephews and cousins and godsons from the far corners of the earth! Two of them, to be exact. Wives and children and lousy pensions and Wilf feels he ought to fit them in if he can. It's a family firm, after all, they're shareholders, and he thinks it's his duty, he's an oldfashioned chap in that way. I must say, I admire him for it, really.'

'You mean that, don't you?' Tottie said.

'Well, of course.' He looked at her in surprise. They were sitting in their tiny garden in the sunshine; he got up, pulled a weed out of the flower bed and examined it with unnatural care. 'I mean, even allowing for pride and all that. Wilf really was frightfully nice about it. Couldn't have been nicer. He said of course he'd never made me any firm promises but he'd understand if I felt let down and wanted to leave. I told him I wouldn't, of course.'

'Why?' Tottie said.

'It would leave him in such a fearful mess if I did. I'm not talking about eventually, but about now. The heirs apparent will be pretty clueless, for a time, anyway.'

'That's his business, isn't it?'

'Yes. But he's an old man and he's been decent to me.'

'An extra half dozen oysters?'

'Don't be silly,' he said patiently. He squatted beside her and took her hand. 'Come on, lady. I can't be angry just to please you.'

'You ought to be angry for yourself. *I'm* angry.'

'Don't be. It's bad in your state of health.' He smiled, blue eyes shining, dropped a kiss in the palm of her hand and folded her fingers over it. 'Oh, I suppose I was fed up at first. But then I thought, driving home, I hadn't any real right to be. It seemed almost immoral, indeed! So many people so much worse off than we are, not just now, I don't mean, but thinking back. Sometimes I wake in the night and remember the war, and think, My God, I've been lucky, I must never forget it. Does that sound priggish?' He waited anxiously until she shook her head, then gave her hand a grateful squeeze. 'I don't mean I'm unaware of the money side. I'll have to look for something else before the baby's born. If I can give old Wilf four months or so, it ought to see him through. If you aren't well enough to work, I'd think again, of course, but you seem so marvellously fit. You are, aren't you?'

'Yes,' Tottie said. 'Yes, I am.'

She was eight weeks pregnant. She felt tired sometimes, an ache in her back, that was all. But the following month the sickness started. Not, curiously, in the mornings, but the middle of the afternoons: regularly, at about three o'clock, she would disappear to the lavatory and retch violently for an hour or more. These bouts left her sweating and giddy:

Ivan, with whom she shared an office, fussed like a kind, maiden aunt.

'You should be in bed, my angel. You are *thirty-three*. Women over thirty should take special care. What is Giles thinking of?'

'It doesn't happen at home,' Tottie said. 'Don't tell him.'

Not that he was likely to. Giles had met Ivan twice, once by chance at a theatre, and a second time when Tottie had invited him to dinner. The early part of the evening had gone easily, Ivan had been sharply amusing and everyone had laughed a great deal, but he stayed on after the other guests had left and he and Giles began drinking what was, for both of them, an unusual amount. That was all right, too, to begin with, until Giles started asking questions about Nikos – 'Which of you does the *cooking*?' – with an awful, arch roguishness that made it plain he was really curious about their sexual habits. Ivan had answered Giles levelly; though his golden eyes darkened a little, he gave no other sign of minding. But he had kissed Tottie roughly in the hallway before he left, bruising her mouth, and when she went back into the drawing room Giles had said, 'Trying to prove something, your little friend?' For the first and only time in their lives, she threw something at him, a heavy, glass ashtray they had bought in Murano. It struck him just beside his left eye and cut him. They stood, looking at each other; then Giles went white and said, 'Oh my God I'm sorry, I behaved disgustingly. Jealous, I suppose, which makes it even more sickeningly ridiculous because I've no cause to be. Not of him.'

He had laughed then, expecting, it seemed, that she would laugh too, but she was too angry. She said, 'How do you know there's no cause?' and he looked at her, blinking.

'Is there, then? I mean, apart from the fact that he makes you laugh more than I do?'

'I don't know.' She really didn't know, suddenly. She said, 'Let's not be silly, Giles. We're both tired.'

She apologized to Ivan. He said, 'Oh, I'm used to it. An occupational hazard, like being a black or a Jew. Though I expect your nice husband would call me out if I said anything about the Chosen Race in his presence.'

Though he seemed, genuinely, to bear no malice, he didn't mention Giles again until Tottie was pregnant and ill. He said, 'You should tell him, you know. It's unfair not to. He wouldn't want you to go on working.'

'We can't afford for me to stop,' Tottie said, and at once felt disloyal. 'It's my fault,' she said. 'I'm greedy, I want things. I spend too much money on clothes.'

She miscarried on the morning of the Coronation. There was television in the hospital ward and when they took the screens from round her bed, she watched the young Queen ride to her crowning. She had not really believed she would lose her baby, she had too much confidence in her own physical hardiness, her powers of survival, and the colourful charade increased her sense of unreality. She felt as if she were in the middle of some curious dream. No one and nothing was real to her. Even when Giles came, in the evening, he was simply a youngish man, handsome in a pink, English way, sitting beside her bed. It seemed absurd that this stranger should hold her hand and weep. He said, 'Darling, I feel so guilty! I'd no idea you'd not been well, why didn't you tell me?' The doctor had told him, she supposed. She knew she should comfort him but felt no desire to: the energy of his self-reproaches exhausted her. She withdrew her hand, withdrew into silence.

It was not until the end of the week that she recovered her spirits. Ivan came to see her, brought flowers and a jar of caviare, made her laugh. Giles, coming in later, found her sitting up with colour in her cheeks. He said, 'I met Ivan going out.' She thought the skin had tightened over his cheekbones the way it did sometimes when he was tired or distressed, but all he said was, 'Oh my love, I'm so glad to see you better.' He sat on the bed and told her he had spent the afternoon with George Golightly and arranged to join the merchant bank. 'I should have done it before – after all, it's hard to keep a good man down in his Uncle's firm! Don't know why I didn't, really – partly silly pride, perhaps, didn't want George to *crow*.' She asked if he had and he said, 'Well, a bit, but he was entitled to, I suppose.' He was not in the least resentful; never was, on his own behalf. Such a nice man, she thought, kind and tolerant – and was ashamed because she felt, suddenly, that she was cataloguing the virtues of some chance acquaintance.

She said, 'Something is wrong, though,' and touched the creases at the corners of his eyes.

He watched her. 'I didn't want to bother you.'

She could do that much for him. She said, 'Please tell me, darling,' and smiled, to show how well she felt, but he still hesitated, searching her face. She said, '*Please*,' again, almost desperately.

'All right. It's frightfully tedious, though.' A pause, a sigh. 'I rather think my mother has gone out of her mind.'

He did think that. It seemed the only explanation. At first he had not really understood what George was trying to tell him, he approached the matter with such lumbering delicacy, and when he did, he could only think his mother had gone mad. For the last two years she had been writing abusive letters to Basil's family, to Azuba, to Thaddeus, to George, to Simon, to Sholto's wife. The letters had begun by being mildly hysterical and had lately become obscene. 'Extraordinary, really,' George said. 'I'd always thought your mother rather *prissy*. But Azuba's just had a letter that turned *me* up. Accusing her of running a brothel for your father's benefit. That's a polite way of putting what she said as you'll see if you care to read it.'

Giles had not cared to, but he did. Read it slowly, putting off the moment when he would have to make some comment. While he read he thought of how his mother had appeared to him recently, busy with her flat, her bridge evenings, one or two charitable activities; a calm, competent woman, growing gracefully older. He and Tottie saw her about once a month. Had it been enough? Giles searched his conscience but was forced to admit that it had seemed so: she had never suggested that they should meet more often, had been content, he had vaguely thought, with Anna's company. They were very close, almost like two girls together. In fact, one of the reasons they hadn't seen more of his mother was that he found the girl's constant presence a little intimidating. Big, dowdy, shy, silent – Tottie had said, 'She'll be beautiful when she finds her style, like a big, glossy young mare,' but Giles hadn't seen it. He liked well turned out, intelligent, talkative girls and he found Anna boring. Perhaps she bored Crystal, too, he thought suddenly; perhaps she had been lonely, driven in on herself, nothing to occupy her but old feuds and bitterness . . .

He looked at George, sitting on the other side of his big, tidy desk, picking his teeth with the nail of his little finger, and wondered what she had written to him. She had nothing against George, surely? He said, 'I had no idea she felt like this,' hoping to show by his tone that he felt she had some excuse for her incredible behaviour. After all, Basil had been unfaithful, and Azuba, Giles knew from things she had said to him, had always been scornful of her. As he had been himself. 'My mother is a silly, self-regarding woman,' he had once told Tottie. He flushed at the memory and said, to George, 'Perhaps she really does feel that the whole family have conspired to reject her.'

But there was no need for a show of loyalty. George was too embarrassed and worried, it seemed on Crystal's behalf. 'Until this letter turned up it seemed best to ignore the whole thing. We thought it was probably menopausal, something like that, and would pass. But this last effort is a bit too much, I think you'll agree. Not just because

111

Azuba's old and it upset her rather, but because it suggests rather more unbalance on your mother's part than we'd thought before.' He paused and cleared his throat; it seemed that his colour rose a little but since his complexion was naturally pink with good living it was hard to tell. 'To be honest, I'd have gone to see her myself if we hadn't had rather an unpleasant passage some years back.'

The dismissive way this was said discouraged questioning. It struck Giles that his uncle's willingness to find him a place in the bank had been slightly increased by the hope that he would perform a disagreeable duty. Not tit for tat, exactly – the job had been offered first – but perhaps the prospect had tipped the balance. He said, rather drily, 'What do you want me to do? Get her certified?'

'Good God, no!' George was so shocked by this suggestion that for a minute or two he neither picked his teeth, nor his nose, nor searched for wax in his ears. He looked at his big, unoccupied hands, palms down on the polished desk in front of him, and said, 'There's no need for that sort of talk, dear lad! For heaven's sake!' He seemed at a loss for words; he lifted one of those workman's paws from the desk and waved it vaguely about as if he might pluck some out of the air. 'I used to be fond of your mother,' he said, in the end. 'She used to be an exceptionally pretty woman.'

'She still is,' Giles felt compelled to say, though it seemed beside the point.

George sighed. 'I can't really believe she's three sheets in the wind. That's what old Simon's wife used to call anyone who was a bit off their head, you know. Died years ago, poor Esther, don't suppose you remember her? But it ought to be looked into and I'm afraid you're the one to do it. Sorry, but there you are. It may just be some sort of silly fantasy that can be put a stop to by a quiet word. If it's more than that, then all I can say is that the family are prepared to help if necessary. Pay for treatment privately, out of the Trust.' He stopped, frowning suddenly, as if disturbed by some echo in his mind. Giles waited, but knowing George, expected no startling revelation: he was probably only probing a tasty tooth cavity with his tongue. When he finally spoke it was in a crisper tone than he'd used before, as if he wanted to get this tiresome item off the agenda. 'Not strictly what it was intended for, you know, but I daresay the Trustees will be glad to arrange something for your mother.'

'I hardly see what my private correspondence has to do with you, Giles dear.'

Crystal sat on the sofa in the drawing room, dressed as if for a garden party, and smiled up at him. Her hair, ash blonde now, was piled high on her head in sweeps and curls and looked like an elaborate hat. Her face, though middle-aged, was healthy, pretty and composed, but her eyes had a vague look as if she were spiritually involved elsewhere. She smiled at her son and said, 'You know you look a little like Philip. I've never noticed it before.'

'Philip who?'

'Oh, darling!' Crystal laughed. 'Turn your face a little to the left. That's it. Something about the jaw line, I think. You know, you'd be very like him, if you lost a little weight.'

Perhaps she *was* mad, Giles thought. He had come prepared to be kind and understanding; a hint, he had hoped, would be enough. But here she sat, apparently oblivious of his carefully oblique approach, and talking about the Duke of Edinburgh.

She said, 'Did you watch the coronation? Anna and I sat all day, glued to the screen. The Queen of Tonga, and poor old Churchill, lurching about in his coach like some dressed up medieval doll! And the actual ceremony was so moving, didn't you think? She looked so solemn and small and *he* was quite wonderful, we thought. To tell you the truth, Anna and I quite lost our hearts! *Lovely* fantasies of his

113

kneeling at our feet and swearing to be *our* liege lord of life and limb!'

Giles stared at her. She said, 'Oh darling, don't be superior. You may think it's just feminine nonsense but there's no need for that potato face!'

He said slowly, 'It was a bit of nonsense that I didn't have time for. I happened to spend most of the day, you may remember, sitting in the waiting room at the hospital. Waiting to see if Tottie was going to *die*.'

She held the back of her hand to her forehead. 'Oh God. Oh Giles, I'm *sorry*.'

She really had forgotten, he saw. But it destroyed his patience with her and gave him a moral advantage.

He said, 'I didn't come here to talk about the Royal Family but about what you choose to call your private correspondence. Though it's not been much of a corres-pondence, has it? Too one-sided. George says . . .'

'Do you prefer to believe George rather than me?' Her voice rose. She controlled herself visibly: sat rather more erect, smiled at him sadly. 'Darling, if you are going to be unpleasant, do keep your voice down. I'd rather Anna didn't hear.'

'She's got the radio on,' Giles said. 'Though how anyone can do their homework with that bloody noise blaring beats me! And *I* wasn't shouting!'

'All right, dear.' Her smile was indulgent now; she put her head a little on one side. 'Let's discuss it calmly, shall we? Without losing our tempers or getting things out of proportion. If I understand you correctly, George has complained to you because I have had the *temerity* to try and keep in touch with some members of my ex-husband's family. What's wrong with that? Am I some sort of *leper*?'

'You know what's wrong.'

'I beg your pardon, I do not.'

He said, gently, 'Darling, I'm sorry. But I saw what you wrote to Azuba.'

114

She looked down at her lap, apparently examining her tinted fingernails with close attention. He saw her throat move as she swallowed. At last she said, 'She treated me very badly. They all did.'

Her tone was light and mild. Indignation remembered in sad tranquillity. She pursed her lips with a small sound of satisfaction.

He said, 'It's an offence to send obscene matter through the post. They could have gone to the police.'

She flinched, but only slightly. As if he had struck her with a feather. 'Are you trying to humiliate me?'

'Of course not. No one is.' He looked at her. She was watching him, her lower lip caught between her teeth. A little girl caught out in some minor naughtiness. He said, 'Look, they've ignored it as long as they could. Get that into your head – they've been very *decent*. Still are being! Dear Christ – George is *worried* about you. He says you must be ill. He even offered to pay for treatment if you were, make some provision out of the Trust.'

She began to cry. 'Giles, how *can* you? How can you turn against me like this, against your own mother? Be so disloyal, so cruel? Oh, I suppose it's my own silly fault, I've brought it on myself, I never told you how they behaved to me. I was too proud and I wanted to spare you. And this is all the thanks I get, my own son taking their side against me! After all I've suffered . . .'

'You've never suffered in your life. You don't know what the word means.' His voice was loud with outrage.

She gasped, 'Oh Giles, you don't know what they did to me . . .' She got to her feet and stood, hands pressed to her face. For a moment he was sorry, could see that this exposure was terrible for her, but when she dropped her hands, he saw the anger in her eyes.

He said, '*What* have they done to you? Come on, tell me. Chapter and verse.'

'What have they done, what have they *done*? You dare

to ask me what they have done? All right, I'll tell you. *Anna* will tell you if you don't believe me, she'll bear me out, she knows what I've been through. And cares, what's more, cares more than you do, my own flesh and blood! She'll tell you how they've despised and rejected me.' Except for her painted mouth, her face was white as a peeled stick and so stiffly distorted that he hardly recognized it. She was a stranger, suddenly; an ageing woman with a ridiculous hair-do and a slashed orange mouth, screaming like some elderly tart at the end of her tether. She threw back her head and shouted, 'Anna, Anna . . .'

'Shut up,' he said in a rough whisper. 'Have you gone *mad?*' Until this moment an unadmitted part of him had been half enjoying this, as he suspected she had been – they both had a liking for drama – but now he was appalled. He said, 'You don't want the child to hear.' He caught her hands but she continued to screech the girl's name, her head twisted sideways, her eyes rolling up. He said, 'You wicked bitch,' and clapped his hand across her mouth.

Anna said, 'Let her go.' He looked up and saw her in the doorway. Crystal gasped and writhed; when he released her she began to scream again and raked her fingers through her piled up hair. He struck her on one cheek, not hard but noisily, with his hand slightly cupped, and Anna flew at him.

The violence of her attack astonished him. Not its suddenness but its quality: this was no childish assault, she was in deadly earnest like a navvy in a street brawl. At first he tried to fend her off, was simply anxious not to hurt her, then, as her fist caught his face, he grew angry and wanted to. She was strong and heavy but no match for him; he pinned her arms to her side and held her tightly against him. She struggled and they swayed together as if in some strange, ritual dance. He was conscious, briefly, of absurdity – what a ridiculous scene, first his mother, now the girl, all those threshing, Sabine limbs – and then of a sharp, sexual pleasure.

It shocked him. He thought of her as a child. But he still held her, even after she had quietened and was merely trembling against him. He said, breathlessly, 'Oh dear, oh dear . . .' And then, 'She was hysterical, I was trying to stop her being hysterical.'

Anna's hair brushed his mouth. It smelled young and clean, of some herb or other, and he found he only wanted to be gentle with her.

He loosened his hold cautiously, telling himself that he still didn't quite trust her. But she stood still, her head bowed. She was wearing school uniform, a blue skirt and a white blouse with ink stains on the collar. She said, 'I'm sorry, I shouldn't have hit you, I'm terribly sorry.' Her voice was low and distressed but it was the look on her face that moved him; her expression of absolute, unqualified shame.

It also humbled him a little. Like her earlier violence, it seemed to have deeper roots than anything he had felt throughout this scene. Beside the passion of her responses his irritated anger seemed almost frivolous. And his mother's apparent despair, mere play-acting.

Crystal was sitting on the sofa, sobbing quietly. Her hair hung in wisps round her face. She stretched out her hands to Anna and the girl ran to her and took them. She kissed the palms and put her arms round Crystal and Crystal looked at Giles over her shoulder and said, 'Tell him, Anna. Go on, tell him.'

What shocked Giles (or so he told Tottie) was not his mother's fantasies, but that she had made Anna a party to them. And not just on one occasion, Anna's retelling had too much detail for that, but persistently, over the months; a daily occasion, even. Knowing his mother, Giles could set the scene: the homework finished, the television switched off, the tray of cocoa, the cosy bedtime tale. All his mother's store of retrospective malice.

Anna said, 'She'd kept it to herself for so long, you see. Once she started, she had to go on.'

And she had no choice but to listen. It made Giles sweat to think of it. That poor child! But Tottie said, 'I don't suppose she minded so much. It's not unpleasant, working up a good, healthy anger on someone else's account.'

Giles thought it unkind of Tottie to diminish Anna in this way. He had been impressed by her championship of his mother. He valued loyalty and Anna was touchingly loyal. Even when Crystal went into the nursing home (accepting, Giles suspected, a fictional breakdown as the only way out of an intolerable situation) she refused to believe she had been told a single lie.

'Whatever you think, I know they drove her there,' she said. 'I don't care if she wrote them beastly letters, they deserved it. They made her terribly unhappy and I shall never forgive them as long as I live. If any of them comes to your house while I'm here, I'm sorry, but I shan't speak to them. I won't be rude, I'll just go to my room, but I think you ought to know, just in case you don't want me to stay.'

She said this, the night of her arrival. Crystal had refused to let Giles take her to the nursing home; Anna had gone with her in a taxi and returned by Tube, first to the flat and then to Chelsea, lugging a heavy suitcase and her satchel, full of books. She put her suitcase down in the hall, marched into the drawing room and made her prepared speech. It was a little stilted, even childish, perhaps, but her manner was challenging. Giles was amazed. He had thought her such a drab and unassuming girl. Incapable of challenging anyone.

'It couldn't have been easy,' he said, when she was unpacking upstairs. 'I mean, for such a mousey child!'

Tottie said, 'She's not a child. She's nearly eighteen.'

'Well. We're almost old enough to be her parents.' He laughed, crinkling his eyes. 'Biologically, anyway.'

Tottie said, 'I never thought her mousey.'

'Shy, then.'

'Not even that. Repressed, maybe. The sort of person who is always more concerned about other people than about herself. There's less guilt attached to it.'

She smiled. Giles remembered that she had said something similar before when he had told her about the scene in the flat.

He said, 'Oh, don't give me that transference stuff!'

'It's called altruistic surrender.'

He sighed with sarcastic patience. 'Sorry, but I'm not one of your smart, literary friends. Just a simple, bluff, banker feller. Isn't it *possible* that she's just a quiet, sweet, unselfish girl who happens to love my mother?'

Tottie laughed out loud. 'Perhaps. It's just that she looked more natural angry. More like herself, somehow.'

She had certainly looked more beautiful. A big, strong, handsome girl with defiant colour in her cheeks, dwarfing their doll's house drawing-room. Her outgrown school coat had been exceptionally unbecoming – the straining buttons over that magnificent chest – but she was young enough for this to be quite unimportant. Giles thought of the way her plump, white, uncreased neck had risen out of the ill-fitting collar and wondered if Tottie was jealous. Tottie was only thirty-three but she had lost her baby and was unlikely to have another. When the doctor had told them this, Giles had felt himself weeping inside. Luckily Tottie had taken it well. But she looked tired and thin, lying on the sofa.

He said, 'She'd make two of you!'

Tottie held out her hand. He shifted his chair closer and took it. He said, 'I hope she won't be too much trouble. It won't be for too long – while Crystal's in the nursing home, and perhaps while she has a holiday, after.' He laughed and squeezed her hand. 'D'you know what Azuba said to George? She said, send her on a world cruise, tell her to find a man. Nothing like a lover to help a woman through the menopause!'

Tottie smiled obediently. One of her front teeth had darkened. Giles said, 'You ought to have that tooth crowned some time.'

They smiled at each other and above their heads Anna trod heavily, making the miniature chandeliers dangle. Giles held Tottie's hand against his cheek and said, 'You will be kind to her, won't you?'

Tottie said, 'Oh, Giles!'

'Well. You know.' He felt uncomfortable. He thought he understood how Tottie might be feeling. It was hard on a woman, growing old. But young girls were so vulnerable and Anna especially so. 'I mean, I know you don't like her all that much but we *are* responsible for her and she's had a simply frightful time with my mother.'

Tottie's face quivered. She might be going to laugh, or to cry. But she did neither; only sighed and said, again, 'Oh, Giles . . .'

Anna said, 'Go on, Tottie. Red-haired people look marvellous in pink. And it's a lovely dress.'

'I don't really need it.'

'That doesn't matter! You should buy things when you see them, not when you need them. That's what Crystal always says. When you really need something you can never find what you want.'

She spoke urgently, as if it was vitally important to her that Tottie should buy this pink dress, displayed in a shop window in Oxford Street. She said, 'Let's go in, at least, and see if it's your size!'

Tottie looked at her curiously. 'I didn't know you were so interested in clothes.'

'Oh, not for myself. I always look awful so there's no

point. But I love shopping with Crystal, she always looks so marvellous in everything.' She smiled at Tottie and added, quickly, 'So do you. I like the things you wear. You look gorgeous in that purple suit. Like a humming bird.'

'I'm not sure that's a compliment.'

Anna flushed. 'I meant it to be. I love bright colours.'

'Why don't you wear them, then?'

'Too big. I'd feel like an elephant going to a party.' She looked shyly at Tottie. 'Have you always been thin? When you were my age?'

Tottie laughed. 'My mother used to make me drink hot lemon and water before breakfast and tell me I would never get a husband! But it was the war, not the lemon juice, that solved my figure problem. I went into the camps a fat girl and came out a thin one.'

'Oh, Tottie!' Anna's expression was horrified. 'I'm so sorry, I didn't *think*, I should never have said that.'

'Why ever not?'

'Well, I mean it was *awful*. To remind you like that. It was terribly thoughtless. Oh, I could bite out my *tongue*.'

Her distress was exhaustingly acute. Tottie was reminded of something her father had once said about an exceptionally humble, elderly aunt. *People who live for others are so wearing*. She sighed and said, 'Everyone has a history, darling. Mine isn't holy ground.'

But Anna's eyes had filled with tears. She blinked at the shop window and whispered, 'Please Tottie, do buy that dress.'

'I saw you in Oxford Street,' Ivan said. 'With that impressive young woman. I hung out of the taxi and whistled but neither of you looked up. How are you getting on?'

'Crystal will be back soon. I'm sorry. I shall miss Anna.'

Tottie was rather surprised to find herself saying this. She had grown fond of Anna but she had felt, sometimes, that living with her was like sitting on a buried land mine. An explosive possibility hidden beneath the gentle grass. She could not explain this feeling.

Certainly not to Giles, who would see it as criticism. *My sister*, he called Anna when he introduced her to his friends, embracing this relationship, it seemed to Tottie, as a cover-up for what he would regard as less admissible emotions. Straight sexual desire was not something Giles could easily accept in himself, especially when the object was a young girl, under his own roof. Perhaps, for him, it could never be the whole story, anyway. He needed to admire before he loved. And (though Tottie found this harder to admit) he liked to love a victim. Anna touched his heart on both these counts: though she had had a wretched time with Crystal, she had remained as true as steel. But sometimes, when Giles became too doting, enlarging on his 'sister's' virtues when he and Tottie were in bed together, Tottie thought she would prefer an honest horniness . . .

She said, to Ivan, 'She's a dear, sweet girl. So kind and thoughtful, it's almost an embarrassment. But it's hard to tell what she is really like.'

'Most young girls are blank pages waiting for Prince Charming to come and scribble on them,' Ivan said. 'That's what makes them boring.'

But he was not interested in Anna. His gold eyes seemed vacant, staring beyond Tottie's shoulder at the big window. Looking at the trees in the square, rustling their dying leaves. Or, perhaps, looking at nothing.

It was the first time Tottie had been to the flat since her miscarriage. The first time, too, she had seen that window uncurtained. Whenever she had been before, the thick, plum-coloured curtains had been drawn, the alabaster lamps lit. Even in summer, Nikos preferred to live underground, like a mole. Now, seeing the rich room for the first time in daylight, the westering sun pouring in, she thought it looked like an abandoned stage set. A look of showy impermanence.

Ivan said, 'All this voluptuous tat.' He was walking about the room, cracking his fingers. He stooped, with an artificial groan, and picked up a couple of cushions. He said, 'Nikos has gone, I suppose it's obvious. He ought to have kept the flat, it was his, after all, and I'm a rotten housekeeper. But it was his last will and testament, so to speak. I could hardly say I'd rather have a bed-sit in East Barnet.'

Tottie said, 'I'm sorry.'

He shrugged his shoulders.

She said, 'When did it happen?'

'You were in hospital. I had the idea of telling you then. Thought it might divert you, but when it came to the point, I didn't think I could be amusing about it. He took it so badly.' He looked at her and she thought his face was sadder and harder. Less boyish. He said, 'I left *him*.'

'I didn't think it was the other way round.'

'Poor Nikos.' He sat down and put his head in his hands, rubbing his temples. Then he looked up. 'What could I *do*? I'd stayed for the last two years because I didn't want to hurt him. It seemed inadequate motivation for the rest of my life.' He stood up again, began pacing. He said, 'There isn't anyone *else*. Just that I wanted to finish it. I suppose I have a distant idea that i might want to get married, have children. I don't know that I do want to. I just wanted a chance to find out.'

'Where's he gone?'

'I'm not sure. He rings up late at night and we have *sepulchral* conversation. Long silences on both sides – on his from emotion and on mine from boredom. I find my-self yawning.' He giggled suddenly. 'Sepulchral. That's the right word, exactly. From the tomb.' He put on a B.B.C. voice. *This is your buried past speaking*. You know, I suddenly thought that, when I picked up the telephone the other night, and it was all I could do to stop myself laughing. I thought, you shallow bastard. I suppose that's the trouble, really. Nikos is a case of still waters running deep and I'm strictly a paddling man.'

He grinned at her, shame-faced; he was unhappier than he wished to seem.

She said, 'What'll he do? Are you worried?'

'Yes, of course, but what's the point? I tell myself that's guilt speaking. Really, I don't know. If he'd made any decisions, I'm the last person he'd tell. It might look as if he were getting over it! No, that's not fair. Maybe he'll go back to America. I suggested it and he said no – he'd just become a derelict in a New York bar. That's the sort of dramatic phrase he employs and it makes me lose patience. It makes him sound false and he isn't. Oh, I suppose all I'm saying is that there is nothing I can do for him and that embarrasses me, in the full sense of the word. I don't love him and nothing short of that is any use at all.' He pulled a funny-sad face. Then looked at Tottie and said, with astonishment, 'Darling, why are you crying?'

'I don't know,' Tottie said. 'I don't know.'

Giles said, 'What's the matter, Tottie?'

He was playing chess with Anna. She wasn't very good but he enjoyed teaching her, liked to watch her smooth young face, frowning at the board.

Tottie's face was screwed up, creased like parchment. She stood just inside the room. Giles said, 'Who was on the telephone?'

'Ivan,' she seemed to be having difficulty in breathing, 'Nikos is dead.'

Giles said, 'Oh, darling.' He got up, put his arm round her, led her to the sofa. She sat stiffly, resisting him.

She said, 'He killed himself because Ivan left him. I don't know how. Ivan just said he left a note and the police came round.'

She was shivering.

Giles said, 'Close the window, Anna.'

Anna jumped up, knocking over the chess board. She said, 'Oh, I'm *sorry*.' She ran to close the window, then knelt, picking up the chess pieces.

Giles poured Tottie a glass of brandy. He said, 'When did this happen?'

'I don't know. He was in a room somewhere in Paddington. He'd made Ivan keep the flat.'

'I didn't know they'd split up.'

Tottie said nothing.

'Did *you* know?' Her silence answered him. He said, in surprise, 'Why didn't you tell me?'

Anna was sitting back on her heels with the chess pieces in her lap. She looked pale and lost. Giles said gently, 'Ivan is a chum of Tottie's, they work in the same firm. And Nikos is – was – a friend of his.'

'His *lover*.' Tottie's green eyes dilated with what seemed scorn, or anger.

'All right, if you must.' Giles glanced at Anna. Though he did not suppose her innocent, he felt awkward about this.

But she said, simply, 'How dreadful. I'm sorry, Tottie.'

'It's not dreadful for me,' Tottie said. 'Only for Ivan.'

But she looked drained and exhausted. Almost as if the news had some fearful relevance for her, Giles thought. He said, 'Ivan must feel terrible.'

'It wasn't his fault.' Her face puckered suddenly, like a little, old woman's, and she rocked from side to side as if in pain, hands pressed between her knees. 'It wasn't his fault. He couldn't help it. He had simply stopped loving him. He couldn't help that.'

Her use of the word 'love' seemed ludicrous to Giles. He said, rather stiffly, 'Of course he couldn't help it, darling.'

She stopped rocking and looked at him with an odd expression on her face. A kind of hostile sadness.

He said, 'Is there anything we can do?'

125

Anna said, eagerly, 'Would he like to come here? He could have my room. I could sleep on the floor in the study.'

Tottie shook her head.

'I don't *mind*,' Anna said. 'Honestly, Tottie. I *like* sleeping on the floor!'

Tottie said, 'There would be no need for that, there is a spare bed in the boxroom. But this house is just about the last place Ivan would come to. Isn't it, Giles?'

The resentment in her tone astonished him. Astonished and hurt him. Had she held that silly incident against him all this while? If she had been his mother, he could have understood it, but it was unlike Tottie! Besides, as he remembered it, he had apologized handsomely at the time.

He said, 'Tottie darling, be *fair*.'

She ignored him. She said, to Anna, in a spiteful voice, 'Giles can't stand Ivan because he's a queer. Queers make his flesh creep, he's incapable of accepting them as members of the human race. Anyone else can be admitted *almost* on equal terms with himself, any minority you like to mention just as long as *he* has the credit for putting them up for his club! Even the S.S. – after all, they were only marginal examples of the cruel instincts present within us all!'

Anna was looking frightened.

Giles said, 'Stop it, Tottie, can't you see you're upsetting the child?'

Tottie threw her head back and began to laugh hysterically. Like a skull laughing – her face and throat were so thin.

Anna said, 'I'm sorry. Oh, *please*. I'm so sorry.'

Giles got into bed beside Tottie. Though he had known she was awake when he came into the bedroom, he had undressed in the dark.

He said, 'Poor Anna! I've calmed her down, I hope, but she really was in a state! All *her* fault for suggesting Ivan should come here, etcetera, etcetera . . .'

Tottie said, in a very remote voice, 'I didn't mean to upset her.'

'Oh, she knows that, darling.'

Giles wanted to put his arms round her. Or wanted to want to. But she lay so still beside him.

He said, 'Dear heart . . .'

She didn't answer.

He said, 'I do love you, Tottie. My green-eyed girl!'

Still no answer. Her silence provoked a mild indignation. She was making this very difficult for him. He said, reproachfully, 'I think she's a quite unusually sensitive girl. And *genuinely* so! I mean, she was upset because she felt her intervention had caused trouble between us, but her own feelings were not uppermost. If I implied that, then I expressed it badly. She's really frightfully devoted to you, Tottie, and admires you enormously. The marvellous way you can look back on everything that has happened to you, quite without bitterness! She said, "I think Tottie is really the most wonderful person I have ever met, I wish I could be even just a little bit like her!" And she meant it, you know, you honestly do have a keen disciple there! I said that of course I agreed with her, but that she mustn't be *too* humble, she had the makings of a pretty fine person herself!'

He laughed in a hopeful way, and waited. Tottie lay still beside him. The few inches of mattress that divided them might have been a bottomless pit; he lay rigid on the edge of it.

At last he said, nervously, 'I do think she has, don't you, Tottie?' and, to his immense relief, she stretched across the gulf that divided them and took his hand and said, in a voice that sounded as if she were smiling, 'I think I would put it slightly differently. I would say you could make her into almost anything that you wanted to.'

Part Three *GILES*

Driving away from the registry office after their wedding, Giles said to Anna, 'If I die now, you'll be my relict,' and laughed, unexpectedly loudly, as if this little joke had solved some mild uneasiness, given her some acceptable status in his mind.

Perhaps, for him, their marriage did have a certain flavour. On their honeymoon, he remembered a coarse remark of his sergeant major's, his early days in the Army. 'One in the family is worth two outside.' He didn't repeat this to Anna; was indeed, slightly shocked that it should have come into his mind. But he did say, one night, 'Do you remember that time you stayed with us when Crystal was ill? I kept calling you my little sister. It was the only way I could keep my hands off you.'

'But you were married to Tottie, then.'

Giles laughed and hugged her. 'Oh, my baby!'

She said, in a horrified voice, 'Did Tottie *know*?'

Feigning innocence?

Tottie had said, 'It was all over before you had any part in it, Anna darling.'

She was living with Ivan in his flat. They had separate rooms. Tottie had bronchitis; she lay, propped up on pillows, in a four-poster bed with purple curtains. Anna had brought her grapes; she sat on Tottie's bed, eating them and weeping. Giles's divorce had been made absolute the week before; he had just asked Anna to marry him. She was nineteen years old.

She said, 'I feel terrible about it.'

'About what?'

'About you.'

Tottie began to laugh, then coughed, holding her side. Anna said, reproachfully, 'It's not funny, Tottie.'

Tottie coughed and coughed. Her eyes streamed. She said, 'Don't make me laugh, Anna, it hurts. There's nothing for you to feel terrible about. I didn't leave Giles because he had his eye on you.' To anyone else she might have said, 'Though perhaps it eased my conscience slightly.' But she was inclined to be gentle with Anna. She had said, to Ivan, 'She wants to come and see me. I think Giles must have asked her to marry him.' And was amused to find herself proved right.

'I didn't mean that.' Anna took another grape. As she ate it, her eyes brimmed with fresh tears. 'He loved you. I mean, I always thought he loved *you*. I knew he was *fond* of me, but I thought – I mean, it wasn't as if you'd left him for another *man*.' She blushed, drew a deep breath. 'I thought he thought you might come back and I was a sort of *stand in*. I suppose that seems naïve, now.'

Or humble, Tottie thought. *I am not worth loving*. Was it possible? Looking at Anna, Tottie felt tired, suddenly. And old as the hills. Giles would not have seduced her; he would have had principles about that. But when he kissed her, pressed her hand, did she think, *how he misses Tottie*? If he was aware of it, Giles was quite capable of encouraging this romantic delusion. Or of not discouraging it, anyway: even honest men enjoy having things both ways. Did Anna?

'I feel so guilty,' Anna said.

So she had come for absolution. This large, sad, beautiful girl, sitting on the end of Tottie's bed eating the grapes she had brought her. She would feel guilty about *that* in a minute. Tottie said, quickly, 'I don't mind your stepping into my shoes if that is what's worrying you. As long as you're sure you want to!'

Anna said, 'Oh, Tottie, of course I am!' But looked startled, as if she had not really thought about this.

132

Crystal said, 'Now you really are my daughter, Anna darling. I'm happier than I can say. For myself, for Giles! He's had such a dreadful time. I know he's been very good about it, wouldn't hear a word against Tottie, but I must say, I thought she behaved very badly. So ungrateful, when you think of all Giles did for her. I know he'd be furious if he heard me say that, but I can't help how I feel. Still, it has all worked out for the best. Certainly for me. I feel as if I had not only gained a real daughter but recovered my son! Perhaps it's unfair to say so and you mustn't repeat it to him, Anna, but I always felt Tottie turned him against me in some way. Made him a bit *hard*. And he's not hard by nature, he was always such a sweet, loving boy, we were so close when he was young. He needed someone like you, Anna, I can see that now by the change in him. Someone gentle and kind and not *cynical*. I always thought Tottie was a little bit cynical!'

Anna said, 'She was very kind to me when you were away.'

Crystal frowned, as if she could hardly remember this occasion.

'When you went on that cruise and I stayed with them. I thought she was a marvellous person. So does Giles.'

Crystal looked at her closely. 'Oh, Tottie was quite a character, I don't deny that. But you mustn't let yourself be jealous of her, darling. Jealousy is such a wasteful emotion. It's a pity, really, that you and Giles have to start off in the Chelsea house. So many reminders. But if that doesn't upset you, I suppose it's sensible. Moving is an expensive business as I'm afraid I'm going to find. But it would be foolish to stay in this flat now you're gone. I thought I might look for something smaller, near Harrods, perhaps. Near enough to you to be useful when I'm needed! I'm looking forward to my grandchildren, darling! There's an admission for you! You know, when Tottie was pregnant, I was really quite upset. To become a grandmother seemed such a terrible *watershed*! Like having all one's teeth out, I suppose, though I'm glad to say *that* is unlikely to happen to me! My dentist says I have the teeth of a healthy young girl! But now I'm prepared to sit back, adjust my shawl, and be a *babushka*, walking my grandchildren in Kensington Gardens!'

'Giles wants to live in the country, eventually,' Anna said.

'Well, I daresay that would be nice. Once he's properly established and doesn't have to work quite such long hours. George keeps his nose to the grindstone, doesn't he? Oh, that family like their pound of flesh!'

'I don't like the country,' Anna said.

Sometimes she had frightening, noisy nightmares. The first time this happened, some months after their wedding, she screamed so loudly that Giles, who was getting out of the bath, slipped on the floor in his panic. When he had picked himself up and reached the bed, she had stopped screaming, but was threshing about like a landed salmon and cursing at the top of her voice. Anna, who never swore! She seemed deeply asleep, her eyes tight shut. He caught her by the shoulders but she was slippery with sweat and he couldn't hold her. He said, 'Anna, *Anna*,' and slapped her thigh. Her eyes came open and she woke up, shouting. 'Damn you for a fucking bastard.'

He kissed her eyes, her hair, her mouth. She shuddered and lay still, looking up at him blankly. He said, 'My goodness, what *language*! What was all that about, my baby?'

She said nothing. He kissed her again. She was soaking wet; he fetched a towel and dried her carefully under her arms, between her full, firm breasts.

She sighed and said, 'I wanted to kill you.'

He mopped between her legs and kissed her there. Then he straightened the twisted sheet and covered her in case she should catch cold.

He said, 'You nearly did. I came a frightful purler in the bathroom. What had I done?'

'I don't know. Yes, I do. You had some other woman. I came in the room. Oh Giles, it was awful. I was so angry, I hated you.'

She had begun to shudder again. He stroked her shoulders. He was too wet himself to get into bed with her. He said, 'Very right and proper.' And then, partly because the thought tickled him, partly to make her laugh, 'Was I actually on the job?'

But she didn't smile. It embarrassed him slightly that she didn't smile. He laughed himself and said, 'You were quite right to be angry if I was having it off with Another.'

The look on her face frightened him. The dumb, stony look of a child who can't say what hurts it. Then he thought – how ridiculous! It was quite clear to him. He said, 'Baby. Silly Baby. You're awake now. I'm here. It's all over.' He was standing up, drying himself, while he said this. He flung the towel down and got into bed. 'That's better, now I can comfort you properly. My warm, lovely girl. My lovely, warm, *jealous* girl. No harm in that, nothing to be ashamed of or get frightened about. But I know what the matter is. I've felt it. Hated myself, sometimes, when I've hit someone, or simply got angry. It's a sort of arrogance, really, as if one thought one was above that sort of thing! But you shouldn't feel it, Anna darling. You've less reason to hate yourself than anyone I know . . .'

The first time he was unfaithful to Anna, on a business trip to New York in the summer of 1960, he told himself that it was because he was so happy with her, sexually. 'I'm really here in bed with you because I love my wife,' he said to the blonde girl whose head was resting on his shoulder.

She said, 'Thank her for me, won't you?' and chuckled. 'It's a novel excuse. Usually it's *the terribly strong Martinis you all drink over heah*! She was a bright girl from Boston and she made a passable stab at a British accent of a plummy, old-fashioned kind.

'I have been drinking Bourbon and I am not drunk,' Giles said, though he was, and it made it easier for him to expand his statement. 'And it's not such a foolish explanation, *actually*. I don't mean I'm just missing her because she's jolly in bed, though she is. Bonny and buxom in bed and at board – that used to be part of the marriage service. No, the real thing is, she treats it – sex, I mean – so marvellously *naturally* that she's taught me to put it in its place. A less important part of life than I used to think it. Not a great performance, you see, but simply a nice, friendly way of continuing the conversation with someone you happen to like and would enjoy being close to. While we were talking in that bar, I thought, well, why not? Whereas a few years ago I would have been frightfully tense and self-conscious before and positively *hangdog* with guilt after. Partly my background, I suppose, my father was a bit of an old goat – I used to suffer agonies when I was a boy in case my mother found out. Or so I told myself. I think now I was simply afraid I might be like him. It bothered me so much that I became a bit of a prude, deliberately imprisoned part of myself. My wife's set me free, you might say. She's such a well-integrated person, she's made me see it's how you behave *altogether* that's important, not what you do with a few inches of flesh!'

He laughed excitedly and clasped the girl from Boston closer. She said, sleepily, 'Will you pass on this pretty compliment when you get home?'

'N-no. I don't think so.' He hesitated, apparently giving this question close attention. He said, in a solemn voice, 'But the important thing is that I *could*. She's younger than I am, a good bit, but she's quite exceptionally understanding and mature.'

She was exactly what he wanted her to be. Being the man he was, anxious above all to form his life into a purposeful and balanced pattern, he did not find this dull. Passion and violence are things only pessimists and failures need, and Giles was neither. He did not want to climb mountains, nor did he necessarily believe the future would bring joy, but he could look forward hopefully because order and compromise were the disciplines he lived by. He saw ahead a cultivated garden and the prospect pleased him more than any conquered peak. And he was not impatient: the present pleased him too, as part of a growing, organic design. His job absorbed him but his marriage was not a background for his working life, it was the framework within which he functioned, safe but free. His house in Chelsea (too small now, really, but marvellously cosy); his two sons, Peregrine and Merlin (not brilliant, either of them, but he was glad of that: brilliance in childhood is so often a flash in the pan); his excellent wife. Where she was concerned, he hardly needed his adaptive talents. She was beautiful and calm and kind, exercised his social conscience by working, voluntarily, for the Prisoners' Aid Society and sitting on School Care Committees (the sort of thing he would have liked to do but had no time for), was endlessly patient with the boys and with Crystal, whom he had begun to refer to, with affectionate pride, as 'my impossible old mother'. And, almost more important, she shared his concern for his friends. When middle age brought its toll of disaster – difficult children, divorce, sudden death – he was proud to see his house become a refuge, the wrecks wash up against his shore, and to know that Anna would perform a salvage operation. 'Anna always has time to listen,' he said, as he, increasingly, had less.

Not that she was his echo. 'Anna has a mind of her own,' he sometimes said, startling people who had not supposed otherwise. He was delighted when she was had up for speeding, driving the Sunbeam Rapier he had bought her to celebrate his forty-second birthday and his appointment to the board, at eighty miles an hour down a restricted stretch of the Portsmouth Road. Anna, who always drove with such elaborate overcaution whenever he was with her! And to crown this absurdity, she had insisted on telling the police officer, 'I'm sorry my speedometer's not working,' and when he said, 'I didn't hear that, Madam,' repeated her statement several times, very loudly, so that he was forced, finally, to bring a second charge against her. 'I thought he was just deaf,' she said.

'Ridiculously innocent,' was what Giles called her. He produced stories to illustrate this quality, sometimes even to strangers in bars, in the way some men bring out family photographs. Once (this was his favourite) she had called on the wife of an old friend of his to take her out to lunch. This visit was unpremeditated; had been, in fact, suggested by Giles only that morning. They had just moved to the country and Giles was proud of his vegetable garden. Since Anna was going to London, why not take some of the new season's asparagus to 'poor old Sue' who had had a minor operation. This was the sort of errand Giles often devised: he liked to do good by proxy. Sue was at home but already engaged for lunch, expecting a woman (no one Anna knew, she said, though Anna had not asked) who was already late. She seemed preoccupied, was only moderately grateful for the asparagus, did not offer drinks. Since she was usually a gushing, ginny girl, Anna was faintly puzzled by this reception, though not offended: she never expected anyone to appear pleased to see her. As she left, hustled out almost, another old friend, a man Giles had known in the Army, came puffing up the stairs (the lift in the antique block of flats was almost always out of order), a bunch of roses in his hand. He was rather a bore, this man, doing something in advertising, had a plain wife and lived in Wimbledon: to say anything more interesting about him would have strained even Giles's loyalty. Anna thought (so she told Giles later), 'Poor old Sue, she'll never get rid of him,' and said, 'What a shame, you've come at the wrong time, like me, never mind, we'll console each other,' and actually bore him away with her to a nearby public house where they had beer and sandwiches together. 'I tried to cheer him up,' she said to Giles when he came home, 'but he seemed terribly glum. Do you think he's lost his job again?'

Of course Giles thought it killingly funny. No one but Anna would have mistaken this situation! It was touching, really! But her later reaction was not so clearly in character. On reflection, Giles found the implications of the story less amusing. Though divorced himself, he was shocked by others divorcing. Perhaps because he had been through the mill himself. He knew that even without children (and in this case there were three boys on one side and two girls on the other) it was a messy and exhausting business. And besides (he admitted this with a wry laugh), he had got to the age when he liked to think of his friends as finally settled. 'But they're not *jellies*,' Anna said. 'And who mentioned divorce? Why shouldn't they just comfort each other? They both have dreary marriages – you know Sue's husband knocks the boys about!' And insisted on visiting Sue (telephoning first this time) not only to apologize for her insensitivity but also to offer to have her children if she and her lover could manage to slip away for a few days together.

Giles was amazed by what seemed to him romantic folly. He knew there were women who enjoyed the flavour of this kind of intrigue but he had never thought Anna one of them, and here she was, actually stirring the pot! And he was also embarrassed on his own behalf. He often lunched with Sue's husband, who was on the Stock Exchange. Of course he wouldn't say anything but suppose *he* mentioned something? To keep quiet, then, would be really lying by default! Anna shrugged her shoulders as if such niceness of principle were unimportant. 'You may regret it,' Giles was reduced to warning her. 'They're awful brats, Sue's boys. You'll have your hands full if she ever takes your offer up.'

'My hands are fairly empty now,' was all that Anna said.

If this was a complaint, a dig at Giles, it was the nearest she ever came to one. She had not wanted her sons to go to boarding school but once the move out of London was decided on, she had to agree that there was really no option. The local schools were simply not good enough. It was not that Giles minded his boys mixing with farm labourers' children (he was no snob, Anna should know that) but his old prep school provided not only higher academic standards but a better education in the full sense of the word. Conventional, perhaps, but one should not take risks with one's children. Independence of mind was the important thing. A boy had to learn to stand on his own feet. Peregrine needed this lesson particularly, he was a shy child, physically timid, but Giles had been shy, too, at his age. It might be hard at first, there might even be a few tears at the station, but as Giles knew from his own experience, children adjust very quickly: once the train had steamed out, he would soon be merry as a cricket. Even Little Oedipus, as Giles sometimes jokingly called his elder son. But the joke was the point. 'It's especially bad for a boy like that to be tied to his mother's apron strings,' he said. 'You'll see, after a couple of terms away, he'll be a different child.' 'That's what I'm afraid of,' Anna said, but admitted, when he took this up, that she was only playing with words.

Of course she was bound to miss them, Giles knew that. He would miss them himself to begin with. But their lives would soon develop a different, and perhaps more rewarding, rhythm. They could live like adults now, have friends for weekends without having to worry about neglecting the children. Anna would have more time for her various committees; time, indeed, to develop any other interest she had a mind to, which was a marvellous luxury, really. 'When you think of it,' he said, 'middle-class wives are really the privileged class of our generation.'

'I envy you,' he said one summer morning. 'This lovely day.'

But she was going to London. Hadn't she told him? 'I'm sure I *did*,' she said, frowning across the breakfast table – quite crossly, Giles thought.

'Oh husbands never listen,' he said cheerfully. 'What are you up to?'

'I thought I'd take Crystal some roses. I told her I would when she rang last night. And I want to do some shopping, Perry needs pyjamas, and perhaps see the exhibition at the Tate. It finishes at the end of the week.' She hesitated and then, for some reason, blushed. 'I may be late home,' she said.

Giles, buttering his toast, was surprised by the amplitude of her answer (Anna rarely specified, he rarely enquired into, the details of her comings and goings), and pleased by the blush. She was often pale in the mornings and colour suited her: he liked to think of her as his ruddy, country girl. And he liked the way she tried to cover her confusion by fiddling with the coffee pot, opening the lid and frowning as if making some momentous decision; whether it was still hot, or if there was enough for another cup. It made her seem vulnerable and feminine and gave him a chance to feel indulgent. He enjoyed feeling indulgent towards women and Anna seldom gave him the opportunity. He would have hated a silly wife, really, but sometimes he wished she would sneak off and buy a foolish, expensive hat. Perhaps that was what was in the wind now, not a hat, Anna never bought hats, but some other extravagance. A present for his forty-sixth birthday next week, or perhaps (this thought pleased him more) a dress she didn't need and so felt guilty about. Red silk, he thought, and wondered if he should suggest it to encourage her: she was, for his liking, too timid about what she wore, choosing dun-coloured materials, olive green or khaki, as if buying a dress were some kind of exercise in camouflage. Not that she ever looked mousey; if one were to use any animal as comparison, it would be a big, beautiful, glossy young mare! In fact that was what Tottie had once called her, Giles remembered, and decided not to mention red silk: Tottie had formed his taste for dramatic clothes and Anna was sensible enough to make the connection.

Having made it himself, he felt guilty. He smiled for distraction, stood up, smiled again at Anna who was watching him, and bent to fasten his cycle clips.

She said, 'Shall I drive you? I can get dressed in a minute.'

He straightened, surprised for the second time this morning. She knew that he only cared to be driven in really bad weather, heavy rain, high wind or snow. He bicycled for his figure's sake; because it set him apart from the other commuters, delivered to the station by their yawning, trousered wives. Because (he recognized this himself and it pleased him to think he was running true to family form) he was getting to the age when eccentricities harden into character.

Anna was smiling at him, lifting her hair with combing fingers as if it felt too heavy for her head. 'I just thought I'd like to.'

'It's a marvellous morning,' he objected. 'Besides, if you're late home, I'll be stuck coming back.'

She had stopped smiling suddenly, as if some dire thought had struck her; was looking very serious. 'But if I know I've got to get back to meet you, then I will, won't I? Or I could pick you up at the office.'

'Nowhere to park. And that bloody exodus at the rush

hour.' Giles felt, all at once, rather testy. 'What's the point, anyway? I like the train, you like to drive.' She nodded but her serious expression remained and his testiness faded. Was this a special day? Some anniversary? He began to check dates in his head – but Anna didn't care about anniversaries. Forget her own birthday if he didn't remind her. The dentist? She was a terrible coward about that. No, not the dentist, she would have told him and he would have remembered. He said, 'Kick me if I'm being obtuse.'

She shook her head and, getting up, came towards him, smiling again. 'It was just I remembered – do you remember, when we were married, you said, *Now you'll be my relict*? Well, I was thinking of that, for no reason, and I was thinking, I'm glad I'm not, not yet.'

He laughed and put his arms round her, round her warm back. He said, 'Well of course, goose, if you really want to pick me up . . .'

But she was pushing him away. 'No, it was a stupid idea. Go on now, you'll be late.'

'There's always the next train.'

She said, 'But you like the nine-fifteen, don't you?'

She came out of the house with him. It was a lovely morning, as he had said: enough mist to make the trees look two-dimensional but a warm sun breaking through. They walked to the garage, Giles in his dark, city suit, white shirt and M.C.C. tie, Anna in her old cotton gown with stains down the front, feet bare on the cool, cropped grass. Giles picked up his bike, wheeled it to the end of the gravel drive, then stopped to look back at the house and the hill rising gently behind it. He kissed Anna but his eyes went beyond her, his heart lifting with pleasure as it always did when he saw his home from this angle, appreciating his achievement (not financially, though the Queen Anne house had doubled in value since he had bought it, repaired the roof, put in heating and bathrooms) but in living terms. This was how a man should live, Giles thought; a house in the country, not too big but solid and handsome; a pony in the paddock for his sons; a lovely, loving, compliant wife. He appreciated her too, even though she was slatternly in the mornings. He said, 'Enjoy your day, darling.'

Her face was lifted for another kiss so he gave her one, on the cheek. He mounted his bicycle, clunked over the cattle grid (no cattle passed down the lane now the farm at the end had been sold for building but Giles liked to keep it because it seemed countrified) and looked back at the house from the bend in the lane. This was another favourite vantage point but Anna stood in the way, blocking a particularly entrancing curve of trees on rising round. He wobbled, trying to see past her, waved, and called out, 'Lovely view . . .'

Anna waved back but didn't turn. She was looking the wrong way, up the hill to the village. From where she stood she could see the new bungalows Giles thought so hideous and would have planted a beech hedge to hide if Anna had not said she liked to see them, liked to know there were people near. When Giles was out of sight she continued to stand, looking at them, hands folded in the sleeves of her gown as if she were cold. A woman came out of the nearest one with a basket of washing; Anna watched her while she hung it out, did not move until she went indoors again. Then she said, aloud, in a mocking voice, 'Ah, come off it, you silly, spoiled cow!' and turned on her heel.

Back in the house she went straight to the kitchen, opened the refrigerator door, deliberated briefly over cold chicken and liver pâté, and then skinned a handful of spring onions to eat with bread and lumps of butter. Standing there, greedily munching away, she heard Mrs Cozens come in the front door, stamp, *stamp*, as if shaking snow off her boots and felt, at once, a sudden, familiar terror. It was as quickly come and gone as a subliminal advertisement on a cinema screen, leaving only the chill behind. She swallowed a sharp crust, hurting her throat, and gasped. Ridiculous to feel guilty – her own spring onions, her own kitchen! She called out, with a faint, breathy tremor, 'Hallo, you're early today.'

Mrs Cozens assumed that whatever people said they meant the opposite, possible because this was her own normal method of communication. To say she was early implied she was sometimes late. 'Whenever I come I always do my time,' she said now, coming into the kitchen with a challenging stare. Anna smiled meekly: she had learned that to explain unguarded remarks only confirmed Mrs Cozens's suspicions. 'I'm going to London today,' she said and added a list of the things she intended to do, as a peace offering. Mrs Cozens liked to be told things and Anna felt, she told Giles, impelled to tell her because she paid her, by London standards, so little. 'My wants are simple, Mrs G.,' Mrs Cozens had said when Anna argued the point. 'You give me what I ask and we won't fall out.' Giles liked this response; he thought Mrs Cozens a marvellous, country character, independent, crusty, outspoken. He treasured the things she said and repeated them to his friends, to Anna's discomfort; it seemed embarrassing to speak of one's daily help as if she were a comic, Dickensian invention. It was only ebullience on Giles's part; he was simply and touchingly delighted to find his new life was turning out so well. But Anna had once said, 'How would you feel if your secretary refused proper payment and demanded information about your private life instead?'

All the same, a kind of nervousness, or guilt, seemed to prompt her into more detail than perhaps Mrs Cozens expected. This morning, as Anna spoke of the Tate Gallery, Mrs Cozens cleared the table and stacked the dishwasher. Politeness prevented her clattering cups, but she hardly seemed interested. Recognizing this, Anna faltered; was relieved when the telephone rang. She ran from the kitchen, closing the door, and ran down the hall. Haste – or excitement, perhaps – made her clumsy; she tripped over the torn hem of her gown and, falling forward, struck her elbow on the edge of the table. She bent over, grimacing with pain, and grabbed the receiver. But it was only Crystal, her clear voice with its pretty, cultivated hesitancy. 'I thought – as you're coming up, darling – I wondered if we might have lunch together and perhaps do the Chagall exhibition. That is, I mean if you'd like it.'

Anna was silent. Not for long, though perhaps it seemed long to her. She stood, cradling her painful elbow with her free hand.

Crystal said, 'Anna?'

Anna said, 'Oh, dearest, I'd love to, but I don't think I can possibly fit it in. I mean, I don't think I'll have the time.'

Honest people lie badly; it is often the measure of their honesty. Or of their pride: they cannot bear to be expert in something that shames them. Even if, being honest, they do not count telling the truth an absolute virtue. 'It's not a moral imperative,' Anna once said to Daniel Parr, 'only a fear of being caught out.'

This delighted Daniel. Anna reminded him of the woman in the Maugham story who acquired a social reputation for outrageous comment by saying, quite simply, what she truly thought and felt. Anna was not in fact like this woman (though she had a certain directness, she was too conscious of other people to be really outspoken) but it placed her for Daniel who often used literature as a sounding board for life. This was partly upbringing – he had been a shy and bookish boy, and though shy no longer was still young enough to cling to earlier habits. And partly a genuinely eager, if rather cold curiosity: he liked to know more than anyone was prepared to tell him. 'Once people get to a certain age, they put on masks and speak like actors in a rather boring play,' he said to Anna the first time they met. 'Telling you nothing worth knowing. Characters in fiction are much more satisfactory. You know not just what they say and do, but why. Think for a minute. How many people at this party do you know as well as you know Emma Bovary, say, or David Copperfield?'

He spoke in a didactic way out of embarrassment. He was at this party, given on a barge moored near Hungerford Bridge by Giles's managing director, because he had recently been involved in a television programme on merchant banks. Earlier, he had been talking to Giles: Anna, trapped against the rail and discussing children with another wife, had watched her husband bending to speak to this short, stocky man with long curly hair and glasses, and been glad to see that Giles was talking so eagerly, was so clearly enjoying himself. Then, a little later, she found the young man standing beside her. He was wearing a pink shirt with a matching tie and a pale seersucker suit. He grinned and said, 'You know, there are some men who tell you *everything*. All the facts, who they are, what they do, all the geography of their lives – and not a bloody thing that means anything!'

He was very young, a little drunk.

'If you mean my husband,' Anna said, 'that's just his party manner. He doesn't really care for this sort of occasion and attack is the best means of defence!'

'That's exactly what I meant. What's he defending, for Christ's sake?' He pulled a comic face, pushed his glasses higher on his nose and made his little speech about characters in fiction. Anna smiled and he sighed elaborately. 'I suppose it's pointless to apologize. You must be Anna. You live in the country in a Queen Anne house that is both charming *and* a splendid investment with the property market the way it is, you have two boys at a fancy school, you do a lot of voluntary social work, you're a marvellous cook and an exceptionally beautiful woman. Your husband told me all these things about you except the last and that proves my point, really, because it could be, for him, the most important.'

Anna said, 'Do you expect people to tell you the secrets of their heart at parties?'

He looked at her gravely, removing his glasses to do so. Without them he looked younger still; his cheeks had a schoolboy bloom. His eyes were almost as dark as Anna's, his mouth soft and full. 'I'd tell you anything,' he said, 'even if I would start, like your husband, by telling you nothing much. Like I shave twice a day and always take five lumps of sugar in my tea. Though you could make deductions from those two items if you chose to. Personal vanity from the constant shaving, working-class background from the sweetness of the tea. I expect your husband drinks china tea with lemon. I owe this knowledge of upper-class habits to three years at Oxford and I speak in this crisp, sardonic way to impress upon you that I care not a fig for such little clues to a man's social standing. You may of course deduce from this remark that I do and that I still feel uneasy in the presence of people who really don't care a fig, even a green one, because their own position is so unassailable and that if I was rude to your husband it was only out of envy.'

Anna giggled and choked over her drink.

'Elephant trick,' he said, whipping a red handkerchief out of his shirt cuff and mopping expertly. 'Don't be embarrassed, it happens to the best people.' He smiled. 'Was that a *good* apology?'

'Beautiful, though there was no need for it. You were only trying to amuse me.'

He closed his eyes and moaned. 'Oh, *cruel* . . .'

She said, 'Giles drinks Indian tea and only without sugar as an example to me because he thinks I shouldn't take it. And he never went to Oxford. Not to any university as it happens. Because of the war.'

He opened his eyes. 'And you?'

She shook her head.

'No. Of course not. You haven't the competitive manner of the seriously educated woman. I mean that as a compliment.' He looked at her closely, head on one side. 'Let me guess. Posh school, all the frills. What after? Not modelling, you're too fat. I *like* it, I hastily add. Secretarial college, then, something to keep the girl out of trouble till she gets married. Mummy in fur tippets and Daddy at the Foreign Office.' He paused. 'I'm only trying to be amusing. Stop me if you find my foolish attempts impertinent.'

'Only wide of the mark. That is, as far as I know, which is almost nothing. Nothing about my father, anyway, and not much about my mother. Except that she came from the East End and was killed in a bombing raid.' She smiled at him shakily.

He said, in a quite different tone from the one he had used up to now, 'I'm sorry. I really am sorry.'

She finished her drink at a gulp and said, with surprise, 'I've never told anyone that before.'

He had a talent, Daniel, for creating intimacy. The illusion of it, anyway. His occupation, perhaps: he called himself a Camden Communicator to those who would understand the term and a jobbing journalist to those who would not, earning his living by expressing modish opinions on television and in literary-political weeklies. He was happy in his chosen environment, darting about in it eager and quick as a young trout in the shallows. He knew they were shallows and would say so, very quickly, if asked. Though he was in fact modest, he was aware of the value of modesty as he was aware of the value of charm:

you never know who may turn out to be useful. Innate good qualities are not necessarily diminished by being used as currency, indeed, in Daniel's case, the dividends were large enough to plough back into the business: naturally kindly, success made him kinder. He was kind to old friends who had not done so well, kind to his parents who were poor and elderly (when she was pregnant with him, his mother had thought she was starting the menopause), buying them a bungalow on the Kent coast and taking them out, once a month, to a theatre and a slap-up meal. If he chose plays that had been running some time and un-fashionable restaurants it was not because he was em-barrassed at the idea of being seen with this old, cockney couple, but because he knew they would be afraid of letting him down in front of his friends. Or he told himself they would be and that he did not want to hurt them.

He did not want to hurt Anna. He was quite unaware that he could do so. She was older than he, married, knew what she was about. If he was mistaken in this it was not his fault: it was a reasonable assumption and all Daniel's assumptions were reasonable. He assumed that whatever people said they usually did, in the end, what they wanted to do, so why beat about the bush, pretend to be better than you are?

For Anna, perhaps, this was a kind of freedom.

She said, 'Oh that was a lovely meal. I'm frightfully greedy. Do you mind? I know it worries Giles, watching me eat sometimes. I know I'm not thin now, but when we got married I really was *fat*. When we're going out I often eat something at home first so I shan't pile my plate too high. Because it really does bother him; he looks nervous if I take a second helping of potatoes! As if he were afraid I might suddenly inflate in front of his eyes, start bulging over the edge of my chair!'

'I like fat, greedy girls,' Daniel said. 'Especially when

I'm buying their lunch. I like to feel I'm getting my money's worth.'

He had taken her to a pub in Wapping. They sat by the window and watched the river. Anna said, 'Oh, I like London, I'm not tired of life. Not only this marvellous river but shabby streets, old newspapers blowing about, smells puffed up from gratings! It seems all I can smell in the country is dead leaves all the year round. A threat to life, not a promise. Giles stands at the window some mornings and says, *God, it smells marvellous*, and I wonder if I'm deficient in some way. Like being deaf to music. Something physically *lacking*.'

She said, 'My mother lived somewhere round here. This end of London. I suppose I ought to want to know where, exactly, ought to wish I could remember her? I know Crystal thought I ought to feel like that. After the war she got a photograph of her for me, from an old aunt she traced in Blackpool. My mother – I say "my mother" because I don't know what else to call her – had apparently spent a holiday with this aunt when she was about fifteen. In the picture, she is standing beside a stuffed tiger on the pier. Crystal said, *You can see your mother was a lovely girl*. I didn't know what to say. I was embarrassed because I thought she looked common, and I was ashamed of thinking that.'

She said, 'That's not true, really. I wanted to belong to Crystal, I didn't want any other mother. When she produced that photograph, I felt she was saying, you're not really my daughter, this is who you belong to! Rejecting me because I wasn't good enough. Though of course that wasn't true, she was only trying to be kind . . .'

She said, 'Oh, she was so kind to me. Giles says she's a silly woman but that's the only way he could get free of her. To teach himself to despise her. I can see why he does but I can't, myself. She was so marvellous to me. I was such a miserable little creature when she rescued me . . .'

She said, with an odd, awkward laugh, 'Rescued! Perhaps that's an over-dramatic word. I don't know. I don't usually talk about myself. I don't know why I am, really. Stop me if I'm boring you.'

Daniel said, 'You wouldn't bore me if you recited a laundry list. It may have escaped your notice, but I am somewhat taken with you.'

He was a cautious young man. And, in spite of his knowing air, something of an innocent. He believed what people told him, on the whole, and not only because it was less trouble.

If Anna considered her husband to be the better man, perhaps this was only guilt on her part. How do you judge 'better' after all? Giles was older, more established, held to certain fixed, old-fashioned principles: he would never seduce a married woman (or had never done so), would never seek advantage through a friend. Perhaps background had moulded them differently, a different set of social checks and learned repressions. Or perhaps Giles had just lived longer, had had more to cut his teeth on. Daniel had been born in 1944, a year to the day before Giles had driven into Belsen in an Army car.

Belsen, to Daniel, was a legend. The war had been fought by old men with crumpled faces. He said, to Anna, 'You might as well feel bitter towards the French because of the Norman Conquest.'

He was startled by the strength of her response. She spoke of Tottie and it was as if she were telling him about a personal experience. She said, 'If you had known her, you couldn't talk like that!'

She saw Tottie; once every six months or so. They had lunch, or she went to the flat. Tottie sent the boys presents on their birthdays.

Anna said, 'Giles likes me to keep in touch with her. He doesn't want to himself but it makes him feel civilized, knowing that I do.'

152

She talked about Giles quite naturally as if he were a common acquaintance whom they both found mildly amusing. If this was not really quite natural, it reassured Daniel who was wary of involvement. He liked women but he was jealous of his time and peace of mind: he did not want to be burdened with someone else's conscience. He said, 'Look. There's no small print at the bottom of my policy. I like a comfortable life. Don't, for your own sake, expect too much of me. I nearly got married once but it fell through and I have been grateful ever since.'

He was not entirely honest about this. He had been engaged to a girl at Oxford. She was not an undergraduate but a pupil at a secretarial college there, a bank manager's daughter from Surrey, prim and pretty and artless as a flower. When Daniel took her to meet his parents she was shocked by their accents and because his father took his new teeth out to eat his tea. She wept in the train going home and said she couldn't go through with it. She said, 'Mummy and Daddy would be so upset, I can't do this to them.'

A lucky escape for Daniel. He was clever enough to see it but young enough to be deeply shocked. It was still a painful memory, too private to be shared. It gave him pleasure, sometimes, when he appeared on television, to imagine her watching him with her family, sitting in their detached house with double garage, Queen Elizabeth roses in the garden and fake Jacobean furniture indoors. And, thinking of her, he sharpened his phrases like weapons. Editing his commentary for the programme on merchant banks he rejected the term 'gentlemen adventurers' and substituted 'latter day pirates of finance'. It pleased him that the Bank registered a mild objection. The class structure was his scene: within it, he fought a private war, with bows and arrows. He knew, intellectually, that no one from Giles's world would have behaved as naïvely as his suburban girl, but emotionally he had identified his enemy.

153

And saw Anna, if only at first and to a very small extent, as their Achilles heel.

He said, 'Hey, stop that! I don't want to send you back to your husband covered in sexual bruises.'

Though the thought pleased him, really. That bland, confident, smiling man! So polite and pleased with himself; talking about money and possessions. *My* house, *my* car, *my* wife . . . He thought, next time I see him at a party, I could take that smile off his face!

Anna said, 'I'm sorry. I wanted you to hurt me.'

She smiled but she was trembling. She sat up, trembling and smiling. They were not in bed, had not made love – had never yet made love. This was their third meeting and they were lying on the grass by the canal in Regent's Park. Daniel was feeling dazed. He had not planned this. He had said, after their lunch in Wapping, 'Come to the Zoo one day. It's the only place human beings can feel superior nowadays. Looking at all those animals they have caught and caged.' It had been a deliberately casual invitation: Daniel had his own rules about married women, leaving it to them to make the running. She telephoned him three days later. She met him at the gates of the Zoo, but had not wanted to go in. Not unless he really wanted to. They had walked to the canal and she had taken his hand and said, 'I would like to sit here, I think.'

Now she was sitting on the bank with grass in her hair, still trembling a little and smiling at him. An Establishment wife with two sons at prep' school and a husband in a merchant bank. A beautiful woman in her thirties. Daniel thought – in some parts of the world she would be considered old!

He said, 'We're too old for this kind of frolic. Too old for parks and the backs of cars.'

But there was nowhere they could go. Daniel had a room in Islington, in a tall, narrow house owned by the widow of a civil servant; a gentle, fading woman, an agoraphobe, who had advertised for a 'quiet lodger'. Daniel did her shopping for her and used her as an alibi. 'My landlady never goes out and she's scared stiff of people. It wouldn't do for her to even meet a stranger on the stairs.' His room was monkishly bare: he retreated to it, as to a fortress or a cell. He entertained his friends in restaurants and girls had places of their own. Flat mates went out for the evening, husbands worked in the daytime. Freelance journalism had its fringe benefits, he often said: you could be free in the afternoons.

He said, to Anna, 'What do you usually do?'

She blushed and said, 'Well . . .'

He said, 'I'm glad you didn't say, *I don't usually.*'

She blushed more deeply. He said, 'You must be about the only grown woman in England who can still blush.' There were leaves among the grass in her hair. He picked them out one by one. He said, 'It's the appearance of virtue most women find hard to give up.'

'Is that a quotation?'

'No. But it's good enough to be.'

They smiled at each other. She said, 'You are pleased with yourself, aren't you?'

'You're supposed to find it attractive. It means you don't have to worry about my feelings because people who are pleased with themselves need not be worried about.'

She said, happily, 'Oh, you are silly, Daniel.'

'I aim to please. Silly people are pleasing because you can feel superior to them. Does that sound like a quotation, too? It wasn't meant to. I am only talking for the sake of talking and not just because I like the sound of my own voice, though I do, but to express my pleasure in your company. There seems no other way of doing so. We would be arrested if I tried a more practical demonstration. Besides, the grass is damp.'

She blushed again, and giggled.

He said, 'You have a lovely, vulgar giggle. Surprising, really. Not in keeping with the rest of you. Taken by itself, or in company with the way you blush, one would think you were about fourteen instead of a mature, experienced woman, heavy with social responsibilities and used to facing up to what, in some circles, are still thought of as moral issues.' He laughed but found he felt oddly nervous. He stood up, took Anna's hands, and hauled her to her feet. He said, softly, holding her, 'You are, aren't you? I mean, you do know what you're up to?'

Anna said, 'Tottie, may I ask you something?'

They were lunching at a fish restaurant near Tottie's office. Ivan had bought a partnership in a literary agency with the money Nikos left him and Tottie ran the foreign rights department. She enjoyed this; seemed to enjoy her life in general. Her copper hair had barely faded; she still looked like a small, bright bird.

Anna said, 'It's rather embarrassing,' and looked round the restaurant which was always full of people Tottie knew. Editors and publishers and authors – sometimes when they lunched together Tottie introduced her and she would go home and say to Giles, 'Do you know who I met today?' It pleased him that Tottie should be happy and successful in a world so different from his own. Sometimes, when his friends' children had literary ambitions, had written a novel or a play, he would say, 'My first wife might be able to help, with advice at any rate. She knows a lot of useful people in that field.'

Tottie said, 'You can ask away. It's a myth that writers are interested in other people's conversations. All they ever listen to are the voices inside their own heads.'

Anna murmured something.

Tottie said, 'I'm sorry? Ivan says I ought to have a deaf aid. Though perhaps an ear trumpet would be more decorative. I can't remember if you ever knew Giles's

Uncle Simon? He used one, though rather as a social weapon. Used to put it down, very obviously, when he was bored with the conversation.'

Anna made a curious sound, half gasp, half groan. She said, 'I never met him. I went to his funeral, though. He died just after we were married.'

Tottie said, 'A dreadful old man, really.'

Anna smiled tightly. Her face was stiff and heroic as if she were awaiting execution. Or about to shoot rapids in a canoe. She said, 'Tottie, may I borrow your flat one afternoon?' Her eyes widened with shock as if she couldn't believe she had said this. She gave a wild snort of laughter and put her hand to her mouth. 'Oh, it's ridiculous, a ridiculous thing to ask, I'm so sorry.'

The colour had drained from her cheeks. Tottie said, 'You look as if you could do with some air,' and beckoned to the waiter.

Close to the restaurant there was a city church with a small, paved garden. Tottie took Anna's arm, as if steering a sleep-walker, and led her to a bench. An old man sat opposite with a bag of bread crusts; pigeons flopped round his feet.

Anna breathed deeply. 'I am so sorry, Tottie. But I couldn't think of anyone else I dare ask. Are you frightfully shocked?'

Her face was a tragic mask. Tottie wanted to laugh. She said, 'Why should I be? Of course I'll give you a key.' She wondered if she could say, 'Don't use Ivan's bed, he wouldn't like it,' but decided not. She said, briskly, like a landlady, 'Ivan and I are never home until six-thirty at the earliest.'

Anna sighed. 'Oh Tottie. It seems hypocritical to say I feel dreadful, but I really do. You see . . .'

'Don't explain, love,' Tottie said, although she would have liked to know more. But she was aware of feeling an element of pleasure in this situation and this shamed her a little. Besides, an elliptical conversation was almost certainly all Anna could bear. She said, 'We're often away at the weekends too, at least in the summer. I told you we had bought a cottage in Wales? Border country. If you ever want that, there's a key in the wash house, on a hook behind the door. I'll give you the address. Only let me know first. There's a woman comes in to clean and I should like to warn her.'

She was amused to see that these practical details horrified Anna. She said, 'Oh Tottie!' and stared miserably at the old man and the pigeons. He stood up, shook the last crumbs out of his bag, and shuffled away. He had long white hair flowing from a bald patch the size of a tea cup at the back of his head. His trousers were tied at the knees with string.

Tottie said, 'He's here most days at this time.'

'What?' Anna's eyes focused on the retreating figure. 'Oh.' She looked at Tottie and said, 'I do love Giles, you know.'

Tottie smiled.

Anna said, 'I really would hate to hurt him.'

Tottie laughed outright. Anna regarded her with pained, dark eyes and then smiled, reluctantly.

Tottie said, 'How *is* Giles?'

'Well,' Anna hesitated. 'The other day he had lunch in a place where he wasn't known and found he'd forgotten his wallet. The man at the next table paid for him but refused to take Giles's address. He said that someone had once paid for *his* lunch in similar circumstances and he had been looking, ever since, for a chance to repay this debt. Giles was frightfully touched.'

Tottie said, rather dryly, 'How sweet.'

Anna looked at her doubtfully. Then the corners of her mouth began to twitch. She said, 'Oh, it's unkind, I shouldn't laugh.' But she began to, a little hysterically. Tears came into her eyes. She said, 'I'm laughing at myself. It seems so foolish in the circumstances that I shouldn't want to laugh at *him* because you might think me disloyal!'

Tottie said, 'A woman I knew who left her husband used to cry her eyes out whenever it rained because he was the sort of man who never thought to change wet socks and was liable to colds. Small things are a useful focus for a sense of guilt.'

She was aware that this was a slightly chilling thing to say. But with Anna, she had often felt a certain ruthlessness was necessary. Indeed, she sometimes seemed to ask for it, playing the innocent girl, too good to be true. Well, she could hardly do *that* any longer, Tottie thought, and smiled at her with a sudden increase of affection.

'Oh, but I don't feel guilty,' Anna said.

Crystal wore a pale mauve trouser suit with a metallic thread in the weave, dangling gold ear rings and high-heeled, gold sandals. She said, 'Anna darling, you do spoil me. What beautiful roses, they smell of summer.' She closed her eyes and inhaled deeply.

'Careful, they're thorny,' Anna said. 'But they're the ones Giles thought you would like best. He sends his love.'

Crystal opened her eyes. 'Tell him to deliver it personally some time!' But this was playfully said: she felt no real grievance. In fact, she was happier discussing Giles with Anna than in his actual presence: his reported messages were more affectionate than any conversation she now had with him.

Anna said, 'He hopes you'll come down to us soon. The garden's looking lovely and the weather is so good just now.'

Crystal said, 'Oh, you don't want an old woman like me!'

'You're not old, how ridiculous!' Anna smiled at her. 'You've done your hair a new way, haven't you?'

Crystal had been waiting for Anna to notice this. 'I have

a new young man,' she said happily. 'He calls himself Luigi, though I expect he comes from Birmingham, really. He says he enjoys doing my hair because it has such a good, natural spring. When I went to him yesterday I said I was wondering about a light perm and he said it would be criminal, in his opinion! But he did want to cut it much shorter, in fact he *almost* persuaded me! I held out, though – it doesn't do to let them have their own way the first time! But I've been wondering since, perhaps he's right? Someone with a fresh approach, looking at me as I am now, not like poor, dear André – he's gone to live in Brighton, you know – as I used to be. It was such a shock when he retired, a sort of *memento mori*, he'd looked after my hair for so long, ever since we came back to London, after the war. I said, 'André, we've grown old together,' and he said, 'I haven't noticed you growing old, Madam, only more beautiful!' I said, 'Oh, André, I'm afraid that is the eye of the beholder!' Which is really what I'm getting at, I suppose. Perhaps it would be more youthful, to go a bit shorter now I've put on a teeny bit of weight round my jaw line. It would lift my face. What do you think, darling?'

'I don't know. You always look very nice.'

There was a flatness in Anna's tone that surprised Crystal, and an echo that hurt her. Her mother's voice – *I don't share your obsession with appearances*. For a moment Crystal felt it keenly, that little stab of remembered pain, but she rallied at once, lifting her chin and smiling gallantly. Old people must not allow themselves the luxury of feeling hurt! She said, 'Darling, you look tired. I do wish we could have a nice, quiet lunch together.'

'I'm sorry. I wish we could, too.' Anna sounded as if she meant this.

'But you've promised to meet Tottie. Don't apologize, darling, you know I'm quite happy to take a back seat! Is she still living in the same flat with that funny little queer?'

'You wouldn't say, funny little heterosexual, would you?'

Crystal did not resent the sharpness in this question: she enjoyed it when Anna bullied her a little. She said, 'Well, darling, that kind of menage must seem a little strange to a woman of my generation. Not that the sexual side was ever very important to me personally – you know poor Basil and I were not really well matched in that way – but I don't know that I should have cared to live with a man who didn't want it sometimes.'

She was excited by her own frankness. It crossed her mind that she might repeat this conversation to Luigi when she next had her hair done. ('I've grown too old to beat about the bush. I'm afraid I often shock my daughter-in-law.') Perhaps she might shock *him* a little with her straight talk. An attractive, older woman teaching a young man a thing or two! She said, 'To live successfully with a man things have to be all right in the bedroom. That's what we were told when we were young and I don't suppose the situation has changed. But I'm afraid I've always been too feminine to understand this modern unisex nonsense.'

Anna was gazing at her lap. 'I think Tottie and Ivan have been happy.'

'I didn't say they weren't *fond* of each other, did I?' Crystal listened to her own laughter, appreciating the merry sound of worldly wisdom. 'But that's not quite the same thing, is it?'

'Oh, they are more than fond,' Anna said. 'They look at life from the same window which is more important than anything else.' She smiled – rather sadly, Crystal thought. 'I would have said they loved each other.'

Anna never said, 'I love you,' to Daniel. He had been on the verge of saying it to her once or twice but had stepped back in time. He had stated his terms in the beginning and

161

she had accepted them, presumably because they were what she wanted. It seemed not only unsophisticated but mildly dishonourable to appear to be trying to change them, if only in a momentary flush of enthusiasm. He told himself he was grateful to her, really, for playing it cool, for preserving their joint, emotional chastity. 'We're both alike, we like to eat hearty but we're not greedy – we take just what we want and no more. It makes for a remarkably comfortable relationship.'

'It's a short step from comfort to boredom,' Anna said. 'Tell me when you're ready to take it.'

Her placid, teasing tone angered him. He said, 'Not yet, you rotten cow,' and twisted his hand in her hair and tugged hard. 'You bored with *me*, is that it?'

She shook her head, gasping. Tears stood in her eyes, and pleasure. He wanted to say, 'Does Giles pull your hair?' but was afraid to sound jealous.

She said, 'Idiot!' and he collapsed with a groan, half on top, half beside her, hot cheek buried in Tottie's soft pillow.

She whispered, against his ear, 'D'you know what I fancy now? Scrambled eggs.'

He said, '*Bitch.*'

'Aren't you hungry?'

'No. Oh, all right, *yes!*' He sat up, rumpled; pushed back his hair, reached for his spectacles from the bedside table, put them on and glowered at her through them. She lay with her hair spread out, naked and smiling. He wished she would cry and cling to him. But he hated women who cried. He said, 'I'm sorry. I'm being perverse.'

'Don't you want scrambled eggs?' Her eyes were dark as well water; he could see nothing in them. 'We could have them fried, if you'd rather.'

He said, 'You're so practical. *That's* over – thank you kindly, dear Daniel – now on to the next thing!'

She laughed. 'You'd hate anything else.'

162

He grumbled, 'How do I know?' But of course she was right. Daniel, the unsentimental lover. He had no right to complain if the role he'd adopted was natural to her. He said, 'Oh, well,' and pushed his glasses higher on his nose. 'My Dad always said you should get up from the table feeling you could manage a little bit more.'

She grabbed at him but he evaded her, getting off the bed at once, and making for the kitchen. Usually she made the bed and tidied the room while he cooked but now, after a brief interval, she followed him; stood with her arms round him and her breasts warm against his back.

She said, 'Daniel, I can't be different. I am what I am.'

'And what's that, may one ask?' He was cracking eggs into a bowl. He had brought them with him; also a French loaf and a bottle of wine and some butter. Anna laughed at him for these domestic arrangements and perhaps it *was* absurd, in the circumstances, to have scruples about Tottie's food, but eggs and wine cost money and, unless you took capital depreciation into account, using beds didn't. Of course such finicky calculations would be foreign to Anna: the circles she moved in, people not only borrowed flats for their extracurricular activities, but expected to find champagne in the ice box! Caviar, even!

He said, 'I know what I am. A decent, honest, working-class boy.'

Perhaps when he'd been at this game as long as she had – when he was going on *forty*, he thought, adding on a few years out of resentment – he would take it as calmly. He wondered how many lovers she'd had – had brought here to this high class pad with painted gold chairs and purple drapes. But once he'd *asked* that, he thought, he'd set himself down as the loser in this situation . . .

She said, 'Daniel . . .' Then, 'Oh, I don't know what I am. Unserious and selfish, even a bit ruthless, I suppose. But I've never pretended to be anything else, have I?'

Her lips were tickling his right shoulder blade. He

finished beating the eggs before he turned round to look at her. At her beautiful, smooth, mocking face. He removed her hands from behind him and stepped back a pace. He said, 'No, you haven't,' and wondered why he felt cheated.

She said, 'Then what is it?' and laughed. 'Do you want a *row*, Daniel? As a diversion?'

He wanted to hit her. She had done nothing wrong and he had never hit a woman in his life, but he wanted to hit her. And she wanted him to – as he jerked back his arm, he saw her eyes spark. Then, in the same split second, the telephone rang and he jabbed his elbow on the edge of the table behind him. The pain was exquisite; he screwed up his eyes and hissed through his teeth.

She said, 'Oh, poor darling.'

He hopped on one foot for distraction, holding his arm. She said, 'Count to ten. Or answer the phone. That'll do just as well.'

He said, 'Oh damn it all,' and padded into the bedroom.

Anna said, behind him. 'She's early, isn't she? It's only ten minutes past three.'

The woman usually rang about four. Some prurient neighbour had been Daniel's first guess, and it embarrassed him horribly: he had been shocked when Anna seemed merely amused by the soft, elderly, gently accented voice, speaking obscenities.

But the abuse was not meant for them, nor was it a neighbour: the caller was a novelist who believed Ivan had treated her badly. The agency had recently been taken over by a city firm and the auditors had advised that a number of unsuccessful writers should be removed from the list. 'Wicked Tory businessmen,' Daniel said virtuously, and was piqued to learn that this particular victim was married to a wealthy industrialist and that her novels were based on her experiences as a titled deb in the 'twenties. 'Poor, dotty old sweet, she did quite well once,' Tottie told Anna.

'But young lordlings on yachts and sweet, giddy girls, and pure love, just don't sell any longer. If you can't bear not to answer the phone, let her run on for a bit or she'll ring back at once. Ivan says about three minutes is the right length, long enough to get it out of her system.'

Daniel thought, privately, that this reported advice was part of an elaborately spiteful ploy on Ivan's part. Why should this madwoman ring his home number at this time of day? Too nutty to take office hours into account? Or had Ivan said, 'If you must speak to me, then I'm at home in the afternoon'? Unlikely, perhaps, but Daniel was paranoic about Ivan, who he felt sure disliked their using the flat. The first time, when Anna had shown him round, they had found his door locked. Daniel understood this (he would have loathed a strange couple romping on his own bed) but it made him uneasy. He had only alluded to this in a roundabout way ('Does he think we'll pinch something?') but Anna had known. Laughed and kissed him and said, 'You're a secret prude, darling.'

Which was true, perhaps. Certainly it was why he always answered the telephone and hated Anna to listen. All that filth pouring into her ear! He usually held the receiver very firmly against his ear for three minutes exactly, listening with a mixture of disgust and pity.

But today his elbow was hurting. It seemed to reflect another, less admissible pain. He crossed the bedroom floor, picked up the phone and said, very loudly and clearly, 'Oh, bugger off, can't you?'

Giles said, 'Is my wife there?'

Daniel recognized his voice instantly. Guilt, perhaps (in some part of his mind he had been expecting this) or perhaps it was only that they had appeared together on television.

He said, 'Oh. Yes. She is.' And stood quite still, feeling his jaw drop as if a hinge had broken.

Giles said, very politely and rather slowly, 'Would you tell her, please, that Peregrine has appendicitis? I shall be leaving my office now and catching a train in fifteen minutes.'

Anna was crossing the bedroom, walking on the balls of her feet. Daniel held the receiver towards her.

Giles's voice said, 'The hospital is St John of the Cross. Past the school, through the village, about half a mile.' He paused, briefly. 'Tell her not to worry. It all seems straightforward.'

Anna held out her hand. Daniel heard the *click*, then the dialling tone. He stood, looking blankly at the receiver until Anna took it gently from him and put it back on the rest. Then she stepped back, looked at him, and began to laugh.

Daniel said, 'Christ! Peregrine!' He thought, *Bloody silly fancy name*!

Anna was standing there. Stark naked and laughing. He said, 'Ought I to slap your face?'

She shook her head, drew a deep breath and coughed, with a wild, whooping sound. She held her side as if coughing hurt her, then began to pick up her clothes from the floor.

Daniel said, 'That's right. You get dressed.' This sounded excruciatingly fatuous. He thought, why not say, 'What about a nice cup of tea?' He pulled his shirt over his head and walked into the kitchen. The wine stood, unopened, by the bowl of beaten eggs. He scraped at the foil round the neck with his thumb nail while he looked round for a corkscrew. He called out, 'Where does the train go from?'

'Waterloo. I can't catch it.'

She had made the bed and was standing in front of the dressing table, twisting her hair up.

He said, from the doorway, 'Will you drive?'

She nodded, her mouth full of pins, looking at him in the mirror. He held the bottle between his bent knees and pulled at the cork.

She said, 'What are you doing?'

'Shock.' He assumed a Scottish accent. 'A wee dram for the nerves.'

The cork plopped out. He went back to the kitchen, poured out a full glass and returned to the bedroom. He said, 'Don't get in a flap now.' His own hand was shaking.

She said, 'I'm not worried.'

He said, 'Giles . . .'

'Bugger Giles.' She sipped the wine, put the glass down, finished her hair. She said, 'He's frightened of pain!'

She was thinking of the boy. That was right, Daniel thought. First things first.

He said, 'They'll have given him something. It's a *simple* job, nothing to it.'

She nodded distantly. She was looking round the room, a gimlet-eyed housewife, checking details. She picked up his jacket and gave it to him. 'I'm afraid you'll have to clean up the kitchen.'

'Stuff *that*.' After all, they could hardly come here again. He was proud to make this practical contribution. He said masterfully, 'I'm coming with you.'

She smiled at him and he kissed her. There was time for that. He said, 'Anna, you're marvellous.' He wanted to add something else. 'I can't leave you to face this alone.' Or, 'It's my job, to explain things to Giles.' But he was afraid she would laugh; think him boyish and quixotic. Which perhaps he was he thought, feeling chilled, suddenly: perhaps she and Giles had some mutual arrangement, went their own way with each other's consent. The signs were all there, her lack of concern, Giles's matter-of-fact voice . . . 'You can do what you like only don't flaunt it, dear! Think of England, the Bank and the Boys and keep up appearances!' Perhaps they even discussed each other's escapades. Lying cosily abed in their quiet country seat, giggling, comparing . . .

He closed his eyes and said, 'Oh God above . . .'

'Daniel?' She touched his hand. 'Come on, if you're coming.'

Waiting at a traffic light in Chiswick, he said, dry-mouthed, 'How did he *know*?'

Her hands moved on the steering wheel, then tightened. 'I suppose he rang his mother. He knew I was seeing her. and I'd told *her* I was lunching with Tottie.' She looked straight ahead, smiling slightly.

The smile bothered him. And the shine in her eyes as she glanced briefly towards him.

He said, 'Would Tottie have said where you were?'

'She's away. At some book fair.'

'Oh.' The lights changed and she accelerated abruptly, jerking him forward.

She said, 'Better fasten your seat belt.'

This was sound advice, the way she was driving. He did up the clips and braced his feet. He said, 'I suppose it was Ivan, then.'

'Suppose so. Poor Ivan, he'd be caught, wouldn't he? Perhaps he just said there was a chance I might be at the flat and hoped I'd make my own explanations. Giles would believe what I told him, you see.'

She sounded smug about this and Daniel thought, *poor old Giles*! A ridiculous surge of male solidarity mixed with relief — at least *she'd* not told him. He said, 'Ivan couldn't have known you'd answer the phone.'

She didn't speak for a minute, taking a roundabout fast and passing a cement lorry on the wrong side. Then she said, 'I don't suppose he'd care, really. Perhaps he'd even be pleased to get his own back.' She laughed, with straightforward amusement. 'Not on me, but on Giles. Though that's an old story.'

And not one Daniel wanted to hear. He felt censorious: how could she be so calm when her child might be dying? *Was* she calm? Quietly exhilarated might be a better

168

description. The exhilaration of being alive and in the thick of the fight.

She said, 'You know, I don't feel surprised. It's as if I'd been waiting for something like this.'

Or hoping for it, he thought. Adulterous women were often galled by a husband's ignorance. He had learned this from books. Had she wanted Giles to find out? Surely not this way? Or was that, too, a relief? A looked-for punishment?

He said, 'It's not a judgment, you know.'

'Poor Perry, of course not!'

'Don't be frightened, love.'

'I'm not.' Her smile made him feel like a little boy who has been told not to be silly.

'What did you mean then? That Giles was likely to guess?'

He laughed, to show that he had accepted this possibility for a long time and been unworried by it.

She shook her head. They were coming on to the motorway after about a mile of thick, crawling traffic. She gave a short sigh and roared into the fast lane.

He said, 'Well, married couples do, don't they? I mean, people who've lived together for years must notice each other's behaviour patterns. Silly, cant phrase and I apologize for it, but it covers a lot of things. I mean, supposing you've not been in the habit of this sort of indulgence, though it's none of my business, of course, if you *have*. But for the sake of argument.' He cleared his throat stagily. 'I'm sorry if this seems an inappropriate conversation. If you'd rather I changed it to politics or literature or the visual arts, just say so. Or if you'd rather I simply shut up altogether.'

'No,' she said. 'Giles and I . . .' And stopped. Daniel waited, but she didn't go on. Minutes passed, and the miles, and she stared ahead, through the windscreen. It had begun to rain, had been raining here for some time by the look of the road and the wet, heavy trees on both sides. Though they had left the motorway now she was still driving almost as fast, along a fairly wide, hilly road with a double white line down the centre.

At last she said, 'I was going to say that Giles and I don't know the first thing about each other. But that's not only a cliché, it's an evasion of the truth. What I mean, I think, is that married people are like actors, trapped in a long run. They get stuck in their roles, go on speaking their lines, long after the sense has gone. Until death, sometimes, but not always. The world must be full of couples who look at each other and think, how amazing, who is this stranger? This partner in deceit? But – and this is my point – it's not the other person they're thinking about at such times, but themselves. What am *I* doing here? There should be some chain of events, some logical steps to retrace, but there's nothing. Just this sense of total bewilderment as if you'd found yourself naked, suddenly, on some lighted stage. The rest of the cast look like strangers but that's only a reflection of your own strangeness to yourself. As if you'd looked in a mirror and seen some quite unfamiliar face.' She paused, for perhaps half a minute. Then said, 'It's bewildering, as I said, but not painful, and not unexciting. You are no longer locked in a box. There is the possibility of release. Of change.'

Daniel had never heard her speak like this before. So slowly and levelly, as if feeling her way in some area of thought, or emotion, that was quite new to her. And seemed to ask for some new response from him. It was that made him uncomfortable – panicked him, really. What was she expecting? Some kind of declaration? He thought – *Oh no, my girl, that's not my scene, you don't catch me that way!* He said, 'I'm sorry to sound flippant. But aren't you hamming it up a bit?'

She glanced at him briefly, without any expression. She said, in her usual, crisp tone, 'Maybe. A crafty female trick, I suppose. Disguising an embarrassing situation with a flow of fancy talk.'

He could hardly have put it better himself. He thought, with relief, *That's my Anna*! But felt, all the same, a queer disappointment. He thought, *perverse bastard*! He said, 'You're bound to feel a bit disorientated. Even I feel a bit awkward and I'm only on the edge of things, you might say. But you'll slip back into your part fast enough when you're fed the right cues by a tight-lipped but civilized husband at the end of this journey. When should we get there?'

'About another fifty-five minutes,' she said. 'Five o'clock, if we're lucky.'

At six-fifteen Giles left his son sleeping and went to telephone his mother.

Crystal said, 'Oh darling, I've been waiting and waiting. Sitting by the telephone hardly daring to breathe.'

'You could have done. They didn't operate after all. The school doctor was mistaken, apparently.'

'What was the matter, then?'

'Constipation.' He smiled. There was humour in this, in the circumstances. He said, loudly, 'Retention of faecal matter producing inflammation. Hence the pain, and the fever.' He laughed out loud.

'Oh, Giles! The poor little boy. It's not funny.'

'No. Not for him, either. He's asleep now but it's been a nasty couple of hours. Humiliation, rather than pain. The enemas didn't work and they had to remove a lump manually.' He felt a certain relish in telling his mother these details.

She said, predictably, 'I can't bear to think about it.'

'It was worse for him, I daresay.'

'Don't be smart, Giles. I know that, of course. He's such a sensitive child. But you don't know how I've felt. Sitting here, helpless and alone and imagining all sorts of horror. And no one to share it with.'

171

'I'm so sorry.'

'It's not important, of course. Though one of you could have telephoned before, perhaps. But I suppose you didn't think of it.'

He said, 'Anna's not here.'

'Oh, darling! But you spoke to her, didn't you?'

'I left a message. I had to catch a train. She should have been here by now.'

'Then where is she?'

He said, 'I really have no idea,' and put the telephone down. And doing so, felt considerably, if shamefully, eased.

His dilemma was a civilized one: he could not admit to feelings he despised. Moral indignation was, of course, out of the question. That was something to be used sparingly among sensible people, reserved for deadlier sins than sexual infidelity. Jealousy and anger? Half an hour ago, sitting by Peregrine's bedside and realizing that Anna should have arrived by now, he had had a sudden, vivid picture of her, sprawled whorishly on another bed, and saying, 'Oh, there's no need to hurry, Giles is a fearful old woman, he always gets in a flap over nothing,' and known this was a pure function of jealousy, to imagine the loved one speaking or behaving in a way she would never speak or behave in life. And been horrified, not because he had been visited by this degrading emotion – that was involuntary, after all – but because he had felt, in that moment, such acute pleasure in it. He had not felt, for a long time, so vigorously and painfully alive.

This elated sensation, with its accompanying guilt, had lasted until he finished speaking to his mother. What he chiefly felt now, emerging into the polished emptiness of the hospital entrance hall, was embarrassment of the peculiarly witless kind that sometimes overtakes people when an immediate crisis is over. Thinking of two things at once – the way he had just used Crystal as a whipping-boy and the peremptory and dramatic message he had sent Anna over the telephone – he sweated and muttered, under his breath, 'Oh dear, oh dear . . .' In this foolish state, it crossed his mind that if Peregrine had in fact been operated on, the situation would be less obviously absurd. At the very least, a seriously ill child, one with peritonitis, perhaps, would have given his parents something important to talk about, bridged the initial awkwardness. To have disrupted his marriage for an attack of acute constipation was nothing less than farcical.

Anna would recognize that, of course; it might even make her laugh. Thinking of the relief that laughter would bring he grimaced, crinkling his eyes and drawing his lips back over his teeth. He thought – *What shall I say? Oh God, I could do with a drink*! It was only a short walk to the village. But then he might miss her . . .

All Ivan had said was, 'It might be worth trying the flat, she sometimes goes there to change or to put her feet up.' There had been no hint in his voice, no warning. Only sympathy. He had said, 'Oh, poor you!' Sounding so camp, Giles had stiffened. Now he thought, perhaps the man who had answered the telephone was some boy friend of Ivan's. Some little playmate. Perhaps the flat was full of people, all putting their feet up! Why had he assumed otherwise? Had Anna guessed? He thought – I can say I didn't think, I was just taken aback. So anxious about Peregrine. He could say, 'I jumped to conclusions, I'm afraid. You ought to be flattered!' She would understand. Christ alive, Anna was his *wife*, not some cold fiend, laughing. She would explain, clear it all up, and of course he'd believe her. They would have a meal somewhere before they drove home. He said, half aloud, 'It'll be all right once she gets here.'

A nursing sister was passing. When he spoke, she turned back. She was about thirty with healthy, shining, grey eyes. She said, 'Your wife here yet, Mr Golightly?'

The use of his name by this stranger surprised him. She said, 'I expect the little boy will be glad to see his Mummy,' and he knew her then, by her voice. She had been there during the worst part of poor Perry's ordeal but he had barely looked at her face, only at her competent hands, her probing, rubber-gloved fingers.

He said, 'No. I can't think what's happened. Rush hour traffic. I'm sorry, I didn't recognize you.'

He knew Daniel's face at once, but from where? Recognition needs a context. Searching for the right one, Giles remembered a foxing conversation in his local pub with a man he knew well but couldn't place because he wasn't behind a counter and wearing his butcher's apron.

The stumbling block in this case was that this vaguely familiar young man was getting out of a police car and Giles knew very few policemen. Standing on the steps, watching for Anna, Giles registered the fact that Daniel was not in uniform, that his right hand was bandaged, and that he appeared to be looking for him. As soon as he got out of the car he came straight for the steps, limping a little. He said, 'How's the boy?'

Giles stared at him. Then said, 'He's all right now.' This television chap at a party, talking to Anna. Parr. Daniel Parr. The party had been on a barge near Hungerford Bridge. A lush affair to sweeten some visiting firemen. A German banker. Anna had said in the car going home, 'He's nice, that telly man, isn't he? Awfully sweet.' He said, 'Where is Anna?'

Daniel said, 'There's been an accident. They've been trying to get you.'

'Who's tried?'

'The police. I don't know why they couldn't.'

Anna dead. Anna dying. Giles thought – I shall have to get a couple to look after the house and the boys in the holidays. A flat in town for myself in the term time. Two rooms in the Barbican. A view of St Paul's, or the river. He said, 'Is she badly hurt?'

'I don't know. She's unconscious. I didn't stay long at the hospital. I thought I should come and fetch you.'

He stuck out his chin as he said this, like a boy owning up. A schoolboy. Giles thought, *I am old enough to be his father*. He said, 'Was it you I spoke to? At the flat?'

'Yes.' Daniel looked at him. 'Oh yes. That was me.'

They sat in the back of the police car. Daniel said, 'It all happened so quickly. That's what people always say, isn't it? The awful truth of clichés. We came over the top of the hill and there was this car coming out.'

'What car?'

Daniel blinked at him. 'I'm trying to tell you. It came out from a drive, or a side-turning. Was already a good way out when we saw it. We hit the back part, I think, and skidded on, down the hill. I think we went over the grass verge, hit something, then sort of bounced back. I can't really be sure. Though I know where we ended up – car on its side in a ditch on the wrong side of the road. Anna was under me.'

Until he said this, he had been speaking rather fast but quite calmly. Now he looked as if he were going to be sick. Giles said, 'Don't worry now. I can hear it all later.'

Daniel swallowed. 'I'm sorry. It's just that I suddenly thought I must have trodden on her trying to get the door open. Which I couldn't do. Jammed, or just panic. . . . Then a lorry driver came along and we did it between us. He hauled me out but she seemed stuck, though we couldn't see how. It wasn't the steering wheel and she was breathing all right. He said we'd better leave her until the ambulance came. His mate had gone on to phone. There were some other people further up the road with the other car.' He closed his eyes as if he did not want to think about this.

175

Giles felt very detached. He thought, in Greek tragedies, the action always happens off stage. It's the aftermath that's important. The effects, not the cause. He said, 'Was anyone hurt in the other car?'

The police driver had slowed to turn right. Giles met his eyes in the mirror, saw him turn his mouth down. He said, 'Just one old lady, sir. She was alone.'

'Badly hurt?'

'I don't know. It looked as if they might be some time getting her free. I took Mr Parr to the hospital.'

Daniel said, 'The car was halfway up a tree. When we went past it, the tree seemed to be growing up through it. . . .' He put his hands up and retched into them. Watery vomit oozed through his fingers.

'Want me to stop?' the policeman said.

Daniel shook his head frantically. He bent forward, making a soft, mewing noise. His glasses came off and hung, dangling from one ear. Giles removed them, said, 'I think we can manage,' and gave Daniel his handkerchief. Daniel fumbled it in front of his mouth, mewed a little more, then sat up and leaned back with his eyes closed. He said, 'Terribly sorry. How repulsively silly!'

Giles wound the window down. The cool evening air smelt of hay though no farm land was visible. This was a sub-rural area, commuter country of a kind Giles particularly disliked. He thought – would not be seen dead living in. The detached houses, glimpsed through silver birch copses, seemed to have county gentry pretensions: the unvarying size of the plots and the rustic name plates betrayed them. Home Wood. Treetops. Birch View. Pretty Hollow. These innocent names, painted in black on wooden boards, some of them shaped like a pointing finger, produced a beautiful, clean, savage hatred in Giles. He thought, *bloody fool* and said, 'Aaaah . . .' A strangled sound, midway between a cough and a groan.

Daniel said, 'Wha'?' and the policeman glanced up.

Giles said, lamely, 'It used to be lovely round here. A pretty village.'

The village had a green, a stagnant pond, a couple of tarted-up pubs, a church and a Baptist chapel with a tin roof. Beyond the chapel three very young, black nurses waited at a bus stop and beyond them, a sign saying *Hospital*.

Giles said, 'Where did it happen?'

Daniel was leaning back, eyes still closed, holding Giles's handkerchief against his mouth. The policeman said, 'Crow Hill. You know the area? The other car must have been coming out of Crow's Acre Lane. There's no other turning.'

'Oh,' Giles said. 'Oh. I see.'

The policeman looked at him in the mirror. He said, 'It's about three-quarters of a mile from the top of the hill to the lane.'

'Yes,' Giles said. 'Yes. I know it.'

Anna was in a cubicle at one end of the Casualty Ward, lying on her side on a high bed with grey blankets over her. Her face was grey, like the blankets; there was a bruise on one side of her forehead and a lot of dried blood round her mouth. There was some degree of concussion and she had lost two front teeth, but there appeared to be no internal injury and no bones were broken. Giles stood, looking down at her, and listening to the doctor telling him these things. His mouth felt dry; he moved his tongue, trying to swallow.

The doctor said, 'The other driver wasn't so lucky.'

She had died instantly, the steering wheel through her chest. An old woman, known to the hospital staff; a retired local headmistress. 'Instantly' was the word the doctor used: Giles wondered if he had thought about it. He said, 'Have her people been told?' and regretted asking this question. He couldn't remember, afterwards, if it had been answered. The doctor was talking and he was looking at Anna and thinking, *I shall have to tell the boys. Speak to my mother. Christ, I feel tired.*

The doctor said, 'Driving nowadays is a pure act of faith. Sometimes when I leave here and get into my car to go home, I feel like a lunatic.'

Giles sat by Anna and held her hand, though there seemed little point in it. She was snoring; from the concussion, he supposed. Or perhaps there was blood in her nose? Unconscious people suffocated sometimes, in their own blood or vomit. There was no one to ask: the doctor had gone and though there were nurses about, hurrying past with squeaking shoes, not one of them had looked into the cubicle. After a while, Giles began to feel indignant about this neglect: he got up, pushed the flowered curtains aside, and looked into the hall. A number of people were waiting, sitting on grey, vinyl-covered benches, most of them staring straight ahead. Their air of hopeless patience seemed dreadful to Giles. He marched to the reception desk and said, in a hectoring tone, 'How long is my wife going to be left lying there?'

The nurse said, 'We'll be taking her up to the wards soon. It's visiting time at the moment.'

He said, 'Is that really relevant?' and was glad to see her colour faintly. She was a pretty child; young skin smooth and unmarked as an egg.

She said, 'I think the police want to talk to you.'

The policeman was at his elbow. Had been waiting, perhaps, for Giles to emerge from the cubicle. 'Just a few questions, sir.'

'Can't they wait?'

'It won't take long. If you'll just come this way.'

Giles felt tired: it seemed easier to do what was expected of him. He said, to the young nurse, 'Please see that someone looks after my wife,' and followed the man into a small office where there was another policeman, rather older, and Daniel, sitting on a low chair, looking angry. As Giles came in, he was saying, 'No, I've told you, she was *not* driving fast. Nor had she been drinking.'

The older policeman said, 'There's no need to take this attitude, Mr Parr. There's been a serious accident. It's my duty to ask you these questions.'

The hostility in his tone amazed Giles. Was everyone involved in an accident automatically a criminal to be bullied? He said, 'What's the point of them? My wife was on the main road, wasn't she? There's no speed restriction there and it was her right of way.'

The policeman, seated behind the desk, looked at Giles in a measuring way. He was about Giles's age and had a broad, very pale face and curiously wideset, pale eyes with shaggy white brows above them. He said, 'Mr Golightly?'

'That is my name.' Giles heard himself speaking in a clipped, upper-class manner. He was only slightly ashamed of this attempt to establish his social ascendancy.

'You were not in the car, were you?'

'I know the road,' Giles said, and the policeman smiled as if this were an admission.

'Then you'll understand that it's hard to see how this happened. On a straight stretch of road. If your wife saw the other car from the top of the hill . . .'

Daniel said loudly, 'I've already explained that I was wrong about that. Or you drew the wrong inference. I said, we saw the car *as* we came over the top of the hill. Not *from* the top. Meaning that we were some way down, quite close to the turning, in fact. There was certainly no time to stop. I'm sorry if I wasn't more exact, but I'm not a driver myself . . .'

'No. And of course you've had time, since you made your original statement, to talk to someone who is.'

'I didn't make a statement. I was only discussing the accident with the policeman who drove me to the hospital. I was very confused at the time.'

'And now you are less so, you can see the implications of what you said then?'

Daniel said, 'I resent that.' He was looking pale and strained and very young. Giles felt protective towards him.

He said, 'Aren't you exceeding your duty, officer?'

'Not in my view.' The policeman smiled at him in a friendly fashion. 'As I see it, people's memories are often adjustable. It is possible that Mr Parr misled us originally. It is also possible that he did not. I understand that your wife was on her way to visit your son who had been taken ill. In these circumstances it is not unreasonable to wonder if she was exercising proper care. But it's our job to find out what happened, Mr Golightly, not to fix the blame.'

'I would like to believe that,' Giles said.

Daniel said, 'Bloody fuzz.'

'Yes,' Giles said. 'Could she have stopped, do you think?'

Daniel stared at him. They were sitting at a small table in a dimly lit bar. They had walked to this pub, which was called The Rising Moon, from the hospital. There was a smell of new paint and piped music moaned softly.

Giles said, very gently and evenly, 'You don't have to protect her from me.'

Daniel swallowed. 'I really can't tell you. Maybe the brakes didn't work. Maybe she thought she could get round the back of the other car, that there wasn't time to do anything else. I'm not a driver, I can't possibly tell you.'

Giles said, 'She will never forgive herself.' He sounded very sure about this. Daniel wondered if he were speaking of how he would feel in this situation.

He said, 'What will the police do?'

'Were there any other witnesses?'

'Not that I know of. They'd have said, wouldn't they?'

'Then it'll depend on what she says when she comes round. She'll tell the truth, even if it goes against her.'

'I suppose so.'

'If she remembers what happened, of course.'

Daniel said, 'Yes.' Then, 'Would you? If you felt you might be at fault? What would be the point, after all?'

'None, possible. Expiation, perhaps.' Giles smiled, rather grimly.

Daniel said, '*Would* she see it that way?' Giles looked at him without saying anything. Daniel gulped his whisky and said, 'Would you like the other half?'

'I'll get them,' Giles said.

He was some time at the bar, talking to the landlord, a fat man with a sad, perspiring face. When he came back he said, 'They've got a room here. I've said that I'll take it. And they'll fix us a meal of sorts.'

'I'm not hungry.'

'Well – I don't suppose it'll be a meal to remember. But you ought to eat something or you'll feel frightful later. I daresay they can rustle up a cab to take you to the local station afterwards. Or all the way home, even. That might be better, you must be feeling pretty shaky.' While he was saying this, with what seemed genuine concern, he was stripping the wrapping from a packet of Gitanes. He said, 'And I really thought I'd given it up. Want one?'

'No. I don't. Thank you.'

Giles smiled at him. 'Do you smoke pot?'

'Not that, either.' Daniel felt vaguely resentful: this seemed a prurient, middle-aged question.

Giles smoked and drank. 'I wonder if they'll legalize it now there's so much unemployment. That would be a dead crafty move, wouldn't it? One way of keeping the young apathetic and servile instead of marching with banners. Opium for the masses is cheaper than a riot squad!' He laughed immoderately, and coughed.

Daniel said primly, 'I'm afraid I don't find the unemployment figures so funny. Though I suppose your lot call it mobility of labour. Free play of market forces.'

181

Giles laughed again. 'My lot? My dear lad – I've voted Labour since 1945, if not always enthusiastically. But if I've had doubts from time to time, this government has settled them!' He stubbed out his cigarette and regarded Daniel triumphantly. 'To my mind, the Tory party has become little more than a focus for the worst kind of atavistic spitefulness. All the petty resentments of boring little people who've got their beastly, clod-hopping feet on the second rung of the ladder and can think of nothing better to do than to kick those on the bottom. Down with the blacks and long haired layabouts, make the poor and the sick and the old stand on their own feet! A kind of unthinking, lower middle class *meanness*.'

Daniel wondered how many members of the lower middle class Giles actually knew. He said, 'Isn't that a bit snobbish?'

'If you object to the term lower middle classes, then of course I withdraw it. I was using it, unfairly perhaps, to denote certain attitudes that I find repellently tasteless and vulgar. And that seem to me to have more to do with sexual frustration than reasoned political assessment, let alone recognized moral behaviour. After all, for the most part, most people try to behave, individually, in a fairly civilized fashion. They temper the wind to the shorn lambs they happen to know. They don't shove them out in the cold and abuse them as they do so!' Giles lit another Gitanes and smiled stiffly. 'I happen to believe that people should be encouraged to behave as well collectively as they do privately. That the same decent principles should inform all levels of their lives.'

Daniel had listened to this curious manifesto with growing amusement. He wondered if Giles were slightly drunk. He said, 'Do you really think most people behave well privately? What "decent principles"?'

'Generosity, tolerance and restraint.' Giles looked at Daniel and then went on, with only a slight hardening of tone, 'As I said, most people *try* to behave well. I may want to push your face in but I think the less of myself for it and have not, in fact, done so. Now, would you like another whisky, or shall we have dinner?'

Giles said to Anna, 'Listen, my love. You don't have to speak to me if you don't want to, but listen, please. I know how terrible you must feel, believe me! You don't live with someone for years and not know something about them, even if it's always less than you think. Perhaps it's salutary to discover that: it stops one being complacent. Perhaps I've been too complacent, too pleased with my life – with *our* life, I should say – but I want you to know I'm not now. And that isn't a bad thing! At the risk of sounding like Dr Pangloss, I would say that when something like this happens, some sort of crisis, there's always the chance to rethink, to try and see what's gone wrong and learn from it. The theory of the curative shock! I'm sorry if I'm putting this badly, I'm tired and I've not slept too well. What I'm trying to say is that everything's going to be all right. Not perfect, perhaps, not the best of all possible worlds, but all right *enough*. At least, on my side. I love you. Nothing that's happened has changed that. And I don't blame you, not for anything. Of course I was angry and hurt to begin with – it would be foolish to pretend anything else – but I'm not now. In fact, thinking it over, I blame myself. I really do. I should have known you'd be bored and restless, stuck in the country with the children gone. But I was so happy, I never thought you might not be. I see that was selfish, now. I don't know what we'll do about this but we'll do something. Move back to London if that's what you'd like. Anything, Anna! I shan't even mind if you want to go on seeing that silly boy. Or I shan't *let* myself mind. I've no right to. I should tell you I've not been *absolutely* faithful, either! Only once or twice when I've been away on a trip, nothing important. I'm telling you, not because I feel guilty, or only very mildly, but because it may make you feel easier. I know what you are, Anna!'

She had recovered consciousness to some extent on the evening of the third day. The nurse who was turning her in the bed had looked up and seen that her eyes were open and watching her. Her eyes were so dark, so fixedly staring, it was hard to say what she saw but she seemed to understand what was said: when they washed or fed her she obeyed simple instructions, moved her body as much as she could. She appeared to be paralysed down one side.

'Hysteria,' the doctor said. 'Which can be, like shyness, a kind of anger.'
    Giles said, 'Anger with herself, do you mean?'
    'Perhaps.' The doctor seemed tired. He stifled a yawn, rubbed his eyes till they squeaked. He said, 'There's nothing physically wrong. Talk to her as much as you can, try to get through to her.'

Giles said, 'Look at me, Anna. Listen. You set such high standards for yourself – too high, perhaps. And now you feel angry because you've let yourself down! Over-conscientious people are like that, but it's a kind of arrogance, really. The sin of pride and all that. But I love you, Anna. Speak to me, darling, *trust* me . . .'

She wouldn't speak to him. She had spoken to the nurses, asked for a bedpan, a drink. But when Giles sat by her bed, she lay with her face averted.
    One afternoon when he came, a new patient had been brought into the ward: a woman who had thrown herself off a railway bridge onto a goods train. She was blinded and had lost both her arms. She lay behind screens, moaning

monotonously, 'Why can't they let me die, why can't they let me die?'

Giles was appalled. When he reached Anna, he saw she was weeping: slow tears beneath her closed eyelids. He went at once to the sister's office and complained angrily. 'No one should be in a public ward in that condition. I know there are no single rooms in this hospital – as you know, if there had been I would have had my wife moved to one. But there must be somewhere you could put that poor creature where she wouldn't distress other patients.'

'Only the corridor,' the sister said.

Giles telephoned Crystal. 'At least we know now that she's aware of what's going on round her. In a way it's a breakthrough – the first emotional response that she's shown. Though it's rather frightful, of course, that it should have come about through someone else's misfortune.'

'But typical of Anna,' Crystal said. 'Poor sweet, she's always been more concerned about other people than about herself, hasn't she? I remember when Peregrine was born, I'd just had that nasty go of pneumonia and Anna rang up and asked how I was, and it wasn't till we'd talked about me for ten minutes that she told me the baby had come! Oh, I felt such a fool, though of course that was the last thing she'd have meant me to feel and of course I couldn't have *known* – he'd taken us all by surprise, hadn't he? Little wretch. Not like his father! You were three weeks late and I was five days in labour – I was quite exhausted by the end! I can see poor Basil now, standing by my bed with tears in his eyes, and the doctor saying, "I'm afraid she can't stand much more." And I was so terribly frightened, I thought, I shall die and I shan't see my baby!'

Giles said, 'I was in Switzerland when Peregrine was born.'

'I remember. Anna was so sorry about that, she was

afraid you'd be upset, missing all the *fun*,' she said. 'Not a single word about what she must have suffered, packing a bag and going into hospital all alone.'

'No,' Giles said. 'No, there wouldn't be.'

He sat beside Anna. He said, 'Darling, I know how you feel. So many terrible things happen – unimaginable things, and never to oneself, only to other people. One feels such shame at always being a spectator. At being so frightfully lucky. One's pity is never pure. It's always mixed with curiosity and a kind of guilty relief – at least, *this* hasn't happened to me! And then one feels such a fearful hypocrite because one knows, in one's heart, that tears can help only oneself. But there's no harm in that, no *blame*, my sweet girl . . .'

After the other visitors had gone, the husband of the woman who had thrown herself onto the train came into the ward. He was a labourer in a flour mill and he had come straight from work, a bicycle ride of ten miles. White dust still clung to his hair and his creased, heavy clothes; his face was theatrically pale, like a bewildered clown's. The sister showed him to his wife's bed and drew the flowered screens round them both.

The injured woman had been quiet since her last injection about an hour before. Shortly after her husband's arrival, the effect of the morphia began to wear off and she started to moan again, *Why don't they let me die?* The nurse who was wheeling round the evening medicine trolley, glanced at the fob watch fastened on her jaunty right breast and smiled brightly as she approached the next bed, thermometer in one hand, two laxative pills in the other. She said, cool fingers feeling the patient's pulse, eyes on her watch, 'She's not conscious, dear, not in any pain. She doesn't know what she's saying.'

The soft keening went on and on, became a ritual, an

accepted background. The women began to talk, though in lower tones than usual. Some put their earphones on and listened to the outside world with bemused faces. Bedpans were brought, and wash bowls, and milky drinks. The flowers were removed from the ward.

All this time, the husband sat silent, his humped form visible through the thin cotton of the screen. When he finally spoke, he stood up and his shadow became monstrous, reaching above the bed, up the wall. He said, 'Why don't you die then, you bloody bitch, why don't you *die*? Finish the job while you're about it. Never could do anything properly, could you? Bloody, rotten, idle *lump*, won't be able to wipe your own bloody ass now, will you? Who's going to do that, d'you think, clean up your shit?'

He began to weep noisily. The sister came running down the ward. She whisked the screens aside, said, 'Come on now, that's enough.' And, as she led him away, holding him by the upper arm like a prisoner, 'Now, you poor man, you know you don't mean a word of that!'

The swing doors closed behind them. There was silence for perhaps half a minute. And then Anna began to laugh.

Walking down the ward the next evening, Giles saw the change in her. She was sitting up in bed, watching him. He said, 'Oh, my darling!'

He would have kissed her, but something in her eyes stopped him. A strange, cold, mocking look. It made him feel clumsy and foolish. He said, almost formally, as he might have spoken to a stranger, 'I'm so glad to see you're better.'

She continued to stare at him. She seemed well and rested; there was colour in her face and her hair was brushed loose round her shoulders.

He said, 'You look so well! I'm so *glad*, sweetheart. I can't tell you!' He smiled, waiting. Then he turned the chair and sat beside her. 'Sister says you had quite a long

talk with the doctor this morning. He's very pleased – *I'm*
so pleased! This is the first time you've been sitting up
when I've come, d'you know that? I'm sorry – if I'd known
I'd have brought flowers and champagne. We could have
celebrated. We'll do that when you come out. That'll be
the day.'

She sat like a statue. A life-size doll, propped up against
pillows. Giles smiled and smiled. His jaw ached and the
skin felt tight on his forehead.

'Crystal wants to come tomorrow again. Do you feel
up to it? If you don't, just say so, and I'll think of a way to
put her off without hurting her. Though if you can bear it,
it would be a kindness, I think.' He crinkled his eyes at the
corners. 'She does love you, you know.'

Anna said nothing. Her silence exhausted him. He felt
so tired, anyway. He had spent the day talking. A boring
board meeting, a long, heavy lunch. His head throbbed; the
lights in the ward seemed too bright. He thought – every
pouch and wrinkle exposed! He said, 'I'm sorry, I'm not up
to much at the moment. I feel so worn out. Rather old,
suddenly. Why won't you speak to me?' He thought he saw
something new in her face. He said, 'Are you angry?'

He was aware of anger himself. At the way she had
escaped everything. Shutting herself up in this fortress of
silence while he dealt with the mess she had made –
the wrecked car, the insurance company, his mother, the
police. . . . He had lied to the police when they called at the
house and asked to see her driving licence. Because he
knew there were two speeding endorsements on it, he had
said that he didn't know where she kept it. He was not sure
how useful this lie was, simply thought it might tip the
balance if they were deciding whether to prosecute, but he
was amazed by how smoothly he told it. Had added, watching his plump, honest face in the mirror, that she had
always been a quite exceptionally careful driver. And he
had lied to his mother, to his friends. 'Luckily she wasn't

alone, she'd been having lunch with an old chum of ours and he'd very kindly driven down with her.'

He said, 'If you're angry, you've no bloody business to be. Not with me, anyway. What have I done? I've stuck by you, I've been *loyal* for Christ's sake, and I don't mean I've just kept up a front before other people. I've not once complained or reproached you, not even to myself, in my heart!'

As he hissed this, leaning forward, his hands on his knees, Anna began to smile. Lifting her upper lip, she showed the dark gap in the front of her mouth. He thought – *Lord, how hideous*! He said, 'What's funny? Am I funny? Do you think – silly, complaisant old fool, is that it? Because I come here, night after night, tell you I love you? Is loving you some kind of frightful weakness that makes you despise me? What am I to do, Anna? What have I *done*? Can't you tell me? How do you think I feel, having to say, "Anna won't speak to me, she talks to the doctor, the nurses, but she won't speak to me"? As if I were a criminal. Some sort of enemy!'

He was shivering. He thought – *like a dog about to be sick*. He disgusted himself. He said, 'Oh, darling, my love, I'm sorry, I'm sorry, of course I don't mean a word of this!'

She leaned back against the pillows and laughed, rolling her head from side to side.

He said, 'Anna, *Anna*. . . .'

Part Four   *ANNA*

I am Anna, of course. Who did you think was writing this? Some God's Eye novelist? They don't exist any longer. People only write about themselves now. To explain, to justify, to discover.

Have I cheated? I don't think so. A few invented scenes and conversations are admissible when you know the actors as well as I do – which is better than I know myself. How could I have written, from the beginning, in the first person? Anna was not me, not as I am now. She was Crystal's daughter, Giles's wife, Daniel's jolly mistress. Always acting the part that was expected of her – was forced on her, perhaps. And aware of it without resentment because the character she was playing was a better person than she knew herself to be.

Perhaps there is a lie in that last sentence. (I must be careful, I want to tell the truth.) Why otherwise should Tottie say to Giles, 'You could make her into almost anything you wanted to.'

But I am being taken in by my own game. Tottie might well have said this but in fact I have only put the words into her mouth just now, years later. At the time, I was quite unconscious of resentment. All I wanted was to be what Crystal (and Giles too, by that point) wanted me to be. Dear, kind, unselfish Anna! I was only afraid, sometimes, of being found out.

I wonder if I have been. The tenderness with which I have treated Anna may have given me away. And – though perhaps this is only obvious to me now because I am ashamed of it – the *use* I have made of Tottie! Writing about her I was, of course, writing about myself. Was free to feel, about her suffering in the camps, what I could not allow myself to feel about mine on that farm.

Is the parallel absurd? Crystal would say yes, no question! 'I know poor old Farmer Owen wasn't very kind to you, but *really* . . .'

To dismiss or to diminish – that was the only way Crystal knew of dealing with unpleasantness that came too close to her. Although I know this now, understand why we never discussed the farm as I grew up, understanding came too late. As a child, as an adolescent even, her silence simply confirmed my fear that my wickedness, for which I had received such punishment, must be too terrible to mention.

And yet Crystal was not, in general, emotionally stupid. When she gave me that picture of my mother, she said, 'I don't know that I care for the tiger, darling, he looks a bit *mothy*, but you can see your mother was a lovely girl.' This was the right note to strike exactly: light but kind. And when I said nothing she didn't question or reproach me as she might have done, quite justly, since she had gone to a great deal of trouble, tracing my mother's old aunt and getting this photograph for me. She said, 'Would you like a frame for it? I've got a silver one somewhere.'

But the pretty girl standing beside the shabby tiger meant nothing to me. Or I didn't want to admit what it meant. Annie-May. Rotting fruit and darkness. I put the picture away in a drawer among a collection of other souvenirs – postcards, locks of hair, shells from a seaside holiday – that Crystal expected me to treasure because she had treasured similar memories when she was young. I never looked at them but I kept them because I wanted to please her and to please her I had to be like her. Or like the person she believed herself to be. Sometimes I thought she looked into my eyes and saw, not me, but a transfigured reflection of herself.

Have I been fair to Crystal? I have, I know, been less than fair to Giles. He sat by my bed and said, 'Anna, Anna . . .' But I couldn't speak to him. Guilt or resentment? Poor Giles . . .

Poor Crystal. She sat by my bed and smiled and smiled until it seemed her face would crack with the effort. Her poor, old lady's face!

'Anna darling, smile for me! Oh darling, when are they going to do something about your mouth? I don't suppose you'll have to have a plate, they can probably make a bridge and you'll never know, once you've got used to it, that the teeth aren't your own. So don't *brood* about it! I said to Giles last night, that's probably upsetting her more than you realize, it may be one of the reasons why she doesn't want to talk. But you know what he's like! "Oh mother, Anna's not like that, she's not vain." And a deep sigh as if I knew nothing at all about anything! I said, "Well, it's hardly a matter of vanity, is it, I expect even the Pope has false teeth", and that made him laugh, for some reason.

'Would you like to see the boys, dear? Giles said not till you're more yourself but I'm sure it would cheer you up. I went to see them last Saturday, did Giles tell you? Peregrine said, "Is Mummy better?" He's growing so like Giles. Merlin is more like poor Basil. He'll look jowly when he grows up if he doesn't watch his weight, he's quite a little roly poly even now. He said, "If Mummy's in hospital, who's looking after my pony?" Though I think he's just as worried as Peregrine, really. It's not always the ones who show their feelings who feel the most, is it?

'Not that Peregrine isn't sensitive just because he appears to be, I didn't mean that. He didn't eat much lunch, just a tiny bit of chicken and his ice-cream. He left his vegetables. I wonder if Giles ought to speak to Matron about that? We don't want that nasty trouble to happen again, do we, and roughage is so important. Anna, darling, why are you laughing?'

I said, 'Do you remember Miss Cooper, the teacher at my school who took us to France one summer? She gave us a little talk before we left. She said, "You may be surprised, girls, to find yourself in an hotel where there is no throne in the lavatory, only two places for the feet and a hole. A toilet in what is called the *ancien mode*. As I say, you may be surprised but you will find this arrangement encourages a more natural posture and therefore a more satisfactory bowel function. So satisfactory, indeed, that you may wish, when you return home, to simulate this position in your own bathroom by the use of a suitable footstool. If you do this as a regular habit you will avoid piles and find it, in the fullness of time, easier to give birth." '

'What an extraordinary woman!' Crystal said. She was looking astonished. 'And what an extraordinary thing to remember! Was Miss Cooper that *big* woman with frizzy hair?'

I nodded. It had been an effort to speak. I had made this effort for Crystal's sake and now I resented it. I thought – *why don't you go away? You silly old woman, you self-satisfied, posturing old fool* . . .

She stayed, of course. Prattling on, so pleased because I had spoken to her. She had 'got through to me' was how she would put it to Giles – rushing to the public telephone with the glad news as soon as she left the ward. 'I just talked to her quite naturally about little things, clothes and the boys and so on, and then she told me a funny story. Not very funny, perhaps, rather crude, to tell you the truth, but you know Anna, how amusingly she can put things sometimes.'

She kissed me fondly when she left. I didn't return her kiss, turning my mouth away. She sighed forgivingly and whispered, 'Oh darling, I'm so glad you are yourself again.'

She was right of course, without knowing it. Watching her walk down the ward, graciously distributing smiles to my fellow prisoners as she went, I saw it all quite plain. I was myself. Not again, but for the first time.

Usually when people say they have 'found themselves' they mean that they have found someone better than they have, up to that point, appeared to be. That was not my situation. I knew myself to be a fake, a cheat, a sham . . .

Had known it always, of course. As a child I had known it, had recognized perhaps most clearly then, the depths of my deceit; as a girl, growing up, I had watched myself join in what now seemed a monstrous conspiracy to give me a personality that was not mine, that was, indeed, totally alien to the person I knew myself to be. And I was not forced into this pretence. I threw myself into it gladly. Believing that if I behaved well I would become good.

A delusion, I saw now. Because the only way I knew of being good was to deny my own true nature and renunciation is not virtue. But if I had not met Daniel I might have come to believe it was, might have gone on, stumbling up that stony path until the end . . .

To say all this – how I felt at that moment in time, lying in the hospital ward and watching Crystal walk away from me – is not a sly cover-up, an elaborately shabby excuse for my recent behaviour. No one takes adultery seriously now, though I suppose Giles's and Crystal's Anna, able to comprehend goodness only in the letter, not the spirit, might have taken it more seriously than most. But I felt none of the things that false, that Other-Anna, should have felt in this situation. No guilt, no remorse, not a twinge! No sackcloth, no ashes! Only a marvellous sense of peace and freedom.

I felt that Daniel had freed me. Or was the instrument that had enabled me to free myself. He had seen me as I was – cold, shallow, sturdily greedy – and had not turned

197

from me in loathing. Because he had accepted me, I had been able to accept myself.

And having come to this acceptance, I had wanted others to accept me too. Had wanted Giles to know, not as Daniel thought (or as I have made him think) because adulterous women are irritated by a husband's ignorance, but because I simply wanted him to see me plain. Wicked Annie-May who steals food and hits people, now love me if you can!

I thought – *is this honest*? I could, after all, have said to Giles, 'Look, I am having an affair with this young man. Only because I want to, no other reason.'

But I couldn't do it. I wanted to be seen plain but lacked the courage to reveal myself directly. The Other-Anna was too strong, perhaps, her fear too deep. Or perhaps I simply knew that he would be 'understanding'; blame himself; forgive me. And I wanted to be recognized, not forgiven.

And to hope for that was no hope at all. *Anna, do you think I don't know you? Better, it would seem, than you know yourself. This is frightfully humiliating for you, I see that, and I feel for you, my darling. I really do, you don't have to twist and turn and hide yourself from me. You haven't deceived me in any important way. It's just a kind of hysteria. You haven't changed, people don't change. I haven't changed.*

Nothing would ever change between us. He was too strong, too firmly rooted. He and Crystal had always been too strong for me, had formed me in their image so that I spoke and behaved as if they were alive within me. I had become their creature out of fear . . .

I thought – what a towering edifice of lies! Hysterical self-pity, Giles is right. All that is wrong is that I cannot bear this humiliation. Saint Anna tumbled off her pedestal at last! And concerned only to build a new and equally blame-less image from the shattered pieces. Retreating into silence, into phoney madness, as Crystal did, that time . . .

I thought – I am copying her even now. Why can't I supply my own answers? Why can't I *die*?

The mutilated woman was dying. Everyone knew this, though no one spoke about it. She had been quiet for two days now. The nurses came and went with silent faces and the walking wounded among us glanced furtively as we passed her bed. But the screens were very tightly closed.

I thought – how does Giles feel about me? Does he wish I had thrown myself under a train like Tolstoy's Anna?

The sister said, 'Your husband phoned to say he might be late tonight. He'll be pleased to see you looking so perky. He's been so worried, the poor man!'

It was five o'clock. This was the Irish sister talking, a rosy girl from Cork. She had really come to tell me that the police wanted to see me. She said, 'Doctor told them you were fit to talk. You do feel up to it? It's nothing to worry about but you know how they like to dot the i's and cross the t's. Might as well get it over with.'

I said, 'Yes, indeed,' and smiled at her.

I saw them in the little office off the ward. I had had a bath and dressed. I didn't know what had happened to the clothes I had been wearing at the time of the accident. Giles had brought me fresh underwear and a light woollen trouser suit that I had never liked. It smelt strange to me, perhaps because it had been hung in a cupboard with other patients' clothes.

There were two policemen. The older one had very wideset eyes that were pale and shiny, like mackerel. He asked me how I felt and if this was my first time out of bed. I made my joke about walking wounded and he smiled. He said they didn't want to tire me but it would be helpful if I would make a short statement. He said, 'Then we shan't have to bother you any more.'

Anything I said would be taken down and used in evidence. I could write my statement, or the policeman would write it for me and I would read it through and sign it. While he was telling me this, I was conscious of an odd elation. It is rare for anything one says to be taken so seriously. He said there was no hurry. I was to take my time.

I said, 'It won't take long. It's quite simple. I was driving fast and I didn't stop.'

He was frowning. 'You mean you didn't see the other car in time?'

I wanted to laugh. This was so ridiculous. I said, 'Yes, I saw it. I didn't stop. That's all.'

There was silence. The younger policeman had gone very red.

The older one pushed back his chair. The scrape set my teeth on edge. He said, very gently, 'Mrs Golightly, do you remember what happened at all?'

I nodded. I began tapping my foot.

He said, 'It's quite usual, you know, not to remember. You were fairly badly concussed. Can you tell me what the weather was like?'

'Dry.' It had been a lovely morning. I had walked with Giles to the gate, picked roses for Crystal.

'You're sure? At the time you hit the other car?'

'Perhaps it had started to rain a little. Does it matter? Because I can't remember the exact state of the weather doesn't mean I can't remember anything, does it?'

He said, slowly and carefully, 'Naturally you were worried, in a hurry to see your son. The other driver was killed. You must have thought about this, anyone would.' He waited. We all waited, sitting in this small, clean room. Then he said, it seemed sorrowfully, 'You are an experienced driver, Mrs Golightly. If you really saw this other car, why didn't you stop?'

He sounded so thoughtful, so painstaking. As if we were

discussing an academic problem. I wanted to laugh. I felt myself smiling tightly. Skin stretched over bone.

'I suppose I wanted to smash something,' I said.

If that had been the truth then, I didn't know. Only that it was the truth now. I wanted to smash my way out of this prison, bring the walls down round me, lie buried in the rubble.

I thought – Giles will never forgive me. That I should have killed an old woman in an accident was one thing. It would be perfectly proper to feel guilty about that for the rest of my life. But to put myself where the law could touch me was another matter, a self-indulgent perversity. Society was ordered to protect people like Giles, not to arraign them. That he would deplore this cosily arrogant view would not prevent him holding it. *Anna, you are inventing out of guilt. I know how you feel, but what is the point of it?*

I couldn't have answered him. All I know is how I felt and what I did, not why.

I thought – I don't belong here, not in Giles's world. I went back into the ward and the Irish sister smiled at me. 'All right? Still steady on your pins?' I nodded, smiling back. She said, 'No hurry to get back to bed. Have a walk, why don't you, it's a lovely evening.'

I went into the grounds. The hospital was on a hill; the sun was setting in a yellow sky. A few patients walked among the flower beds. Some sat on wooden seats before the chapel. Although the air was warm there was a little breeze and this was the most sheltered place. I thought – at least I am alive.

The car park was on the top of the hill. I walked up there, wanting air. To feel the wind in my face.

Nothing else was in my mind at all. I sat in the driver's seat of the old Morris simply because the window was open and I felt tired suddenly. It was a family car – ash trays full of toffee papers, a smell of bananas, an old rug on the back seat for the dog. A careless, superstitious family. The ignition key was in the lock; a St Christopher medal dangled from the ring. It was an unusually pretty one, made of beaten silver.

I drove towards the westering sun and thought I had never seen the sky so beautiful. I can remember thinking that. And later, when my headlights turned up a familiar lane – *if I feel anything now, I will go back.* I pulled to the side, onto the grass verge, and waited. Somewhere behind the lit windows of the converted Victorian mansion, my sons were bathing, or eating supper, or going to bed. Two little boys I had given birth to. Two graceful strangers with straw-coloured hair. I waited, called on my love for them, thought of the meals I had fed them, the games we had played, the name tapes I had stitched on their clothes, but nothing stirred in me.

I left the car in a back street in a village near Oxford. Since I did not want to leave the side lights on and run the battery down, I left it under a lamp post with two wheels on the pavement. I removed the St Christopher medal from the key ring and put it on the driver's seat before locking the door and leaving the key itself under the back wheel where the police might think to look for it but a casual thief would not. And worried, as I walked away, because I had not filled the petrol tank as a kind of hiring fee.

I had a cheque book but little money. Under a pound. I walked along the main road to a lorry driver's café and ordered tea while I waited.

My driver was a small, compact, silent man, in his early thirties, perhaps. A young, weathered look. He had brick-coloured hands with tufts of stiff, dark hair on the backs of his fingers. He was going to Wales which was where I wanted to go. The decision had seemed to me like a revelation though I suppose hiding the car key had reminded me of Tottie's cottage, with the key on a hook behind the wash house door.

Since I was clearly too old to be a student, I told the driver that my mother was ill, there was no suitable train, and my car was out of action. I would have elaborated further but he hardly seemed to care. He said, 'I don't mind a bit of company,' but seemed disinclined, once we were on the road, to take advantage of mine.

I slept off and on. It was uncomfortable in the cab of the lorry but I was so tired I could have slept on nails. I dreamed that I was lying in bed in a prison hospital. I had killed someone and was to be hanged for it. The only way I could escape was to have a baby. They would not hang me if I were having a baby. I lay in the hospital bed, coarse, grey blanket drawn up under my chin, and planned how I could get out of the ward, find a man, get pregnant . . .

I woke, sweating. The dream had no relevance to my present position. They hanged no one nowadays, and it was an old dream, anyway; one that I used to have years ago, when I was a girl. What it had meant then, I didn't know, nor what it meant now. Only that it was the same dream, exactly the same in every detail; the same, grey blanket, the same terror.

I found that I was sexually roused. I thought – perhaps this explains those earlier dreams. To need to become pregnant to avert my own death was the only way I could admit that kind of sensation!

This made me want to laugh. I looked at my silent companion and thought – suppose he were to say, 'Why not stop by the road for a bit?' We could do it in the bushes at the side of the road. I would get pregnant, go to Tottie's cottage, live there alone, have my baby. I would find some job or other. I was strong and competent and young enough. I would cut myself off, be reborn with my baby's birth, start a new life. Giles would not want me back with a lorry driver's bastard.

But my driver made no sexual advances. He barely spoke to me except when we stopped at an all night pull-in near Ludlow. We ate beans on toast for which he paid. He said, 'You don't look too well,' but quite impersonally, as if he were commenting on the weather. And, when he dropped me where our roads parted, a little later, 'Sure you'll be all right?'

'Oh yes,' I said. And when he still hesitated, looking down at me from the cab, 'This is absolutely perfect, you have been *marvellously* kind.'

Perhaps there was an element of calculated histrionics in all this. I was acting out despair in a way that made me seem, if not innocent or mad, at least not quite responsible. I see this now; perhaps, in some artful byway of my mind, I even knew it then. Was aware that my behaviour had, to any sympathetic eye, cancelled out my wild statement to the police; provided evidence of such a state of shock that nothing I had said could be believed. Or not believed entirely.

But this is hindsight. My despair was real enough. More real, ironically, once I had expressed it as a kind of fiction – clothed it, as it were, in a theatrical gesture – than it had been before. Now that I had seen myself despairing, I could admit despair.

And by admittance was purged of it, to some extent, though perhaps pain and exhaustion played a larger part. I know that for the rest of that dreadful night, and for several days afterwards, I was as impervious to emotion as a leper is to heat or cold.

Tottie's cottage is a short walk from the village up a narrow, rutted lane. The view from the back windows is of

204

a bare hill; pale rock and purple heather. A bleak, cloud-shadowed landscape, as empty as I felt myself to be. I sat, for long stretches of time during that first week, staring out at it and feeling nothing . . .

This is a fantasy, of course. The fantasy we are all prone to when our lives become intolerable. A dream of limbo . . .

In fact, I was fully occupied. I put logs on the fire, slept deeply, fed myself. Tottie's idea of rustic retreat was much like Marie Antoinette's: although there was a tiny butter churn in the larder, there was also an amazing selection of tinned food, much of it from Fortnum and Mason. I found the woman who looked after the cottage for her (or, to be more exact, she found me, coming the first afternoon to investigate the smoke from the chimney), and arranged with her to cash a cheque and to buy eggs and milk and butter.

I wrote to Tottie briefly, and at greater length to Giles. I did feel something for him, even if only a dry and distant sense of obligation, but the motive behind my letter was purely selfish: I wanted to be left alone. I wrote draft after draft until I had achieved what seemed the most effective mixture of apology and plea, couched in terms he would respect and understand. I assured him I was well, that he need not worry on that score. I described the cottage in 'amusing' detail – the butter churn, the expensive, hand-thrown pots, the copper warming pans. I told him that he was not to blame himself, to feel that he had failed me; that he was kind and good and always had been. If his kindness felt like a reproach to me that was my fault, my inadequacy, not his, and I was ashamed of asking him to extend his kindness further. I said, 'If you come here we will both talk too much. And you will tell me what I think before I have a chance to think it for myself.' I implied that what I wanted to 'think out', in part, was my relationship with Daniel, but suggested, too, that I had a grander purpose in my solitude. I said, 'To live by other people's standards, as on other people's money, makes you bankrupt in the end. I need to find my own before I can make sense of anything. I have lived falsely for too long. I want truth now, not dignity.'

It was a cold letter, being so worked-over, and ultimately a lying one; little more than an elaborately cunning device to stop Giles following me. I had no purpose other than to get away, no plan . . .

The weather was beautiful; a golden, late September. Tottie's country clothes were too small for me; I borrowed a sweater and a pair of jeans of Ivan's, and went walking. This was some forty miles from where I had lived with Crystal, from the Owens' farm, but the landscape was similar, soft, sheep-cropped turf and dry-stone walls, and my imagination peopled it, so that several times, returning to the cottage in the steel-blue dusk, I half expected to find Crystal there. *Annie-duckie.* And once, again at dusk, walking down a twisting lane, I came upon a man lifting milk churns from a stand, and saw Farmer Owen's face. *Annie-May.*

But I was Anna now. And the man was not Farmer Owen. I smiled and said, 'Good evening.' I felt nothing, or thought I felt nothing. But after I had passed him I began to run, and remembered running home from school, heart pounding, cheeks shaking, sobbing, 'Crystal, Crystal, Crystal,' as a magic incantation; believing that if I stopped it for a single second I should see him, waiting for me in a gateway or behind a tree.

Sometimes past and present fused together in my mind so that neither seemed entirely real. I visited the dentist in the village. He came twice a week to a lock-up surgery over the general store; an elderly man with a moustache like drooping wire and liver-spotted hands. The second time I went, I lay in the chair half asleep and he sat beside me, holding my bridge in place while the cement hardened. I thought, *what an absurdly intimate thing for one stranger to do to another*, and, at that moment, he touched my breast with his free hand. So light a touch, it could almost have been a mistake, but when I opened my eyes I saw his shamed and guilty look. And, to my amazement, it excited me.

Crystal had said, 'Doctor Davies is coming to have a look at you, Annie-duckie. He's a bit gruff but you mustn't mind, you mustn't be scared of him. I'll tell you a secret, if you like. He's a little in love with me, the poor old man.' And though I didn't understand why, I had seen that this excited her.

I was the same age now that Crystal had been then. And perhaps because of that, she seemed more real to me than Annie-May. This dismayed me because it seemed a kind of treachery and I tried to remember her, to forge a link between us, but the more I thought, the less real she became. I thought – one day I will hire a car and go there. Look at the cottage, drive up past the farm.

I didn't go. There was no point. One farm was much like another. And one neglected child . . .

Some years ago, the police brought a case against a man who had kept his eldest son locked in a hen house for a year. He had other, younger children: a girl of three and a small boy. There was a picture of him in the newspaper, sitting with the baby on his knee, the little girl leaning against him. He looked an ordinary man, an affectionate father, but he had chained a seven-year-old child to an iron staple driven into the ground and left him, naked except for a piece of sacking, lying in his own filth.

I read the report at breakfast. Prosecution and defence. The child had been wild, destructive – uncontrollable since his mother had been taken to a mental hospital after the birth of her third child. The father was inadequate, in need of help. I knew all this, accepted this civilized judgment. There was no point in punishment; I was ashamed of wanting it. Of sitting there, palms sweating, in a dream of vengeance.

Perhaps it is only possible to see oneself through other people. The only way of defining and resolving one's own situation. Or perhaps I can only see myself that way.

Now that I was alone, I could not see myself at all. I could only see Giles, Crystal, Tottie. Their history was my history, I had no other. They were real and I was nothing, only the stage on which they moved; the actuality of their lives mocking the shadow play of mine.

I thought – this isn't true! They don't exist except through me. I pull the strings and they gesticulate, open their mouths and speak on my behalf. I am the puppet master, the manipulator. Not only in fiction, but in life.

I thought – I am their creator and destroyer. I battened on Crystal like some fledgling cuckoo, forced my way into her life, employed the art of helplessness to make her care for me. I destroyed Tottie's marriage, not, as I had sometimes thought, because I loved and admired her so consumingly that I had to be like her, marry Giles because she had married him, but because I hated her for being what I could never be. Someone who had suffered and survived, was integrated, whole.

I thought – do I hate Giles? Have I destroyed him too? Am I going mad?

I walked no more. I let the fire go out. The mist descended from the mountain and the house grew cold. I did not feed myself, or dress, or wash. I stayed in bed, shivering under blankets.

I thought – I don't hate them, I only hate myself. Not for my parody of virtue but for my dream of freedom. I had dreamed there was some force that slept within me; an imprisoned spirit; a coiled spring, waiting. Had felt, on that drive from London, free at last, as if a lid had lifted or a gate had opened. But all that was released had been an agent of destruction.

I remembered Giles's story about the man who had paid for his lunch. It is always a stranger who pays, an innocent. I had killed an innocent stranger. If it was vengeance I had dreamed of, I had been monstrously avenged.

The postman brought letters, plodding up the lane through the mist and knocking until I got out of bed and opened the door.

I was amazed to receive these letters. This evidence that the people I had begun to think of as my creatures still had life without me.

Tottie wrote: *Dear Anna, stay as long as you want. We shan't be coming down again this year – as soon as autumn comes, Ivan insists he is a city boy! I was so sorry to hear from Giles about the accident, so hope nothing tiresome comes of it, and that you're feeling better now.*

I left Giles's letter lying unopened on the table while I put my clothes on, made coffee, lit the fire. I had imagined what he would do so often. He would ignore my letter, come to find me – I had been surprised he had not come already. Perhaps this letter was to say that now I had made the break he wasn't sorry, that he wanted a divorce. Or that he would come at the weekend. Or that he would come and bring the boys: it would be easier for us both if they were there. Or that he would send Daniel. That would be like Giles, to suggest that I would rather see that silly boy!

None of these things. He hoped I was rested now. He had known I was all right, of course: he had asked Tottie to telephone the woman who looked after her cottage as soon as he received my letter. Before that he had been fairly desperate, naturally, but that was over now.

He should have known how desperate *I* felt. He was ashamed of his stupidity. He understood that I wanted to be left alone, would not come until I felt I wanted him. If he said he hoped I would, quite soon, then that was not a plea, only a statement of his own position.

There was no word from the police as yet. He wasn't sure whether this was a good sign or a bad. He thought they were unlikely, anyway, to bring a serious charge. There had been no witnesses apart from Daniel – and Daniel had certainly convinced *him* that I had not been to blame.

He wished he could think it would be as easy to convince me. He knew how I must feel. Or how he would feel if he were me. Which was, he supposed, all one could ever say.

It was a careful, caring letter. If it disappointed me, fell short of something I had hoped for, then perhaps my life was always likely to. Or so I told myself. I had a violent nature, however tamed and corseted, and Giles was not a passionate man. There was no dark side to him. He was a reasoning, civilized, moral being, as he assumed I was. As, for most of the time, I tried to be.

I knew, even as I put the letter on the fire and watched it burn, that I would behave in a reasonable and civilized way. I would recognize that I was unlikely to have killed anyone deliberately and that doubt was no excuse for wallowing in useless guilt. Today – or tomorrow or the next day – I would clean the house, wash Ivan's jeans and sweater and the sheets I had slept in, carry in logs from the shed, replace what tins could be replaced from the village store and make a list of those I would have sent from London. I would telephone Giles and tell him there was no need to fetch me, look up trains, order a taxi, shut the windows, lock the doors, put the key in the wash house . . .

As I thought about these things and saw myself doing them, tears poured down my face. Tears of rage and pain. *I'm so unhappy – it's not fair – he should have known – someone should have known – they shouldn't have left me here alone so long – they don't love me, no one loves me, or someone would have come.*

And wept, for this simple, childish hurt, as I had never wept for any grief of mine before.

I was cleaning the bedroom window when Crystal came. I looked up and saw her.

The taxi must have refused to bring her to the door. It had been raining since the mist cleared, not hard but steadily, and the rutted lane was slippery with mud. Crystal picked her way carefully up the grassy, central spine. She was wearing knee-length, fawn boots, a fawn suit with a paler, fur collar, and a large-brimmed, dark brown hat.

She stopped when she was a little way from the gate and glanced up at the cottage. If she had been wearing her glasses she would have seen me at the window but she is too vain to wear them in public. Satisfied that she was unobserved, she opened her bag and put them on now, in order to examine her face in her compact mirror. She did this at some length, lifting her chin, smoothing back the loose skin at the side of her jaw, and appraising the effect of this temporary face lift before applying powder and lipstick.

I stood quite still and watched her. A ridiculous old woman, powdering her nose in the rain before rushing in (as she would doubtless put it) where angels fear to tread . . .

I thought – *is* it so ridiculous? What are we, apart from what we appear to be?

And gave her time to compose her scarlet, loving smile before I ran down to the door.

VIRAGO MODERN CLASSICS
&
CLASSIC NON-FICTION

The first Virago Modern Classic, *Frost in May* by Antonia White, was published in 1978. It launched a list dedicated to the celebration of women writers and to the rediscovery and reprinting of their works. Its aim was, and is, to demonstrate the existence of a female tradition in fiction, and to broaden the sometimes narrow definition of a 'classic' which has often led to the neglect of interesting novels and short stories. Published with new introductions by some of today's best writers, the books are chosen for many reasons: they may be great works of fiction; they may be wonderful period pieces; they may reveal particular aspects of women's lives; they may be classics of comedy or storytelling.

The companion series, Virago Classic Non-Fiction, includes diaries, letters, literary criticism, and biographies – often by and about authors published in the Virago Modern Classics series.

'Good news for everyone writing and reading today' – *Hilary Mantel*

'A continuingly magnificent imprint' – *Joanna Trollope*

'The Virago Modern Classics have reshaped literary history and enriched the reading of us all. No library is complete without them' – *Margaret Drabble*

VIRAGO MODERN CLASSICS
&
CLASSIC NON-FICTION

Some of the authors included in these two series –

Elizabeth von Arnim, Dorothy Baker, Pat Barker, Nina Bawden,
Nicola Beauman, Sybille Bedford, Jane Bowles, Kay Boyle,
Vera Brittain, Leonora Carrington, Angela Carter, Willa Cather,
Colette, Ivy Compton-Burnett, E.M. Delafield, Maureen Duffy,
Elaine Dundy, Nell Dunn, Emily Eden, George Egerton,
George Eliot, Miles Franklin, Mrs Gaskell,
Charlotte Perkins Gilman, George Gissing,
Victoria Glendinning, Radclyffe Hall, Shirley Hazzard,
Dorothy Hewett, Mary Hocking, Alice Hoffman,
Winifred Holtby, Janette Turner Hospital, Zora Neale Hurston,
Elizabeth Jenkins, F. Tennyson Jesse, Molly Keane,
Margaret Laurence, Maura Laverty, Rosamond Lehmann,
Rose Macaulay, Shena Mackay, Olivia Manning, Paule Marshall,
F.M. Mayor, Anaïs Nin, Kate O'Brien, Olivia, Grace Paley,
Mollie Panter-Downes, Dawn Powell, Dorothy Richardson,
E. Arnot Robertson, Jacqueline Rose, Vita Sackville-West,
Elaine Showalter, May Sinclair, Agnes Smedley, Dodie Smith,
Stevie Smith, Nancy Spain, Christina Stead, Carolyn Steedman,
Gertrude Stein, Jan Struther, Han Suyin, Elizabeth Taylor,
Sylvia Townsend Warner, Mary Webb, Eudora Welty,
Mae West, Rebecca West, Edith Wharton, Antonia White,
Christa Wolf, Virginia Woolf, E.H. Young.

Also by Nina Bawden

IN MY OWN TIME
Almost an Autobiography

'A joy' – **David Holloway**

'A born story-teller, a gift as evident in this autobiography as in her novels' – *Independent*

Nina Bawden's acclaimed career spans twenty adult novels and seventeen for children. Hugely admired as a novelist who unravels the complex emotions that simmer beneath family life, she now turns to her own story. In deceptively simple vignettes she takes us through her life and, fascinatingly, reveals the origins and inspirations of her many books. We learn about her childhood evacuation to Suffolk and Wales, and of her years at Oxford where she met Richard Burton and Margaret Thatcher. Perhaps most moving of all is the courageous account of her oldest son Niki, who was diagnosed a schizophrenic. *In My Own Time* is a tribute to the great talent and quiet heroism of a very special woman.

GEORGE BENEATH A PAPER MOON

'I like it as much as any novel I've read this year. The comedy lies, as in the best and subtlest of comedies, in the exquisite patterning, the way in which events bounce and reverberate' – *New Statesman*

George is an unusually successful travel agent, providing other people with the adventures he dare not risk. Though content to wrap himself in fantasies, he is haunted by the belief that he fathered the daughter of his best friends. A holiday in Turkey snaps his private world when George finds himself in the midst of intrigue and murder and is forced to acknowledge that life is not the fairy-tale he'd imagined. In this superbly constructed and mercilessly observed novel – part comedy, part thriller – Nina Bawden exposes the fictions we impose on our lives.

THE ICE HOUSE

'Nina Bawden's great talent is to be able to take you along a perfectly ordinary street, rip the façade away and show the strange and passionate events that go on behind closed doors' – *Daily Telegraph*

At fifteen, Daisy, confident and cherished, is appalled to hear that Ruth's father locked her in the old garden ice house as a childhood punishment. The revelation of that primitive cruelty cements a friendship to last for many years. Friendship, love, marriage and, above all, the scorching effects of adultery, come under the microscope in this dextrous novel. Journeying from a terrifying suburban household to its unexpected conclusion in the Egyptian Pharaohs' tombs, *The Ice House* is startling, tragic and humorous by turns.

Books by post

Virago Books are available through mail order or from your local bookshop. Other books which might be of interest include:–

☐ The Birds on the Trees	Nina Bawden	£4.99
☐ Familiar Passions	Nina Bawden	£5.99
☐ Family Money	Nina Bawden	£5.99
☐ George Beneath a Paper Moon	Nina Bawden	£6.99
☐ Grain of Truth	Nina Bawden	£5.99
☐ The Ice House	Nina Bawden	£5.99
☐ In My Own Time	Nina Bawden	£7.99
☐ A Little Love, A Little Learning	Nina Bawden	£5.99
☐ Tortoise by Candlelight	Nina Bawden	£5.99
☐ Walking Naked	Nina Bawden	£5.99
☐ A Woman of My Age	Nina Bawden	£5.99

Please send Cheque/Eurocheque/Postal Order (sterling only), Access, Visa or Mastercard:

☐☐☐☐☐☐☐☐☐☐☐☐☐☐☐☐

Expiry Date: _____   Signature: _____

Please allow 75 pence per book for post and packing in U.K.
Overseas customers please allow £1.00 per copy for post and packing.

All orders to:
Virago Press, Book Service by Post, P.O. Box 29, Douglas,
Isle of Man, IM99 1BQ.   Tel: 01624 675137.   Fax: 01624 670923.

Name: _____

Address: _____

_____

Please allow 20 days for delivery.
Please tick box if you would like to receive a free stock list ☐
Please tick box if you do not wish to receive any additional information ☐

Prices and availability subject to change without notice.